...ocalypse, and a cling-... why haven't you read *Angelfall* yet?'
theprettybooks.wordpress.com

'Devotees of the paranormal will get their angel fix here'
Voice of Youth Advocates

'An explosive, pulse-pounding journey . . . A frickin' fantastic read.'
Star

'Explicit, vivid, gritty and evocative . . . A book that defies the
labels and boundaries of its genre, and a wonderfully spine-
chilling read.'
keepcalmandreadabook.wordpress.com

'Completely enthralling . . . It deserves to be a hit.'
Sunday Mirror

'A fantastic combination of action, horror and romance . . .
A thrill to read.'
thebookbag.co.uk

It's rare to read a book that is so intoxicating that it is all
you can think of . . . Susan Ee really has created something
of a masterpiece.'

Susan Ee is the author of the *USA Today* bestselling books in the Penryn & the End of Days trilogy, *Angelfall* and *World After*. Her books have been translated into over twenty languages, and her short films have played at major festivals. She used to be a lawyer but loves being a writer because it allows her imagination to bust out and go feral.

Visit her at www.susanee.com, find her on Facebook at facebook.com/AngefallOfficial and follow Susan on Twitter @Susan_Ee.

By Susan Ee

Angelfall
World After
End of Days

END OF DAYS

SUSAN EE

HODDER

Originally published in the United States by Amazon
Publishing, 2015. This edition made possible under a license
arrangement originating with Amazon Publishing.

First published in Great Britain in 2015 by Hodder & Stoughton
An Hachette UK company

A CIP catalogue record for this title is available from the British Library

Paperback ISBN 978 1 444 77855 7
eBook ISBN 978 1 444 77856 4

Typeset by Hewer Text UK Ltd, Edinburgh
Printed and bound by CPI Group (UK) Ltd, Croydon, CR0 4YY

Hodder & Stoughton Ltd
Carmelite House
50 Victoria Embankment
London EC4Y 0DZ

Hodder & Stoughton policy is to use papers that are natural, renewa-
ble and recyclable products and made from wood grown in sustainable
forests. The logging and manufacturing processes are expected to conform
to the environmental regulations of the country of origin.
www.hodder.co.uk

Dedicated to readers like Penryn who have it tough at home, who had to grow up fast due to life circumstances, and who have no idea how much potential they really have. You are being fire forged, just like Penryn. And like her, you can turn your greatest trials into your greatest strengths.

1

Everywhere we fly, people scatter below us.

They see the great shadow of our swarm above them, and they run.

We fly over a cityscape that has been charred, broken, and mostly abandoned. San Francisco used to be one of the most beautiful cities in the world, with its trolley cars and famous restaurants. Tourists used to stroll Fisherman's Wharf and cruise the crowded alleys of Chinatown.

Now the grungy survivors fight for scraps and harass terrified women. They scurry into the shadows and disappear as soon as they spot us. The only ones left are the most desperate who choose to stay out in the open, hoping to escape the gangs for the few seconds it takes us to fly by.

Below us, a girl hunches over a dead man lying with limbs spread wide. She hardly notices us, or she simply doesn't care. Here and there, I see light glinting off something in a window, signs that someone is watching us through binoculars, or maybe aiming a rifle at us as we pass.

We must be quite a sight. A cloud of scorpion-tailed, man-sized locusts blotting out the sky.

And in the middle of it all, a demon with enormous wings carrying a teenage girl. At least, Raffe must look like a demon to anyone who didn't know he was an archangel flying on borrowed wings.

They probably think he kidnapped the girl he's holding. They couldn't possibly guess that I feel safe in his arms. That I'm resting my head on the warm curve of his neck because I like the feel of his skin.

'Do we humans always look like that from above?' I ask.

He answers. I can feel the vibrations in his throat and see his mouth moving, but I can't hear him above the thunderous buzz of the locust swarm.

It's probably good I didn't hear him anyway. Angels probably think we look like roaches scurrying from one shadow to another.

But we're not roaches or monkeys or monsters, no matter what the angels think of us. We are still the same people we once were. At least, we are on the inside.

I hope so, anyway.

I glance over at my cut-up sister who is flying beside us. Even now, I have to remind myself that Paige is still the same girl I've always loved. Well, maybe not exactly the same.

She's riding on the shriveled body of Beliel, which is being carried like a palanquin by several locusts. He has blood all over him and looks long dead even though I know he's still alive. It's no worse than what he deserves, but there's still a part of me that wonders at the primitive cruelty of it all.

A gray island of rock appears ahead of us in the middle of San Francisco Bay. Alcatraz, the notorious former prison. There's a whirlwind of locusts above the island. It's a small part of the hive that didn't come when Paige called for help on the beach a few hours ago.

I point to an island behind Alcatraz. It's bigger and greener, with no buildings that I can see. I'm pretty sure that's Angel Island. Despite the name, any place has to be nicer than Alcatraz. I don't want Paige on that hellish rock.

We veer around the locust whirlwind and head to the larger island.

I motion to Paige to come with us. Her locust and the ones closest to her follow us, but the majority join the swarm above Alcatraz, swelling the size of the dark funnel above the prison. Some seem confused, following us at first, then changing direction and heading back to Alcatraz as if compelled to be part of the hive.

Only a handful of locusts stay with us as we circle Angel Island for a good spot to land.

The rising sun highlights the emerald greens of trees surrounded by the bay. From this angle, Alcatraz sits in front of the wide panorama of the San Francisco skyline. It must have been a breathtaking view once. Now it looks like a jagged line of broken teeth.

We land by the water on the west shore. The tsunamis left a rubble of bricks on the beach and a mass of splintered trees on one side of the hill while leaving the other side mostly intact.

When we reach the ground, Raffe lets me go. I feel like I've been curled up against him for a year. My arms are practically frozen in place around his shoulders, and my legs are stiff. The locusts stumble around when they land like they're having the same issues.

Raffe stretches his neck and shakes out his arms. His leathery bat wings fold and disappear behind him. He's still wearing his mask from the party-turned-massacre at the aerie. It's deep red shot through with silver, and it covers his entire face except for his mouth.

'Aren't you going to take that off?' I shake the numbness out of my hands. 'You look like red death on demon wings.'

'Good. That's how every angel should look.' He rolls his shoulders. I suppose it's not easy having someone cling on to you for hours. Despite trying to relax his muscles, he's on full alert as his eyes scan our eerily quiet surroundings.

I adjust the strap around my shoulder so that my sword, disguised as a teddy bear, sits against my hip for easy access. Then I step over to help my sister off Beliel. As I near Paige, her locusts hiss at me, jabbing their scorpion stingers in my direction.

I stop, my heart pounding.

Raffe is beside me in an instant. 'Let her come to you,' he says quietly.

Paige climbs off her ride and pets a locust with her small hand. 'Shh. It's okay. That's Penryn.'

It still amazes me to see these monsters listening to my baby sister. Our stare-down lasts a moment longer until the beasts lower their stingers under Paige's gentle crooning. I let out my breath, and we back away, letting Paige soothe them.

Paige bends to gather up Raffe's severed wings. She had been lying on them, and the stained feathers look crushed, but they begin fluffing almost instantly in her arms. I can't blame Raffe for cutting them off Beliel before the locusts could suck them dry along with the rest of the demon, but I wish he hadn't had to do it. Now we'll have to find a doctor to reattach them to Raffe before they wither.

We start up the beach and see a couple of rowboats tied to a tree. The island must be occupied after all.

Raffe motions for us to hide while he heads up the slope.

It looks like there used to be a row of houses on one side of the hill. On the lower ground, only the concrete foundations remain, littered with smashed boards stained with water and salt. But on the higher ground, several boarded-up buildings are intact.

We skitter behind the nearest building. It's large enough to have been barracks of some kind. Like the others, it's sealed up with white painted boards. They look like they'd been shut up long before the Great Attack.

The whole thing feels like a ghost settlement except for the house on the hill overlooking the bay. It's a perfectly intact Victorian, complete with a white picket fence. It's the only building that looks like a family home and the only one with color or any sense of life.

I don't see any threats, certainly nothing that the locusts can't scare off, but I stay out of sight anyway. I watch Raffe as he leaps to fly up the hill, moving behind the cover of barrack to tree, barrack to tree, working his way toward the main house.

When he gets there, gunfire shatters the peace.

2

Raffe flattens himself against a wall.

'We're not here to harm you,' he shouts.

Another gunshot answers from an upstairs window. I flinch, my nerves about as taut as they can be.

'I can hear you talking in there,' shouts Raffe. He must think we're all deaf. I guess compared to angels, we are. 'And the answer is no. I doubt that my wings will be worth as much as angel wings. There is no chance of you being able to take me on, so stop fooling yourselves. We just want the house. Be smart. Leave.'

The front door slams open. Three burly men step out, pointing their rifles in different directions as if unsure where their enemies are.

Raffe takes flight, and the locusts follow his lead. He sweeps the air with his impressive demon wings, looking intimidating before dropping back down beside the house.

The locusts fly toward him, diving in and out of the tree line with their scorpion stingers curled behind them.

As soon as the men get a good look at what they're up against, they run. They crash through the trees across from the locusts. Then they circle around the rubble toward the beach.

As the men run, a woman scampers out of the house like a beaten dog. She races in the opposite direction of the men. She looks back to see where they are, looking more like she's running from them than from the winged creatures.

She disappears into the hills behind the house, while the men take the rowboats and head out on the bay.

Raffe walks around to the front of the vacated house and pauses, listening carefully. He waves for us to join him as he walks in.

By the time we reach the Victorian, Raffe yells, 'All clear.'

I put my hand on Paige's shoulder as we enter the yard through the white picket fence. She clutches Raffe's feathered wings like a security blanket as she stares at the house. The Victorian is butter colored with maroon trim. It has a porch with wicker furniture and looks a lot like a dollhouse.

One of the locusts drops Beliel beside the picket fence. He lies there like a piece of meat. The ropey flesh of his body is the color and texture of beef jerky, and blood still trickles from wounds where Paige bit chunks out of his cheek and arms. He looks pitiful, but this is one locust victim I don't feel sorry for.

'What should we do with Beliel?' I ask Raffe.

'I'll take care of him.' Raffe walks down the porch steps toward us.

Considering all the awful things that Beliel has done, I'm not sure why Raffe didn't kill him instead of just cutting his wings off. Maybe he thought the locusts would do it or that Paige's attack on him at the aerie would be fatal. But now that he's made it this far, Raffe doesn't seem inclined to finish him off.

'Come on, Paige.' My sister walks beside me up onto the wooden porch and into the house.

Inside, I expect dust and mold, but instead, it's surprisingly nice. The living room looks like it used to be an exhibit. A lady's dress from the 1800s is displayed in the corner. Beside it, museum ropes on brass stands are bunched together, no longer needed to keep the public away from the antique living room furniture.

Paige looks around and walks over to the window. Beyond the warped glass, Raffe drags Beliel up to the fence gate. He dumps him there and walks behind the house. Beliel seems dead, but I know he's not. Locust-stung victims are paralyzed enough to seem dead even though they're still conscious. That's part of the horror of being stung.

'Come on. Let's check out the rest of the house,' I say. But Paige continues to stare out the window at the shriveled form of Beliel.

Outside, Raffe walks back into sight with his arms full of rusty chains. He makes quite the intimidating picture as he wraps the chains around Beliel, forming loops around his neck, the fence post, and his thighs. He padlocks them together in the center of his chest.

If I didn't know better, I'd be terrified of Raffe. He looks merciless and inhuman as he handles the helpless demon.

Strangely, it's Beliel who keeps pulling at my attention, though. There's something about him in chains that keeps catching my eye. Something familiar.

I shake it off. I must be on the verge of hallucinating from exhaustion.

3

I was never a morning girl, and now that I've had a few
nights with no sleep, I feel like a zombie. I want to crash
onto a couch somewhere and sleep for a week.

But first, I need to help my sister settle in.

It takes me an hour to clean her up in the bathtub.
She's covered in Beliel's blood and gore. If the frightened people at the Resistance thought she was a monster
when she was in a clean flower-print dress, they'd definitely turn into torch-bearing, lynch-mob villagers if
they saw her now.

I'm afraid to actually scrub her because of all her
stitches and bruises. Normally, our mom would do this.
She was always surprisingly gentle when it came to
handling Paige.

Maybe thinking the same thing, Paige asks, 'Where's Mom?'

'She's with the Resistance. They should be at the camp by now.' I dribble water over her and dab gingerly between stitches with a sponge. 'We came to look for you but got caught and taken to Alcatraz. She's all right now, though. The Resistance came to rescue everyone on the island, and I saw her on the boat as they were escaping.'

Her bruises still look angry, and I don't want to accidentally pop a stitch. I wonder if these are the kinds of stitches that dissolve or if a doctor needs to take them out.

That makes me think of Doc, the guy who sewed her up in the first place. I don't care what his situation was. No decent human being would have mangled and mutilated little kids into man-eating monsters just because Uriel the megalomaniac angel told him to. I want to kick Doc to pieces when I see how bruised and abused Paige is.

So how crazy is it that I'm nursing a small thought that maybe he can help her?

I sigh and drop the sponge into the water. I can't stand to look at her ribs sticking out of her stitched skin anymore. She's about as clean as she's going to get anyway. I drop her blood-stained clothes in the sink and walk into one of the bedrooms to see if I can find something for her to wear.

I rummage through the antique drawers, not really expecting to find anything. It seems like this place was some sort of historic tourist site rather than anyone's house. But somebody has stayed here. Maybe even decided that this could be home.

There's not a lot, but at least one woman had settled here, at least for a while. I reach in and pull out a white blouse and linen skirt. Thong underwear. A lacy bra. A sheer camisole. A cropped T-shirt. A pair of stretchy men's boxers.

People were funny during the early days after the Great Attack. Even when they evacuated their homes, they took their cell phones, laptops, keys, wallets, suitcases, and shoes that would have been great for tropical vacations but not for running on the streets. It was as if people couldn't accept that it wouldn't all blow over in a few days.

Eventually, though, those things ended up abandoned in cars and streets or, in this case, in the drawers of a museum house. I find a T-shirt that's almost as big as Paige. There's no chance of finding a pair of pants for her, so a T-shirt dress will have to do for now.

I tuck her in upstairs and leave her shoes beside the bed in case we need to go in a hurry.

I kiss her forehead and tell her goodnight. Her eyes shut like a doll's, and her breath deepens almost immediately. She must be absolutely exhausted. Who knows the last time she slept? Who knows the last time she ate?

I head downstairs to find Raffe leaning over the dining table with his wings laid out in front of him. He's taken off his mask, and it's a relief to be able to see his face again.

He's grooming his wings. It looks like he has washed the blood out of them. They lie on the table, damp and limp. He plucks out the broken feathers and smooths the healthy ones.

'At least you have them back,' I say.

The light hits his dark hair, showing his highlights.

He takes a big breath. 'We're back to square one.' He sits on a wooden chair, almost wilting into it. 'I need to find a doctor.' He doesn't sound optimistic.

'They had some stuff on Alcatraz. Angelic surgical supplies, I think. They did all kinds of experiments there. Could any of that stuff be useful?'

He looks at me with eyes so blue they're almost black. 'Maybe. I should probably scope out that island anyway. It's too close for us to ignore.' He rubs his temples.

I can see the frustration stiffening the lines of his shoulders. While Archangel Uriel is creating a false apocalypse and lying to the angels to get them to vote him in as their Messenger, Raffe is stuck trying to get his angel wings sewn back on. Until then, he can't return to angel society to try to straighten things out.

'You need some sleep,' I say. 'We all do. I'm so tired my legs just want to give out.' I sway a little. It was a long night, and I'm still surprised we all made it through alive to see the morning.

I half expect him to argue, but he nods. It just confirms that we need the rest that badly, and maybe he needs time to figure out how to find a doctor who can help him.

We trudge upstairs to the two bedrooms.

I turn to Raffe in front of the doors. 'Paige and I will—'

'I'm sure Paige will sleep better alone.'

For a second, I think that maybe he wants to be alone with me. I have a moment of crazy awkwardness mixed with excitement before I see his expression.

Raffe gives me a stern look. So much for my theory.

He just doesn't want me to sleep in the same room as my sister. He doesn't know that I already shared a room with her when we were with the Resistance. She's had plenty of chances to attack me.

'But—'

'You take this room.' Raffe points to the room across the hall. 'I'll take the couch.' His voice is casually commanding. He's obviously used to having everyone obey him.

'There's no real couch. Just an antique settee made for ladies half your size.'

'I've slept on rocks in the snow. A cramped settee is a luxury. I'll be fine.'

'Paige isn't going to hurt me.'

'No, she's won't. You'll be too far away to tempt her while you're asleep and vulnerable.'

I'm too tired to argue. I peek into her room to make sure she's still asleep before walking into my own room across the hall.

The morning sun shines its warmth through the window of my room and onto the bed. There are dried wildflowers on the bedside table, adding a splash of purples and yellows. The scent of rosemary wafts in through the open window.

I take off my shoes and lean Pooky Bear against the bed within easy reach. The teddy bear sits on top of the gauzy dress that covers the sword's scabbard. I've felt a tinge of emotion coming off it ever since we've been back with Raffe. It's both happy to be near him and sad to be forbidden to him. I stroke the soft fur of the bear and give it a little pat.

Normally, I sleep in my clothes in case I need to run. But I'm sick of sleeping that way. It's uncomfortable, and the welcoming room reminds me of what it was like before we were scared all the time.

I decide this will be one of those rare times when I can sleep comfortably. I pad over to the chest of drawers and rummage through the clothes I found earlier.

There's not much of a choice, but I make the best of what's there. I choose the cropped T-shirt and the men's boxers. The T-shirt is loose but fits okay. It comes down to the bottom of my ribs, leaving my midriff bare.

The stretchy boxers cling to me perfectly even though they're for guys. One leg is frayed and unraveling, but they're clean, and the elastic isn't too tight.

I crawl into bed, marveling at the silky luxury of sheets. The second my head lands on the pillow, I begin fading away.

The soft breeze flows in from the windows. Part of me knows that it's sunny outside and warm in the way that October can be sometimes.

But another part of me sees thunderstorms. The sun melts into this rain, and my room with the garden view turns into storm clouds as I drift deeper into sleep.

I'm back where the Fallen are being dragged away to the Pit in chains. The spikes in their necks and foreheads, wrists and ankles drip blood as the hellions ride them.

It's the same dream I had through my sword when I was at the Resistance camp. But a part of me remembers that I'm not sleeping with the blade this time. It's leaning against the bed but not touching me. This doesn't feel like a sword memory.

I'm dreaming about my own experience of being in the sword's memory. A dream about a dream.

In the thunderstorm, Raffe glides down, brushing hands with a few of the newly Fallen as he heads toward the earth below. I see their faces as Raffe touches hands with them. This group of Fallen must be the Watchers – the elite group of angel warriors who fell for loving Daughters of Men.

They were under Raffe's command, his loyal soldiers. They clearly look to him to help save them despite their choice to break angelic law by marrying Daughters of Men.

One face catches my eye. His bound form is familiar.

I strain to see him better, and eventually, I do.

It's Beliel.

He looks fresher than I'm used to, and his usual sneer is gone. There is anger in his face, but behind that, there's genuine pain in his eyes. He grips Raffe's hand for a moment longer than the other Fallen did, almost shaking it.

Raffe nods to him and continues toward the earth.

Lightning flashes, and the sky rumbles as rain drips down Beliel's face.

When I wake up, the sun has moved across the sky.

I don't hear anything unusual, so hopefully, Paige is still asleep. I get up and walk toward the open window. Outside, it's still sunny, with the breeze blowing through the trees. The birds sing and the bees buzz as though the world hasn't completely changed.

Despite the warmth, though, when I look outside, I get chills.

Beliel still lies chained to the garden gate, shriveled and tortured. But his eyes are open, and he stares right at me. I guess he could be completely thawed from his paralysis by now. No wonder I had a nightmare about him.

But it wasn't really a nightmare, was it? It was more like a memory of what the sword showed me. I shake my head slowly, trying to make sense of it all.

Is it possible that Beliel could have been one of Raffe's Watchers?

4

The room is warming from the sun. I guess it's probably around noon. It feels glorious to have a break from all the craziness.

I'm not prepared to give up on my precious sleep yet, but a glass of water sounds good. When I open my door, Raffe is sitting in the hallway with his eyes closed.

I frown. 'What are you doing?'

'I was too tired to walk to the settee,' he says without opening his eyes.

'You're keeping watch? I would have taken my turn if you'd told me. Who are we worried about?'

Raffe snorts.

'I mean, any specific enemy at the moment?'

He's sitting facing Paige's door. I guess I should have known.

'She won't hurt me.'

'That's what Beliel thought.' His eyes are still closed, and his lips barely move. If he wasn't talking, I would have thought he was asleep.

'Beliel is not her big sister, and he didn't raise her either.'

'Call me a sentimentalist, but I like the idea of you in one piece. Besides, she's not the only one who might be interested in your tasty flesh.'

I tilt my head. 'Who told you I was tasty?'

'Haven't you heard that old saying? Tasty as a fool?'

'You made that up.'

'Huh. Must be an angelic saying. It's to warn the foolish about things that go bump in the night.'

'It's daytime.'

'Ah. So you don't deny that you're foolish?' He finally opens his eyes with a grin. But his expression goes slack when he sees all of me.

'What are you wearing?' He scans over my outfit.

I was so comfortable that I'd forgotten I'm wearing the cropped T-shirt and stretchy shorts. I glance down at myself, wondering if I should be self-conscious. I'm reasonably covered except for my midriff, and I guess I'm showing more of my legs than usual.

'This coming from a guy who runs around shirtless all the time?' Of course, I kind of like him shirtless and showing off his six-pack abs, but I don't mention that.

'It's hard to wear a shirt when you've got wings. Besides, I haven't heard complaints.'

'Don't let it get to your head, Raffe. You haven't heard compliments either.' I want to say that we have plenty of guys who look just as good as he does, but that'd be a total lie.

He's still scrutinizing my outfit. 'Are you wearing men's shorts?'

'I guess so. But they fit.'

'Whose are they?'

'Nobody's. I found them in a drawer.'

He reaches over and pulls a thread off the frayed leg. It unravels, slowly winding its way around my thigh and incrementally shortening the already short shorts.

'What would you do if you had to make a run for it?' His voice is husky as he stares, mesmerized, at the unraveling thread.

'I'd grab my shoes and run.'

'Dressed like this? In front of lawless men?' His eyes drift up to my midriff.

'If you're worried about pervs breaking into the house, it's not going to make a difference whether I'm in this outfit or in baggy jeans and a sweatshirt. Either they're decent human beings or they're not. Their actions are on them.'

'It'll be tough for them to take any action while I'm pummeling their faces. Disrespect will not be tolerated.'

I half smile at him. 'Because you're all about respect.'

He sighs as if a little disgusted with himself. 'Lately, I seem to be all about you.'

'What makes you say that?' I wish my voice didn't sound so breathless.

'I'm sitting on the hard floor outside your door while you take a cozy little nap, aren't I?'

I slide down the wall to sit beside him on the hallway floor. We sit with our arms almost touching, letting the quiet settle around us.

After a while, I say, 'I think sleep would do you some good. You can take the bed. I'll keep watch for a bit.'

'Not a chance. It's you who's at risk, not me.'

'What is it that you think is going to get me?' My arm rubs against his when I shift to look at him.

'The list is endless.'

'Since when did you become so protective?'

'Since my enemies have determined that you're my Daughter of Man.'

I swallow. My throat is dry.

'They have?'

'Beliel saw us together at the masquerade. Even with my mask on, Uriel knew it was me on the beach with you.'

'So am I?' I whisper. 'Your Daughter of Man?' I can almost hear my heart pounding. It beats even harder when I realize that he can probably hear it.

He looks away from me. 'Some things just can't be. But neither Uri nor Beliel understand that.'

I let my breath out – slowly, controlled. He might as well have said that I don't understand it either.

'So who exactly would be coming after me?' I ask.

'Aside from the usual suspects, the entire host of angels saw you with me when I cut the wings off Beliel. They think you're traveling in the company of a mask-wearing "demon" who cuts wings off "angels." That's enough to come after you, if only to find me. Besides, you're an angel killer now, for which the penalty is an automatic death sentence. You're quite the popular girl.'

I think about that for a minute. Is there really anything I can do about it? 'But we all look alike to them, right? How can they even tell us apart? They all look the same to me. They're all so darned perfect in every way – perfect Olympian bodies, perfectly beautiful faces, even perfect hair. If it wasn't for you, I'd think that angels were all totally interchangeable.'

'You mean because I'm beyond perfect?'

'No. Because you're so humble.'

'Humility's overrated.'

'So is clear self-assessment, apparently.'

'Real warriors don't stand for psychobabble.'

'Or for rational thinking.'

He glances at my naked legs.

'No, not that rational, I admit.' Raffe stands up and puts out a hand to me. 'Come on. Get some sleep.'

'Only if you do too.' I grab his hand, and he pulls me up.

'Fine. If that will quiet you down.'

We walk into my room, and I crawl onto the bed. I lie down on top of the covers, thinking he's making sure that I get some sleep. But instead of leaving, he climbs onto the bed beside me.

'What are you doing?' I ask.

He lies his cheek on the pillow next to mine and closes his eyes with some relief. 'Taking a nap.'

'You're not going downstairs?'

'Nope.'

'What about the settee?'

'Too uncomfortable.'

'I thought you said you've slept on rocks in the snow.'

'I have. That's why I sleep on soft beds whenever I can.'

I expect him to lie there full of tension like me, but his breathing quickly turns deep and slow.

He must be exhausted. Even aside from his lack of sleep and being constantly on red alert, he's still recovering from his wing injuries, both the initial amputation and the surgery. I can't imagine what he's going through.

I lie there, trying to sleep beside him.

The scent of rosemary wafts in through the window along with the warm breeze. The buzzing of the bees near the plants below sounds distant and soothing. The buttery sunshine glows through my closed eyelids.

I turn away from the bright window and end up

facing Raffe. I can't help but open my eyes to look at him. His dark lashes lie in a crescent against his cheek. Long and curved, they would be the envy of every girl. The line of his nose is strong and straight. His lips soft and sensual.

Sensual? I almost giggle. What kind of word is that to pop into my head? I'm not sure I've ever thought of anything as being *sensual* before.

His muscular chest rises and falls in a steady rhythm that's mesmerizing. My hand twitches, wanting to stroke his smooth muscles.

I swallow and flip over to my other side.

With him at my back, I take a deep breath and let it out slowly, like I'm trying to calm myself in a fight.

He moans softly and shifts. My movements must have disturbed him.

I feel his warm breath on the back of my neck. He must have turned onto his side, facing me. He's so close I can feel the electric tingle of almost touching along my spine.

So close.

His breathing maintains a deep, steady rhythm. He's totally asleep while I'm hyperaware of him lying beside me in bed. What's up with that? Isn't it supposed to be the other way around?

I try to shove this whole confusing mess of emotions

into the vault in my head. But either the vault is full or this bundle of emotions is too big or too stubborn or too thorny to shove into the vault.

In the meantime, my body slowly arches back until we touch.

The second my thigh touches his, he moans and shifts, throwing his arm around me. He pulls me back toward his hard body.

What do I do?

The entire length of my back is now pressed against his chest.

What do I do?

Hard. Warm. Muscular.

Perspiration prickles my forehead. When did it get so hot in here?

The weight of his arm presses my body against him and pins me down onto the bed. I have a moment of panic where I think about jumping out of bed.

But that would wake him. A flood of embarrassment hits me at the thought of him seeing me all hot and bothered while he's been sleeping.

I try to calm down. He's holding me like a teddy bear while he sleeps peacefully. He's probably so exhausted that he's oblivious to me.

His hand is hot on my ribs. I'm exquisitely aware that his thumb lies along the bottom of my breast.

A thought slips into my head. I can't seem to get rid of it no matter how hard I try to shove it aside.

What would it be like to have Raffe's hand on that part of my body?

I'm seventeen years old, going on eighteen, and I've never had a guy caress my breast. The way things are going, I probably never will, at least, not in a good, loving kind of way. In an apocalyptic world, violence is guaranteed and good experiences are just a dream. That makes me want to feel it in a good way all the more. Something gentle and sweet that should have happened in due time with the right guy if the world hadn't gone to hell.

While my head rages in argument and confusion, my hand covers his. Gently, oh, so gently. What would it be like to have Raffe's hand caress my nipple?

Really?

Am I really thinking this?

But thinking is not the right word for what's going on inside me. It's more of an . . . urge. An irresistible, undeniable, pounding, trembling, panting urge.

I slowly inch his hand up so that his thumb presses against the soft flesh of my breast.

Then I nudge it up just another fraction.

Raffe's breathing is still steady. He's still asleep.

A little more. Just a fraction . . .

Until I can feel the warmth of his hand spreading over my chest.

And then everything changes.

His breathing becomes ragged. His hand pushes up and begins kneading my flesh. Demanding. On the verge of hurting, but not quite. Not quite. An incredible sensation runs through me, starting from my breast and flooding out from there.

I'm panting before I know it.

He moans and kisses the nape of my neck. He works his way up to my mouth. His lips land on mine, hot and wet and sucking. His tongue sweeps in, teasing mine.

My whole world is a mass of sensations – the soft sucking of his lips, the warm slipperiness of his tongue, the hard pressure of his body against mine.

He flips me onto my back and moves over me. The weight of his body presses me down against the mattress. My arms slip around his neck, and my legs and hips shift restlessly.

I'm whimpering or moaning or mewling, I'm not sure which. I'm so deeply lost in the vortex of sensations that the only thing that matters is the here and now.

Raffe.

My hands run over the muscles of his chest, his shoulders, his bulging arms.

Then he pulls away, leaving me gasping.

I groggily open my eyes, feeling drugged, reaching out for him.

He looks at me with intense eyes. Distressed but swirling with want.

He pushes back away from me.

He turns to sit with his back to me. 'Christ.' He rakes his hair with both hands. 'What just happened?'

I open my mouth to answer, but the only thing that comes out is 'Raffe.' I can't tell if it's a question or a plea.

He sits with his back ramrod straight, his muscles stiff, his wings folded tightly along his back. I touch his shoulder, and he starts as though I shocked him with electricity.

Without another word, he gets up and walks briskly out of the room.

6

I hear Raffe's footsteps clomp down the wooden stairs. The front door opens and slams shut. Then I see a snowy wing tip sweep the air outside my window as he takes off.

I shut my eyes in utter humiliation.

How can the world end in a giant fury of biblical proportions yet still leave room for embarrassment?

I lie there for what seems like forever, wishing I could blot out what happened. But I can't. Massive confusion swirls through me. I get it. He's not supposed to . . . Daughter of Man . . . blah, blah, blah.

Can't anything be simple? I sigh and stare at the white ceiling.

I might have stayed there all day if I hadn't glanced through the door that Raffe left open on his way out.

Across the hallway, Paige's door is open and her bed is empty.

I sit up. 'Paige?'

No answer. I grab my tennis shoes, slipping them on while walking down the hallway.

'Paige?'

I don't hear anything. She's not in the kitchen, dining room, or living room. I look out the living room window.

There she is. Her little body is curled up on the ground beside Beliel, who is still chained to the picket fence.

I run outside. 'Paige? Are you all right?'

She lifts her head, blinking sleepily at me. My heart slows down, and I exhale, letting out the tension.

'What are you doing out here?' I'm careful to walk beyond Beliel's reach. Paige lies just out of his reach too. She may be strangely attached to him, but she's not stupid.

Beliel the demon lies still. He's raw and red where the chunks were taken out, although he's not bleeding anymore. I'm pretty sure he's come out of his paralysis, but he hasn't moved since we were at the aerie.

His skin is pruned. His breathing is raspy, as if his lungs are bleeding. He's not healing as quickly as I expected him to. But his eyes follow us, alert and hostile.

I put my arm under my sister's shoulders and lift her up in my arms. Until recently, she had been getting too big for me to do that, but the Great Attack changed all that. Now she's no heavier than a stuffed doll.

She squirms, looking around. She's making sleepy toddler noises, making it clear she doesn't want to be taken away. She reaches out toward Beliel, who just sneers. He doesn't seem bothered or confused by her inconsistent attitude toward him.

'Your voice sounds familiar,' says Beliel. He hasn't moved, hasn't blinked. He's like a dead body that can move its eyes and lips. 'Where have I seen you?'

I'm a little creeped out that he's thinking the same thing I thought when I first saw him in chains.

I walk away from him with Paige in my arms.

'Your angel doesn't have much time left to get his wings back,' says Beliel.

'How do you know? You're not a doctor.'

'Raphael ripped a wing almost completely off my back once. I had to have that puny human doctor sew it back on. He warned me that I wouldn't have much time if they came off again.'

'What puny doctor? Doc?'

'I ignored him. But now that I think of it, the little puke was probably right. Raphael has done nothing but make us both wingless.'

'He's not wingless.'

'He will be.' He gives a grim smile, exposing his bloody teeth.

I keep walking onto the porch. I'm almost at the door when he speaks again.

'You're in love with him, aren't you?' he rasps. 'You think you're so special. Special enough to catch an archangel's love.' He makes a dry, rattling noise that I think must be a laugh. 'Do you know how many people have thought they could win his love over the centuries? That he'd be loyal to them just as they were loyal to him?'

I know I should ignore him. Nothing he says can be trusted – I know that – but curiosity burns through me anyway. I put my sister down at the open doorway.

'Go back to your bed, Paige.' After a little coaxing, she walks into the house.

I turn and lean on the porch railing. 'What do you know about him?'

'You want to know how many Daughters of Men he's gone through? How many hearts do you think have shattered over Raphael, the great archangel?'

'You're telling me he's a heartbreaker?'

'I'm telling you he's heart*less*.'

'You're going to tell me that he did you wrong? That you don't deserve to be chained up like a rabid animal?'

'He's not a good guy, your angel. None of them are.'

'Thanks for the warning.' I turn to go back into the house.

'You don't believe me. I can show you.' He says these words quietly like it doesn't matter to him whether I believe him or not.

I pause at the doorstep.

'I'm not a big fan of creepy guys offering to show me anything.'

'That sword you carry around hidden under the stuffed animal,' he says, 'it can do more than just look shiny. It can show you things.'

I get goose bumps. How does he know?

'I can show you what I experienced at the hands of that archangel you're so enamored with. We just both need to be touching the sword.'

I turn back toward him. 'I'm not stupid enough to give you my sword.'

'You don't need to give it to me. You can hold it while I just touch it.'

I look at him to see if there are any tricks. 'Why should I risk losing my sword just to see if you're telling the truth?'

'There is no risk. The sword will not allow me to lift it or to take it from you.' He's talking to me like I'm an idiot. 'It'll be perfectly safe for you.'

I envision myself being in a memory trance within easy reach of Beliel. 'Thanks, but no.'

'Afraid?'

'Not stupid.'

'You can tie my hands, chain me, bag me, put me in a cage. Do whatever you like to ensure your safety from an old demon who can't even get up on his own anymore. Once you do that, you know the sword won't allow me to take it, so you'll be perfectly safe.'

I stare at him, trying to see through his game.

'Are you really afraid of me harming you?' he asks. 'Or maybe you just don't want to know the truth about your precious archangel? He's not what he seems. He's a liar and a betrayer, and I can prove it. The sword won't let me lie – it doesn't pass on pretty words. Just memories.'

I hesitate. I should be turning around to leave, and he knows it. I should be ignoring everything he says.

But instead, I stand rooted to the porch. 'You have your own agenda that has nothing to do with showing me the truth.'

'Of course I do. Maybe you'll let me go after you realize that he's really the bad guy, not me.'

'You're the good guy now?'

Beliel's voice turns cold. 'Do you want to see it or not?'

I stand in the sunshine, looking at the beautiful view of the bay and the green hills beyond it. The sky is blue with only a few puffy clouds.

I should explore more of the island to see if there's something here we could use. I should be coming up with a plan to get my sister better. I should be making myself useful instead of flirting with disaster.

But my dream keeps coming back to me. Could Beliel have been one of Raffe's Watchers?

'Were you . . . did you used to work with Raffe?'

'You could say that. He used to be my commanding officer. There was a time when I would have done anything for him. Anything. That was before he betrayed me. Just like he's going to do to you. It's in his nature.'

'I know you lied to my sister just for sport. I'm not a lonely, scared seven-year-old, so drop the evil manipulation act.'

'Suit yourself, little Daughter of Man. You wouldn't have believed what you saw anyway. You're too loyal to the archangel to believe that he was the source of so much misery.'

I turn around and walk into the house. I check to see that Paige is sleeping in her room. I check the cupboards in the kitchen to take stock of the few cans of soup left by the men who were camped here before us.

While wandering around, the desire to see what Beliel is offering nags at me. Maybe he'll show me something that brings me to my senses about Raffe. Maybe I'll snap out of it and move on with my life – my life with other human beings, where I belong.

I can't even think about what happened earlier with Raffe without my face flaming in embarrassment. How am I supposed to look at him when he comes back?

If he comes back.

The thought twists my gut into a knot.

I kick a decorative pillow on the floor, getting no satisfaction out of seeing it bounce off the wall.

Okay. Enough.

It's just peeking into Beliel's memory. Obi's men are risking their lives every day, trying to spy on the angels for tiny scraps of intel. And here I am with the best spying device in the world, plus an offer to go into an enemy's memories. I'll have my sword with me the whole time, and it's true that he won't be able to use it against me.

I'll just get it out of my system and move on. I'll be extra careful.

Regardless of what Beliel has to show me, Paige and I will leave the island afterward, and we'll go back to the Resistance. We'll find Mom and see if we can find Doc. Maybe he can help Paige eat normal food again.

And then, after that, we'll . . . survive.

Alone.

I go upstairs to grab Pooky Bear, then walk outside to Beliel. He's lying near the fence post, curled in the exact same position he was in when I left. I can see in his eyes that he was expecting me to come back.

'So what do I do?'

'I need to be touching your sword.'

I lift my sword, pointing it at him. It shines in the sunlight. I have the urge to ask it if it wants to do this. But I don't want to sound stupid in front of Beliel.

'Come closer.' He holds out his hand to grab it.

I hesitate. 'Do you need to hold it, or can you just touch it?'

'Touch it.'

'Okay. Turn around.'

He turns on the dirt without protest. His back is roped with strings of dried muscle. I don't want to touch him with a ten-foot sword. But I press the tip of my blade into his back anyway.

'One wrong move and I'll stick you right through.' I'm not sure if the connection is enough with only the tip touching his back, but he doesn't seem concerned about it.

He takes a deep breath and lets it out slowly.

I feel something opening in my head.

It's not like the other times when I suddenly found myself somewhere else. This one is weaker, lighter, as if I could choose not to go there if I wanted, as if the sword isn't so sure about this particular voyage.

I take a deep breath too. I make sure my feet are in proper fighting position and brace myself for an attack.

And then I close my eyes.

7

I feel a moment of dizziness, then I land on firm ground.

The first thing that hits me is the overwhelming heat. Then the stench of rotten eggs.

Under a black-purple sky, a chariot is drawn by six angels harnessed like horses. Blood and sweat stream down their shoulders and chests where the harness cuts into them. They strain to drag the chariot and the giant demon who drives it.

The demon has wings of course. He could just fly to his destination if he wanted. Instead, he rolls slowly through his domain.

The demon is so big he makes Beliel look like a child. His wings flame with what looks like real fire reflecting off his sweaty skin.

He carries a stick with a circle of shriveled heads at the top. On the heads, the eyes blink and the mouths try to scream. Or maybe they're drowning and gasping for air. I'm not sure, because no sound comes out. Each has long blond hair that flows up and around the heads like seaweed waving in a current.

Once I get past the horror of the heads, I realize that the eyes are all the same shade of green. How many heads would you have to choose from to be able to collect a group with the exact same shade of eyes and hair?

The ground is covered in broken glass and shards of bone. Each wheel is draped with two angels as if the monster demon didn't want his shiny wheels marred by the rough ground. The Fallen angels are chained to the wheels and are stuck through with all kinds of shards sticking out of their skin.

Beliel is one of these Fallen chained to a wheel.

His wings are the color of a dying sunset. They must be his original angel wings. They're half stretched out like he hopes to be able to keep them from being crushed. But many of the feathers are already scorched and broken.

I hadn't thought about how demons become the way they are. Maybe there's a transition time between being an angel and becoming a demon. Since Beliel still has feathers, I'm guessing this probably means that it hasn't been long since his fall.

His face is recognizable, although somehow smoother, more innocent. His eyes lack that stinging, harsh quality that I've come to know. He looks almost handsome without his usual smirk and bitterness, though there's pain.

A lot of pain.

But he bears it without a whimper.

The wheel rolls, crushing his body against the bone shards covering the ground, making him endure the weight of both the vehicle and the monster riding on it. His face is focused and determined, looking like he's clenching his jaw to keep from screaming.

His wings tremble with the effort to hover above the ground. That protects them from the worst of the damage, but they still drag along the field of sharp bone and glass.

As the wheels roll, the angels who are chained to them are getting their wings slowly crushed and splintered. They still carry their empty scabbards, which clank and drag against the rough ground, reminders of what they've lost.

The giant demon cracks his stick above his head, and it unspools, whipping through the air. The shrunken heads begin shrieking as soon as they're let loose. They shoot toward the harnessed angels with hair streaking through the air in front of them like snaky spears.

When they hit the angels pulling the chariot, the sharp hair begins to shred their skin.

The heads open their mouths wide and frantically gnaw on the Fallen. One of them manages to burrow halfway into the back of an angel before the whip gets pulled back.

These Fallen angels look starved and are covered in festering wounds. I suspect even angels need their nourishment to fuel their speed healing.

Then, in the middle of all this, a pack of hellions with their bat faces and shadowy wings slink toward them. They're bigger than the ones I saw in my sword's memories. Beefier and with spotted wings, as if they had disease blooming on them.

These hellions have a crafty gleam in their eyes that make them look more dangerous than the ones I've seen before. They look around, aware, moving with purpose. The modern hellions seem to have devolved into smaller, weaker, dimmer versions of these.

Still, these hellions are nothing compared with the demon lord. They're shadow creatures against the towering thing riding the chariot, and they're clearly afraid of him.

Maybe they're not the same species. They don't look anything like him. The hellions look like toothy bat-winged animals with squashed faces while the giant looks like an angel gone ugly.

The hellions are dragging someone behind them. She was probably once pretty, with mahogany hair and gray eyes, but now she looks like a used-up doll. Her eyes are empty, her face blank, like she's sent her inner self away somewhere.

They pull her along the rough ground by her ankles. Her arms drag behind her head, and her tangled hair gets snagged on the spiky bones that tug at her. Her dress is torn into rags, and every bit of her is filthy and bloody. I want to help her up, to kick the hellions off her, but I am just a shadow here in Beliel's memory.

I see faint smudges of the Halloween paint that the Watchers' wives had on that night when I saw Raffe fighting for them. I don't recognize this girl, but she must be one of the wives that the hellions were given. Raffe managed to save some but not all. I was there to see how much he tried. Maybe she was one of the ones who ran in panic.

The hellions drag the poor girl around all of the chariot wheels, staying far away from the demon while still being close enough to see the angels. They tremble when they have to come near the demon and keep looking up at him, as though afraid that he'll strike out.

The demon hisses at them, and the air suddenly becomes more foul. Did he just breathe a whole lot of stinky sulfur toward the hellions the way a skunk might aim its scent? No wonder the air smells like rotten eggs here.

Half of the hellions run off in terror. But the other half stays, curling up and trembling until the demon loses interest.

They carefully resume their walk around the chariot. They're looking at the expressions of each angel as they pass.

The Fallen tense up when they see the girl, staring with fascinated horror. They all look carefully at the girl as if they're trying to see if they recognize her. Many shut their eyes when they see her, like their thoughts torture them even more than what's actually happening to them.

When the hellions finally catch Beliel's attention, his eyes grow wide in horror.

'Mira,' he rasps.

The woman blinks when she hears her name. Her eyes seem to focus. She turns her head. 'Beliel?' Her voice is vague, sounding like her inner self is still far away. But when she sees him, her face morphs from a blank mask to recognition. Then it turns to pure anguish.

She reaches out for him. 'Beliel!'

'Mira!' he screams, terror in his voice.

The hellions sense it, and they hop with excitement. They chatter, nearly clapping their hands together in delight like little children.

Then they bare their sharp teeth threateningly, showing Beliel that they're about to harm Mira in ways he can't imagine.

'No!' Beliel thrashes against his chains, screaming threats against the hellions. 'Mira!'

Then the hellions dive on the girl.

Beliel's scream is horrifying. Mira finally breaks and screams too, her cries becoming wet and gurgling.

Beliel begins calling out in a broken, defeated voice, 'Raphael! Where are you? You were supposed to protect her, you worthless traitor!'

I finally peek to see if I can get out of here. I can't take this anymore.

The hellions have dragged the girl farther up to keep pace with the chariot to make sure that Beliel continues to see what they're doing to his woman.

Beliel thrashes against his chains. He's so frantic I think he might actually have a shot at breaking free. These are not the screams of an angry man. These are the nightmare screams of someone having his soul torn to pieces right in front of him.

Beliel breaks down and sobs. He sobs for his Daughter of Man. For the girl who even now looks to him to rescue and protect her. Maybe even for their children, who are likely being hunted and killed by someone he thought was his friend. A friend like Raffe.

8

I'm so preoccupied with watching the plight of the two lovers that I haven't been paying attention to anything else. But now, the back of my neck prickles. My sixth sense is urgently whispering to me, trying to get through all the noise of what's happening in front of me.

I look around. And that's when I see that the demon lord riding the chariot is staring right at me.

How can he see me? I'm just a ghost in Beliel's memory.

But he stares right at me. His eyes are bloodshot, looking like he lives in a world of perpetual smoke. His face is curious and angry at the same time, as if he's offended by an intruder watching him.

'Spy,' he hisses. 'You don't belong here.' His words sound like a hundred slithering snakes, but I can still understand him.

As soon as the demon says the word *spy*, the hellions all look at me. Their eyes widen as though they can't believe their luck. It doesn't take me long to figure out that I'm not invisible anymore.

The demon takes a good look at me with his blood-shot eyes. Then he whips his stick in my direction. The heads – the screaming, drowning, bloody heads – shoot out toward me at the end of his unspooling whip.

Their expressions are a mix of despair and hope. They're desperately delighted to be heading my way, with their fractured teeth showing in their gaping mouths. Their hair, which should be flying back, reaches toward me.

At the same time, the hellions leap at me, all claws and fangs.

I stumble backward.

I try to turn and run, but the uneven ground trips me, and I'm falling onto the sharp glass and shards of bone.

The heads scream as they race toward my face.

I'm falling.

Falling.

* * *

I stumble backward and fall onto my butt.

I'm back on the island. Beliel, wingless and shriveled again, lies on the ground in front of me.

Then a hellion jumps out of Beliel's back. It leaps at me with extended claws.

I scream, crab-crawling backward.

It swipes my shoulder as it flies past me. Blood flows down my arm.

The tip of my sword is still buried in Beliel's back. I try to pull it out. There's resistance, like someone is pulling on the other side. Revulsion reverberates through my arm as though the blade is an extension of me.

Two more hellions shove through along my sword like conjoined twins. They pop out of Beliel's back, which is bleeding from the slit where the hellions came out.

They're leaping out of his memories.

I finally yank out my sword and scooch back as fast as I can away from Beliel.

The hellions land in the garden with a thump. They roll and land on their feet, shaking their heads and moving drunkenly as they look around the small yard. They squint against the sunlight and lift their hands to shield their eyes. That gives me a second to get on my feet and catch my breath.

But then they jump. It's all I can do to lift my sword and swipe blindly in front of me.

I'm in luck because they seem disoriented, and one even trips over its own feet. They change course and stay out of range of my blade.

But their disorientation doesn't last long. They circle me until they get their bearings, gauging my moves with crafty eyes. These hellions are smarter than others I've fought in my sword dreams.

One feints while the other tries to get behind me. Where's the third?

The missing hellion leaps out of a bush and comes at me from the side.

I spin, bringing my sword up to slice the beast. My arms adjust as I move – my angel sword wielding me instead of the other way around. The blade adjusts into a perfect position to cut through the hellion's torso. It lands on the grass, shuddering and bleeding out.

I finish my spin and kick the one trying to get behind me.

It lands on the far side of the fence. It pushes itself up and hisses at me.

The two surviving hellions back off, keeping their eyes on me.

Then they run off and take flight, disappearing into the trees.

Beliel chuckles. 'Welcome to my world, Daughter of Man.'

'I should have known you were going to trick me,' I pant as I put pressure on my shoulder to stop the bleeding. The blood feels slick on my fingers as it soaks through my shirt.

Beliel sits up, chains clinking. He's a lot more mobile than I thought. 'Just because hellions came after you doesn't mean what you saw wasn't the truth. How was I supposed to know they could get through?' He doesn't sound at all surprised.

'What happened to Mira,' he says, 'that'll be you someday soon. And your precious Raphael will be responsible for it. I once thought of him as my friend too. He promised he'd protect Mira. Now you know what becomes of people who trust him.'

I get up shakily and head for the house. I don't think I can trust myself to be in the same space with that horrible creature for much longer.

I could kick myself for listening to him in the first place, but I guess I don't have to. He already did it for me.

9

I'm washing the blood off my shoulder in the kitchen when Raffe comes back.

'What happened?' he asks, dropping a plastic garbage bag on the floor and rushing to me.

'Nothing. I'm fine.' My voice is stiff and standoffish. I think about covering up the wound, but my shirt is torn, so I can't. The old cropped T-shirt is hanging off my wounded shoulder by a thread. No doubt it would be sexy if it weren't for all that blood.

He brushes my hand aside and leans into me to look at the gashes on my shoulder.

'Are these from the dead hellion in the yard?' He's close enough that his breath caresses my neck. I step away, feeling awkward.

'Yeah. And his two friends.'

He clenches his jaw so hard I can see his cheek muscles twitching.

'Don't worry,' I say. 'Being around you had nothing to do with it.'

He cocks his head at me. 'What makes you think I was worried it had to do with me?'

Oops. Did he ever mention hellions to me? Or do I know he worries about them coming after me because I peeked into his memories through Pooky Bear?

I could lie, but . . . I sigh. We all have to accept our faults eventually. And mine is that I'm a terrible liar.

'I – um . . . saw things through your sword. Not intentionally. Not at first.'

'Things?' He crosses his arms and glares at me. 'What kind of things?'

I chew my lip as I think about what to say.

He then looks at his old sword lying on the counter. The shine on Pooky's blade seems to dim a bit under his glare.

'My sword showed you her memories of me?'

My shoulders relax a little. 'So you know that she can do that?'

'I know that she used to be loyal to me and that I trusted her.' He's talking to Pooky Bear, not me.

'I think it was an accident. She was just trying to

teach me how to use a sword. I mean, I had never held one before.'

Raffe continues to talk to his sword. 'It's one thing to be forced to give up on a bearer because you think he may have fallen. It's another to expose his private moments.'

'Look,' I say. 'It's weird enough having a semisentient sword without being in the middle of an argument between you two. Can you please just let it go?'

'What did she show you?' He holds up his hand. 'Wait. Don't tell me. I don't want to know that you've seen me dancing in my underwear to my favorite music.'

'Angels wear underwear?' Oh, man, I wish I hadn't said that. I'm just digging myself in deeper and deeper today.

'No.' He shakes his head. 'Figure of speech.'

'Oh.' I nod, trying to get the image out of my head of Raffe dancing to some rock song, possibly buck naked. 'Well, speaking of weird things, the hellions came through the sword.'

'What?'

I clear my throat. 'That hellion you saw on the lawn and two others crawled out of Beliel through the sword.' I still have hope that I won't have to confess it all, but he must have gone through angel interrogation school because he gets it all out of me.

He frowns and paces around the kitchen as I tell him what happened.

When I finish, he says, 'You can never trust Beliel.'

'That's what he says about you.'

He rummages through the trash bag he dropped earlier. 'Maybe he's right. You shouldn't trust anyone.'

He shoves a mix of canned food and first aid supplies out of the bag. He plucks bandages, ointments, and tape and walks over to me.

'Where did you get those?'

'Alcatraz. Thought they might be useful.'

'What else did you find there?'

'An abandoned mess.' He probes his finger gently along my wound. I flinch. 'I just want to make sure there's nothing broken,' he says.

'Did you know that could happen? That hellions could come out through an angel sword?'

'I've heard stories but always thought they were myths. I suppose a demon might have some insight into such things. Beliel must have figured he could try to lure some hellions out to help him.'

His hand is gentle as he wipes antibacterial lotion on the cuts. 'You need to be careful. The hellions are going to be everywhere you are from now on.'

'What do you care? You'll be out of my life the second you get your wings back. You've made that pretty clear.'

He takes a deep breath. He presses a gauze pad on my shoulder. I wince. He gently strokes my arm.

'I wish it could be different,' he says, taping up the gauze. 'But it's not. I have my own people. I have responsibilities. I can't just—'

'Stop.' I shake my head. 'I get it. You're right. You have your life. I have mine. I don't need to be with someone who doesn't . . .' Want me. Love me.

I have enough of those people in my life. I'm a girl whose dad left, leaving us with an out-of-service phone number and no forwarding address, and whose mom . . .

'You're a very special girl, Penryn. An amazing girl. An I-didn't-even-know-someone-like-you-existed kind of girl. And you deserve someone who treats you like you're the only important thing in his life because you are. Someone who plows his fields and raises pigs just for you.'

'You're matching me up with a pig farmer?'

He shrugs. 'Or whatever it is that decent men do when they're not at war. Although he should be able to protect you. Don't settle for a man who can't protect you.' He rips a piece of tape from the dispenser with a surprising amount of force.

'You're serious? You want me to marry a pig farmer who knows how to use his pig poke to protect me? Really?'

'I'm just saying you should pick a man who knows that he's not worthy of you and who will dedicate his life to provide for you and protect you.' He presses another piece of gauze next to the first one. I wince again. 'And make sure he's kind to you and treats you with respect in every way. Otherwise, he can expect a visit from me.' His voice is hard and unmerciful.

I shake my head as he rips off another piece of tape. I don't know whether to be mad at him or to joke with him.

I move away from his touch, hoping that might take the edge off my confused emotions.

Raffe sighs. He reaches out and runs his fingers gently along the last piece of tape that he put on my bandage.

I wait for him to continue. When he doesn't, I wonder if talking about what's happening between us makes any difference at all. Maybe what I really need is a little space to figure things out. I grab the sword and a can of tuna and head out the back door.

10

Outside, I stand in the sun and let the warmth soak into my bones. I take a deep breath full of the scent of rosemary and slowly let it out.

My dad used to say there's magic in the warmth of sunlight. He used to tell us that if we close our eyes, take a big breath, and let the sun soak in, we'll see that everything is going to be okay. He usually said that right after Mom had a day-long freak-out session of yelling and throwing things around the condo.

Hell, if Dad's technique can work for one of Mom's marathon fury sessions, then it should work for the apocalypse. Guys, though, that's another matter. I'm pretty sure that Dad wouldn't have a technique that could handle what's going on with Raffe.

There are tiny yellow flowers dotting the hillside of the island, reminding me of the park that we used to go to with my dad before he left us. The only thing out of place is the small group of monstrous scorpion-tailed beasts and the little stitched-up girl with bruises all over her body.

Among the tall grasses, my sister puts a bandage on a monster's finger as if it were her pet instead of a biblical locust designed to torture people in true apocalyptic style.

Beneath her oversized T-shirt, I know that Paige's ribs stick out in clear lines. It hurt to see them this morning when I put her to bed. She has circles around her eyes, and her hands are nothing but bones as she plays nurse to the monster.

She sits in the grass beside her pets. I've noticed she sits every chance she gets. I think she's conserving energy. I think she's starving to death.

I have to force myself to walk toward them. No matter how much time I spend with the locusts, I can't get comfortable around them. As I near, the locusts fly away, much to my relief.

I sit beside her on the grass and show her the can of tuna. 'Remember the tuna sandwiches Dad used to make for us? They were your favorite before you became a vegetarian.' I pull open the pop-top can and show her the pink fish inside.

Paige leans away from the can.

'Remember how Dad used to plop the tuna onto the bread and make a smiley face with it? That used to make your day.'

'Daddy come home?'

She's asking when he'll be coming back. The answer is never. 'We don't need him.'

Wouldn't it be great if that were true? I'm not sure I'd come back if I were him. I wonder if he thinks of us.

She looks at me with doe eyes. 'Miss him.'

I try to think of something soothing to say, but I just don't have it in me. 'Me too.'

I pick out a piece of tuna with my fingers and put it up to her mouth. 'Here. Try a piece.'

She shakes her head sadly back and forth.

'Come on, Paige.'

She looks down at the ground like she's ashamed. The hollows in her cheeks and between her collarbones scare me.

I put the tuna in my mouth and slowly chew. 'It's good.'

She peeks at me from beneath her hair.

'Are you hungry?' I ask.

She nods. For a second, her eyes dip down to the bandage on my shoulder. It's spotting with blood.

She looks away as if ashamed and gazes up at the

locusts circling above us. But her eyes keep drifting back to my bandage, and her nostrils flare like she smells something good.

Maybe it's time for me to go.

I'm putting the can down when I hear an animal calling. It sounds like a hyena. I'm not sure I've ever heard a hyena, but my bones recognize the sound of a predator in the wild. My hackles rise on the back of my neck.

A shadow jumps between the trees to my left.

Another shadow leaps between branches, then several more.

And as the next one jumps closer to the nearest tree, I see the shape of teeth and wings.

Hellions.

A lot of them.

The trees around us begin to boil with shadows leaping from tree to tree, getting closer. The mad hyena laugh keeps up its steady call as the mob of shadows leaps toward us.

Paige's locusts fly toward the hellions. But there are too many of them.

I grab Paige's hand, and we run toward the main house. The skin along my spine prickles, trying to sense how close unseen claws are to sinking into me.

I yell toward the house. 'Hellions!'

Raffe looks out the dining room window.

'How many?' he calls out as we run to the house.

I point to the shadows hopping closer to us from the woods. Raffe disappears from the window.

A second later, he bursts out the front door and thumps down the porch, carrying a backpack with a blanket bundle strapped to it.

As he runs by the picket fence, we both look at Beliel's broken chain hanging off the post. Beliel is nowhere in sight.

I assume the hellions freed him. They may not like each other, but they're still on the same team. Isn't that why Beliel invited me to look into his past, so he could lure the hellions to help him?

Raffe tosses the backpack to me. I assume the bundle attached to it is his wings.

I slip on the backpack while a couple of Paige's locusts land beside her. They hiss at the shadows gathering around them.

I take a step back. I still can't bring myself to get too close to those scorpion stingers. 'We gotta go, Paige. Can you get them to fly us?'

My heart races at the thought of being held by one of these monsters, but I'm more comfortable with that idea right now than being in Raffe's arms. He's made it pretty clear how he feels about me – about us – and the fact that there is no us.

Raffe throws me a dirty look. He bends over and swipes his arm behind my knees, lifting me up in his embrace.

'I can go with one of the locusts.' I stiffen in his arms and try to lean as far away from him as I can.

'The hell you will.' He runs a couple of steps before spreading his wings.

With two sweeps of his wide wings, we're up in the air.

My arms wrap around his neck. I have no choice but to lean close and hold tight. This isn't the time to argue.

The locusts are just behind us with my sister.

Shadows leap toward us through the trees. Angel Island must be some kind of hellion convention center. Either that or these new hellions are far too good at organizing.

Raffe leads the way toward San Francisco. Behind us, a cloud of hellions bursts out of the trees after us.

11

As usual, there's a swarm of locusts funneling over Alcatraz. My hair whips my face from the wind generated by their wings. As we near, a stream of locusts heads our way.

They join our little group until we swell into a swarm of our own. The creatures aren't nuzzling us, but they're not attacking either. They seem to be joining us on our flight by sheer instinct.

The hellion cloud behind us pauses. It's nowhere near the size of the locust swarm. It hovers in place for a few seconds as if assessing the situation, then the cloud turns around and shrinks into the distance.

I take a deep breath and let the tension out. We're safe for the moment.

Raffe watches them go with a frown, deep in thought. I look back at the hellions retreating and realize what the problem is. The hellions aren't behaving as stupidly as they should.

I have a nagging worry about what just happened. What did I release into the world?

The funnel over Alcatraz becomes thinner as more of the locust swarm peels off and heads toward us.

This new group flows in a spike formation led by a locust with an extra large scorpion tail curled over his head. Something about that makes me nervous. They're just following my sister out of instinct, aren't they?

I dismiss the uneasiness as a reasonable reaction to the sight of a large locust swarm coming in our direction.

But a second later, the leader proves my worries right. He's close enough now for me to see the white streak in his long hair. I turn cold when I recognize him.

He's the one who toyed with me by shoving me against the rollup gate of the shipping container filled with desperate people who had been starved for sport. This is the one Beliel said they bred and trained to be part of the locust leader group.

He's bigger than the others, and I remember Beliel saying the leader group got better nutrition. Why is he here? Can Paige order the locusts to turn on him? This one is too twisted and dangerous to live. I don't want him anywhere near us.

When he reaches us, he grabs the arm of the locust Paige was tending to earlier, jerking him to a stop in midair. White Streak looks almost twice the size of Paige's locust.

White Streak rips off a wing and tosses the screeching locust toward the water.

Paige screams. She stares wide-eyed as her pet help-lessly beats the one wing he has left as he falls like a rock toward the water.

He makes a tiny splash in the dark bay. The water swallows him up as though he never existed.

White Streak roars at Paige's other locusts, jabbing his oversized stinger menacingly into the air.

Paige's small band of locusts buzzes in circles, looking confused. They look to White Streak and steal glances at Paige, who is crying over her murdered pet.

White Streak roars again.

All but four of Paige's locusts flutter reluctantly into the insect swarm behind White Streak.

White Streak's locusts tighten their circle around us. The roar of their wings is deafening, and our hair blows everywhere. White Streak swings back and forth, staring down Paige.

She looks like a little stitched-up doll in a monster's arms with an even bigger monster stalking her.

Raffe must feel my tension, because he flies in White Streak's path toward Paige. Raffe's demon wings claw the air around us with every stroke. He pauses in front of White Streak, letting his crescent-shaped wing blades flash in the sun.

White Streak widens his eyes like a crazed man. I wonder what he was in the World Before? A serial killer?

He puffs up at the sight of Raffe, assessing him. He glances at me, probably wondering whether Raffe will drop me to fight him.

He roars at Paige's locusts, not daring to take on Raffe directly, at least not right now. He may be a killer when it comes to starved prisoners and little girls, but he's not willing to fight an angel demon.

He turns and swipes his tail at one of Paige's remaining locusts. He doesn't sting, just uses his stinger to slice Paige's locust across the face, drawing a line of blood across his cheek. The smaller locust cringes, looking like he thought that the bigger one meant to slit his throat.

White Streak turns his back on us as if to show that he's not afraid. He grabs Paige's pet by the hair and flies away, with the smaller locust awkwardly fluttering his wings to stay up.

The unsure beast turns and gives Paige a distressed

look. He doesn't want to go. But all Paige can do is reach out her hand as he fades farther away from her.

This is some kind of leadership challenge, and the swarm seems to be waiting it out to see who they're supposed to follow. Whatever it is she did last night to rally the locusts against the angels, it's not working against White Streak.

A serial killer versus a seven-year-old girl. No contest. I'm just glad he didn't make a move to hurt her, thanks to Raffe.

Paige is left with the locust who carries her and the two flanking her. Our smaller group probably makes it easier for us to fly without being noticed and shot at, but I don't like the feeling of being bullied, especially by that marauding insect.

We move on.

I can see worry in Paige's eyes. I'm guessing she doesn't care about having her power taken, but she hates to see her locusts getting punished.

12

'We need to go to the Resistance,' I say as I cling to Raffe's neck. 'Maybe Doc is there. He might be able to help both you and Paige.' My mother should also be there, waiting for us.

'Human doctor?'

'Trained by angels. I think he sewed on Beliel's wings – I mean, your wings onto him.'

He's quiet as he sweeps his large demon wings through the air.

'I don't like it either,' I say. 'But what choice do we have?'

'Why not?' He sounds resigned. 'Might as well fly into the heart of the enemy where the primitive natives can tear me to pieces, sell my body parts for money, and grind the rest to be consumed in teas for sexual potency.'

I tighten my arms around his neck. 'We're not that primitive anymore.'

He arches his perfect eyebrow at me, sending waves of skepticism.

'We have Viagra now.'

He gives me a sideways glance as if he suspects what that is.

We fly over the water and down the East Bay landmass as the sun sets. Steering clear of the aerie, we take the long way around toward Resistance headquarters. There is a surprising number of angels in the air today. They fly in formation from every direction toward Half Moon Bay, where the new aerie is located.

When we see a particularly large group in the air, we land in front of a mall and lie low beneath the awning of a Macy's department store.

'They must be flying in for the Messenger election,' says Raffe. There's worry in his voice as he watches the host of angels flying above us.

I unwrap my arms from his neck and step away from his warmth. It feels chilly on my own under the department store awning. 'You mean there are more angels coming into the area? Like we didn't have enough on our hands.'

From this distance, the angels look like they're inching across the sky. Raffe watches them fly overhead. His body twitches just a little, looking like he's making an effort not to jump into the air and join them.

'What was it like to be one of them?' I ask.

He gazes at the sky for a long moment before saying anything. 'My Watchers and I were on a mission once to clear the area of a demon invasion. Except we couldn't find any demons. But Cyclone, one of my Watchers, was so worked up for a battle that he wouldn't accept that there was no one to fight.'

He nods toward the angels flying in the distance. 'We were flying in formation like that when Cyclone suddenly decided that if he could just cause a big enough scene, then the demons would be attracted to the noise and destruction and they'd come to us. So he started flying in circles as fast as he could, sure that he would cause a cyclone.'

He smiles at the memory. 'Half of us joined him as a lark while the rest of us landed to watch and heckle. We started throwing things at him – twigs, leaves, mud, whatever we could find – because everyone knows that a tornado should have debris.'

He has a mischievous look in his eyes as he remembers. 'The ones in the air, they flew over to a tree that I swear must have been diseased, because it had these rotten oranges still on the branches. They started throwing them at us, and it turned into a giant mud and orange fight.' He chuckles as he gazes up at the sky.

His face is relaxed and happy in a way I've never seen. 'We had orange pulp caked in our ears and hair for days after.'

He watches the angels flying away from us.

I can almost see the lonely years creeping back to him like shadows at the end of the day. The happiness seeps out of his face, and he's back to being a hardened outsider traveling in an apocalypse.

'You're sure this human doctor can transplant wings?' he asks.

'That's what Beliel said.' Of course, Beliel said a lot of things.

'And you're sure he's at the Resistance camp?'

'No, but I'm pretty sure he was rescued off Alcatraz by the Resistance. If he's not there, maybe someone will know where he is.' I have all kinds of worries about going to the camp and trusting the doctor who messed up Paige in the first place.

I sigh. 'I can't think of a better plan. Can you?'

He looks at the angels for a little longer before turning and heading into Macy's.

It's not a bad idea. Paige and I both need to change into some real clothes, so we might as well go shopping while we wait for the sky to clear. We leave the locusts outside and follow Raffe into the store.

Inside, the electricity is out, but there's enough sun coming through the huge windows to light up the front part of the store. Many of the racks are drunkenly leaning or scattered on the floor. Clothes of all colors and fabrics spill into the aisles. In the windows, naked mannequins lie on top of each other in sexual poses.

Someone has sprayed graffiti on the ceiling. A crude knight stands alone with his sword drawn against a fire-breathing dragon that is ten times his size. The dragon's tail disappears into darkness where the window light fades deep into the store.

Beside the knight are the words 'Where Have All the Heroes Gone?'

It looks to me like the artist thought the knight didn't stand a chance against the dragon. I know just how he feels.

I look around and try to remember what it was like to go shopping. We walk through the special-event dresses. The racks and floor are covered in silky sparkle and shine.

This would have been my year for the prom. I doubt anyone would have asked me, and even if someone had, we couldn't have afforded one of these dresses anyway. I run my hand through the shimmery fabric on a rack of full-length gowns, wondering what it would have been like to go to the prom instead of a masquerade ball full of killers.

I catch Raffe watching me. The light behind him halos his dark hair and broad shoulders. If he were human, the girls at my school would have died just to be in the same room with him. But of course, he's not human.

'That would look good on you,' he says and nods to the movie-star dress in my hand.

'Thanks. Do you think it'll go well with combat boots?'

'You won't always be fighting, Penryn. There will come a time when you'll be so bored that you'll wish you were fighting.'

'I can only dream.' I pull out the dress and lay it against me, feeling the soft, sparkly fabric.

He steps over and scrutinizes me in my pretend dress. Then he nods his approval.

'How do you think things might have been . . .' My voice dries up. I swallow and keep going. 'If you were human, or I was an angel?'

He reaches out as if he can't help himself and runs his forefinger along the shoulder of the dress. 'If I were human, I'd plow the nicest farm for you.' He sounds completely sincere. 'Better than anyone else's. It would have golden pineapples, the juiciest grapes, and the most flavorful radishes in the entire world.'

I just stare at him, trying to figure out if he's joking. I think he's serious. 'You haven't been to a lot of farms, have you, Raffe? Most of us aren't farmers anymore anyway.'

'That wouldn't diminish my little human commitment to you.'

I smile a little. 'If I was an angel, I'd tickle your feet with my feathers and sing angelic songs for you every morning.'

He scrunches his brow, looking like it pains him to try to envision this.

'Right.' I nod. 'Neither of us have any idea what it would be like to be in each other's world. Got it.'

He looks down at me with sincere eyes. 'If I were human, I would have been the first in line for you . . .' He looks away. 'But I'm not. I'm an archangel, and my people are in trouble. I have no choice but to try to set things straight. I can't get distracted by a Daughter of Man.'

He nods a little to himself. 'I can't.'

I hook the dress carefully back on the rack and make myself listen to what he's telling me. I just need to accept the situation.

I take a good look at him, steeling myself to see deter-mination and maybe even pity. But instead, I see turmoil. There's a battle raging behind his eyes.

A tiny light of hope flares in my chest. I don't even know what I'm hoping for anymore. My brain can't seem to keep up with my heart.

'Just this once,' he says almost more to himself than to me. 'Just one moment.'

Then he leans down and kisses me.

It's the kind of kiss that I've been dying for since I was born.

His lips are supple, his touch tender. He strokes my hair gently.

He licks my lips – a probing, wet glide – then touches my tongue with his. Electric sensations zip from the tip of my tongue down to my toes and back again.

I feel like I'm drowning in him. Who knew such a thing existed? I open my mouth and grab him tighter, almost climbing into his arms.

We kiss wildly for what seems like a year, for what is only a millisecond. My breath is ragged, and it feels like I can't get enough air. My insides are melting, flowing like lava through my body.

Then he stops.

He takes a deep breath and steps back, holding me at arm's length.

I groggily take a step toward him on pure instinct. My eyelids feel heavy, and I just want to get lost in the sensation that is Raffe.

There's a mix of longing and sadness in his eyes, but he's not letting me get any closer.

Seeing that brings me back to myself. Back to the here and now.

The invasion. My mom. My sister. The massacres. They all come rushing back. He's right.

We're at war.

On the verge of an apocalypse filled with monsters and torture in a nightmare world.

And I'm standing here, a moonstruck teenager pining for an enemy soldier. What am I, crazy?

This time, I'm the first to turn away.

13

The vault in my head feels full, and my churning emotions need a break.

I wander deeper into the store, away from Raffe. In the dim area before the store gets really dark, I find a display platform to sit on. It's bright enough for me to see but dark enough to be just one of the shadows if anyone else is watching. Sometimes, I feel like my whole life is lived in this twilight space between sunshine and darkness.

I sit and brood over the fallen racks and broken pieces of our old civilization. When I get tired of that, I look into the dark part of the store. I can't see anything but keep imagining things that may or may not be moving. But then, as I look around, I do see something.

Behind a tilted sign near a sea of shoes and several fallen mannequins is a small flashlight. It's on, but it's weak, casting more shadows than light.

I put my hand on the soft fur of Pooky Bear and debate whether to run away or to investigate. I don't feel like running to Raffe, so I hop onto my feet and walk quietly in the direction of the flashlight.

Before I can get there, someone steps into the light.

It's Paige. She's still in her oversized T-shirt that hangs crookedly off one shoulder and falls past her knees. Her tennis shoes are almost black with dried blood.

The dim light hits the hollows of her face, emphasizing her skeletal features beneath the stitches and casting long shadows from her hair onto her neck. She walks toward the mannequins like she's sleepwalking. She looks mesmerized by something on the floor.

I take another look at the mannequins and realize that one of them is a man.

He's lying on his back on top of the scattered shoes with his head and shoulders mixed with mannequin limbs, as if he collapsed onto them. One pale hand stretches toward the fallen flashlight while the other clutches a scrap of paper over his chest. He must have died of a heart attack.

Paige kneels down beside him like she's in a trance. She'll see me if she looks up, but she's too preoccupied with the man. Maybe she smells people now the way a predator might smell prey.

I know what she's about to do.

But I don't stop her.

I want to. Oh, Christ, I want to.

But I don't.

My eyes burn and sting with tears. This is too much for me. I want my mom.

All this time, I've been thinking that I'm the strong one, that I'm making the hard choices and carrying the weight of responsibility for my family on my shoulders. But I realize now that the toughest choices, the ones that will haunt us for the rest of our lives, are ones that my mom is still sheltering me from.

Isn't that what happened when the Resistance caught Paige like an animal? I was still trying to feed her soup and hamburgers while my mother already knew what she needed. Wasn't she the one who took Paige out there to the grove so she could find a victim for her?

I can't even look away. My feet feel leaden, and my eyes refuse to close. This is who my sister is now.

Her lip curls, flashing the tips of her razor-grafted teeth.

I hear a faint groan. My heart almost stops. Did that come from the man or from Paige? Is he alive?

Paige is close enough to be able to tell. She lifts his arm up to her mouth, showing all of her razor teeth.

I try to call to her, but what comes out is just a puff of breath. He's dead. He must be. Still, I can't look away, and my heart pounds in my ears.

She stops with his arm in front of her mouth, her nose crinkled, and her lips drawn back like a growling dog.

The piece of paper the man is still holding is now in front of her face. She pauses to stare at it.

She pushes the man's hand out to get a better look.

The skin of her nose straightens, and her mouth closes, hiding her teeth behind her lips. Her eyes warm as she stares at the paper. Her mouth begins to tremble, and she moves his arm back onto his chest. She leans away from the man.

Paige puts her hands up to cradle her head, swaying gently back and forth like a worn-out woman with too many problems.

Then she spins and runs off into the darkness.

I stand in the shadows, my heart slowly tearing over what she's going through. My baby sister is choosing to be human against all her new animal instincts. And she's doing it at the cost of starving to death.

I walk over to the man and bend down to see what he's holding. I step around high-heeled shoes and makeup jars to reach him. He's still breathing but unconscious.

Still breathing.

I sit down shakily next to him, not sure if my wobbly legs will hold me up.

His clothes are dirty and worn, and his beard and hair are scraggly, as if he's been on the road for weeks. Someone once told me that heart attacks can last for days. I wonder how long he's been here.

I have the craziest urge to call an ambulance.

It's hard to believe that we used to live in a world where complete strangers would have given him medicine and hooked him up to machines to monitor his condition. They would have looked after him around the clock. Absolute strangers who knew nothing about him. Strangers who wouldn't have even rummaged through his stuff to steal useful items.

And everyone would have thought that was perfectly normal.

I lift his arm to see what's on the paper he's holding. I don't want to take it out of his hand, because whatever it is, it must have been important enough for him to get it out and grip it as he's dying.

It's a torn and stained piece of paper with a kid's crayon drawing. A house, a tree, a stick figure adult holding the hand of a stick figure kid. Scrawled along the bottom in shaky block letters are the words 'I Love You, Daddy' in pink crayon.

I look at it for a long time in the shadowy light before I put his hand back down gently on his chest.

I drag him as carefully as I can until he's lying flat on the carpet instead of on the pile of mannequins on the tiled floor.

There's a backpack nearby that I also bring and set beside him. He must have taken it off when he started to feel bad. I rummage through and find a water bottle.

His head is warm and heavy on my arm as I tilt it for the water. Most of it spills out around his lips, but some of it trickles into his mouth. His throat reflexively swallows, making me wonder if he's completely out.

I put his head down, making sure there's a folded jacket to cushion it. I can't think of anything else to do. So I leave him to his business of dying.

14

I find the most normal clothes I can for Paige. A pink shirt with a sparkly heart, jeans, high-tops, and a zip-up sweater. I make sure everything but her shirt is a dark color so she won't be seen at night. I also make sure that the sweater has a big enough hood to shadow her face in case we need to go unnoticed.

For me, it's black boots, black jeans, and a maroon top that will hide the blood that's bound to stain it. I just hope that blood will be someone else's instead of mine. I might as well dress postapocalyptic practical. I also grab a down jacket that's as light as a . . . I put it down and pick a dark fleece jacket instead. I'm not in the mood for angel reminders right now.

Raffe has found a baseball cap and a dark trench

coat that covers his wings. He looks good in a base-ball cap.

I mentally roll my eyes at myself. I'm such a dork. The world is coming to an end, my sister is a man-eating monster, there's a dying man in the store with us, and we'll be lucky to survive another night. And I'm here drooling after a guy who doesn't even want me. He's not even human. How messed up is that? Sometimes, I wish I could take a vacation from myself.

I shove his coat and cap into my backpack with more force than necessary.

By the time we get out of the store, the angels are gone. Raffe moves to hold me for flight.

I step back. 'You don't have to. I'll catch a ride with one of the locusts.' I have to force the words out. The last thing I want to do is be in the arms of a scorpion-tailed monster.

But Raffe has made it all too clear that this – what-ever this is that we may or may not have between us – is a nonstarter. He's made it clear that he's leaving. And if there's one thing I've learned, it's that trying to make someone stay with you when he doesn't want to is a recipe for heartbreak. Just ask my mom.

I clench my teeth. I can do it. So what if it's utterly creepy to walk into the arms of a nightmare creature with a needle-sharp stinger that almost killed you? A girl's gotta have some scrap of pride, even in the World After.

Raffe watches me as if reading my thoughts. Then he looks at the locusts. His lip curls as he assesses them, his eyes scanning from their thick legs to their insectile torsos to their iridescent wings. He looks at the curled stingers last.

He shakes his head. 'Those wings are so flimsy I wouldn't trust them to carry you. And those overgrown nails – you'd catch an infection if they scratched you. You can ride one when they improve on the design.' He steps forward and, in one smooth motion, lifts me into his firm embrace. 'Until then, you're stuck with me being your air taxi.'

He takes flight before I can argue.

There's a wind blowing from the bay, and it's pointless to try to hold a conversation. So I relax my muscles and tuck my face into the curve of his neck. Maybe for the last time, I let his warm body shelter me.

As the sun sets, I catch a few fire glows below us, probably hidden campfires that got out of control. They look like tiny candles in a shadowy landmass.

We have to land four times on the way south to avoid being seen by angels. I've never seen so many in the air before. Raffe tenses every time we spot the flying formations.

Something serious is going on with his people, but he can't get anywhere close to them, much less get involved. With every passing minute, I can feel his urgency to get his feathered wings reattached so he can dive back into his world.

I try not to think about what will happen in my world when he does.

Eventually, we fly over the Resistance headquarters – otherwise known as Paly High. It sits like every other deserted group of buildings, with no indication that it's anything special.

In the parking lot, every car faces the street so it won't have to do a U-turn to get out. Assuming Obi's escape plan has been executed properly, the cars are gassed and ready to go, with keys in the ignition.

As we descend, I see bodies hunched behind tires and trees and lying out in the open like the dead. A few people scramble here and there in the moonlight, but they look the same as people moving everywhere else in the World After. Obi has done a nice job of training people not to bring attention to their headquarters, even though the camp must be overflowing now that they've rescued the Alcatraz refugees.

We circle above the grove across the street from Paly.

The moon is rising in the twilight shadows, letting us see without being seen. There's still enough light to see a few shadows scattering into the bushes as we come down. I'm surprised there are people out here at dusk, considering how spooked everyone is of the monsters in the dark.

When we land, Raffe lets me go. The night air feels cold on my skin after being held by him for so long.

'You stay here out of sight,' I say. 'I'll see if I can find out whether Doc is here or not.'

'Not a chance.' Raffe reaches for my backpack and pulls out his trench coat and cap.

'I know it's hard for you to wait while I scope out the situation, but I can handle it. Besides, who's going to watch Paige?' As soon as I ask this question, I know it's the wrong thing to say. You don't tell an elite soldier to stay behind and watch the kids.

'Her pets can babysit.' He puts on his coat, carefully shifting his shoulders until the wings settle beneath the fabric. He slips on the backpack for good measure. His feathered wings are wrapped in a blanket and strapped to the pack, looking like an ordinary bedroll. His demon wings can mold themselves to his back, but the pack hides any unusual bulges that might catch someone's eye.

Everything about this situation makes me nervous.

Raffe is walking into a camp full of hostiles. Paige shouldn't be so close to people who wanted to tear her to pieces. And the last time I saw Obi, he had me arrested.

There's also a part of me that doesn't want Raffe eavesdropping on people. Of course, I've repeatedly trusted him with my life, but that doesn't change the fact that he's one of the enemy. Any minute now, we might have to choose our loyalties. When that happens, I'd be an idiot to think we'll be on the same side.

But my instincts tell me that out of all the things to worry about right now, that's low on the list. My sensei always told me to trust my instincts, that my gut knows things my brain doesn't and can figure things out faster.

Of course, my instincts have told me things about Raffe that haven't panned out. My cheeks warm at the thought of what happened with him earlier today in bed.

He flips the collar on his coat and buttons it all the way up to cover his bare chest, then puts on his cap. Even though we had a warm day, the October night is chilly enough that he won't look suspicious. California nights can easily be twenty degrees colder than the days.

'Stay here, Paige. We'll be back soon, okay?'

Paige is already busy quieting her locusts and hardly seems to notice us. I don't like leaving her, but I can't take her into camp either. The last time she was here, the frightened Resistance people lassoed her like an animal, and who knows what they would have done if the locusts hadn't attacked. I can't expect the angry villager attitude to have changed since then.

As soon as we start moving, I feel eyes watching me. I keep looking around, but I don't see anything. On the edge of my vision, though, I see shadows shifting.

'Locust victims,' whispers Raffe.

I'm guessing this means that they haven't been accepted into camp. I don't think they're dangerous, but I rest my hand on Pooky Bear, taking comfort in the soft fur. Then I take a deep breath and continue through the dark grove.

15

The school grounds are quiet and seemingly deserted. I guesstimate that there must be a few thousand people here now. But you'd never know it.

Obi has done such a great job of setting up the refugee camp that even the new people follow the rules. They know not to walk out in the open. The amount of trash here is no greater and no worse than trash floating anywhere else in Silicon Valley. The entire campus is so quiet that I'd almost be surprised if I saw anyone here.

But once we get close enough to the buildings, we can see the dim lights glowing inside. The windows are covered by blankets and towels, but some have been put up sloppily, letting light and motion slip through the edges.

I step up to a window and peek through a crack. The room is jammed with people. They look reasonably well fed, some almost clean. I don't recognize them – they must be the Alcatraz refugees. I look through another window and see the same. With this many new people, the whole place must be filled with chaos and confusion.

I see a guy through one window who comes into a classroom with a bag of food. He passes it out, and it's gone in no time. He puts his hands up and says something to the people still reaching out to him even though the food is gone. There's an argument, but the man slips out of the door before it can get too heated.

The lucky ones gobble up their food as fast as they can while the others watch with an intensity that's uncomfortable. The crowd mills around, churning until a whole new group of people stand in the prime spot near the door, probably waiting for the next batch of food.

'What are you doing?' asks a harsh voice.

I spin around to see two guys in camouflage holding rifles.

'Just . . . nothing.'

'Well, do your nothing inside where the birds can't see you. Weren't you listening during the orientation?'

'I'm looking for someone. Do you know where the twins are? Dee and Dum?'

'Yeah, right,' says the guard. 'Like they have time to talk to every teenage girl crying for her lost puppy. Next thing you know, you'll be asking to see Obadiah West. Those guys have a whole camp to run. They don't have time for stupid questions.'

I can only blink at them, probably convincing them that yes, I was planning on asking some stupid questions. They point us to the nearest door.

'Get back to your assigned room. Someone will be bringing food as soon as they can, and you'll be shipped to a nice hotel room when it's dark enough to hide the envoy.'

'Hide from what?'

They look at me like I'm nuts. 'The angels.' One gives the other a look that says *duh*.

'But they can see in the dark,' I say.

'Who told you that? They can't see in the dark. The only thing they can do better than us is fly.'

The other guard says, 'They can hear better than us too.'

'Yeah, whatever,' says the first guy. 'But they can't see in the dark.'

'But I'm telling you—' I stop when Raffe taps me on the arm. He nods toward the door and begins walking. I follow.

'They don't know that angels can see in the dark.' I

forgot that I know things about the angels that maybe other people don't. 'They need to know.'

'Why?' asks Raffe.

'Because people need to know that angels can see us if we ever try to' – *attack them* – 'hide in the dark.'

He eyes me as if he read my thoughts, but of course, he doesn't need to read my mind. It's pretty obvious why it would benefit the humans to know the angels' powers.

Raffe walks beside me up the steps to the doors. 'You can talk until your lips fall off, but it won't do you any good. These are foot soldiers. Their job is to follow orders. Nothing else.'

And he would know. He's a soldier himself, isn't he? A soldier for the wrong army.

It dawns on me that even though Uriel is creating a false apocalypse and is out to kill Raffe, that doesn't mean Raffe is willing to help humans win the war against his own people. I've had plenty of humans try to kill me since the Great Attack, but that doesn't mean I'm willing to help the angels wipe out the humans. Far from it.

The guards watch us until we walk into the building.

As soon as we get inside, I have to fight a wave of claustrophobia. The hallway is crammed with people moving in different directions. When you're my size, being in a crowd means all you can see are the torsos and heads of the people nearest you.

Raffe looks even more uncomfortable than I feel. In a crowd this tight, he can't help but have people brushing up against his blanket-wrapped wings strapped to his backpack. We can only hope that no one notices anything strange.

He stands stiffly with his back to the door without moving in. He looks so out of place that I almost feel sorry for him. He shakes his head at me.

I try to blend in as best I can. We shouldn't have to be here long before the guards leave the area.

Obi must have his hands full with all these new people. I sprung the Alcatraz rescue on them at the last minute, so it's a wonder he even managed to collect boats and organize people to rescue the captives on the island. Of course he didn't have time to prepare for them once they got here.

I imagine it's been quite a day for the Resistance. Obi's not just running freedom fighters anymore. He's had to put together a refugee camp full of scared, hungry people while still keeping the organization as stealthy as possible.

I have my issues with Obi. I can't say he's going to be my best friend or anything, but I have to admit, he's taken on a lot that no one else would.

I consider going deeper into the building to try to see if I can find Doc or Dee-Dum. The twins are sure to know where Doc is. But it's too crowded and chaotic in here, and I don't like the idea of being trapped in the middle of a building full of panicking refugees if something happens.

I'm about to tell Raffe we should go as soon as the guards move on when I hear my name. It's not a voice I recognize, and I can't tell who said it since no one is looking at me. Everyone looks busy having their own conversations.

Then someone else says my name on the other side of the hallway. Still, no one is looking at us.

'Penryn.'

I see the guy who spoke. He has curly hair and wears a huge shirt that hangs on his scarecrow shoulders and a pair of oversized pants held up by a cinched belt. It's as if he's used to being extra large and hasn't mentally adjusted to his postapocalyptic weight. He's several people away from me down the hallway but still close enough to hear. I don't recognize him or anyone around him.

'Penryn?' asks the woman speaking to the guy. 'What kind of name is that?'

They're not calling me. They're talking *about* me.

The guy shrugs. 'Probably some foreign name that means angel slayer.'

'Yeah, right. So do you believe it?'

'What? That she killed an angel?'

How did they know about that?

He shrugs again. 'Don't know.' He lowers his voice. 'All I know is that it would be amazing to have a safety pass from the angels.'

The woman shakes her head. 'No way would they keep their word. How would we even know if they're really putting a bounty on her head?'

I exchange glances with Raffe at the word *bounty*.

'Some street gang could've just made this whole thing up to kill her,' she says. 'Maybe she's one of their enemies or something. Who knows? The whole world's gone crazy.'

'I know one thing,' says another guy closer to me. He wears glasses with a big crack on one lens. 'Whether it was the angels or gangs or demons from hell who put the bounty on that girl, it ain't gonna be me who turns her in.' He shakes his head.

'Me neither,' says another man nearby. 'I heard it was Penryn who saved us from that nightmare on Alcatraz.'

'Obadiah West saved us,' says the woman. 'And so did those funny twins. What were their names?'

'Tweedledee and Tweedledum.'

'That can't be right.'

'I kid you not.'

'Yeah, but it was the girl Penryn who told them to do it. She's the one who got them to rescue us.'

'I heard she threatened to sic her monster sister on them if they didn't.'

'Penryn—'

'She's a friend of mine,' says one woman I've never seen before. 'We're like sisters.'

I lower my head, hoping no one recognizes me. Luckily, no one even notices us. As I make my way toward the door, I see a flyer taped to it. The only thing I catch as I pass are the words 'Talent Show.'

I have visions of amateur tuba players and tap dancers. A talent show is an odd thing to have during the apocalypse. But then again, it's an odd thing to have at any time.

Raffe pushes through the door, and we head back into the night.

16

Outside, the air is fresh and quiet compared with the stuffiness and noise inside. We skulk in the shadows until we reach the adobe mission-style building that Obi uses as his headquarters. This door has the same flyer. I pause to read it.

TALENT SHOW

Don't miss the biggest thing since the last Oscars!
Bigger than the Great Attack! Bigger than Obi's
ego! Bigger than Boden's BO!
Come one, come all
To the greatest show of all!

Win a custom-made, bulletproof, luxury RV!
Filled with every survival supply imaginable.
Yup. Even that.

Next Wed. at noon at the Stanford Theater on
University Ave.

Amaze your friends. Befuddle your enemies. Show
off your talents.
Auditions every evening
Ladies welcome

The usual betting rules apply on the contestants.

~ Brought to you by You Know Who ~

This flyer has comments scrawled all over it in different
handwriting:

'Nothing could be bigger than Obi's ego.'

'Is that what the ladies are calling it? Hey, Obi – leave
some women for the rest of us, would ya?'

'Obadiah West is a great man. A hero. Even I'm
thinking about giving him a kiss.'

'It's the talentless show!'

'Be nice or I'll crack open your skull and drink the sludge inside.'

'Will the contestants be wearing clothes?'

'I sure hope so. Have you seen the men here? Hairy, dude. Seriously hairy.'

I'm guessing these guys miss the Internet.

Raffe pulls open the door, and we step into a dimly lit hallway. The main building is busy with people but far less crowded than the first building. The people here walk with confidence, whereas the group in the other building looked lost and unsure.

These are probably old-timers compared with the Alcatraz refugees in the other building. I even recognize a few faces here and there. I duck my head, hoping my hair will hide my face.

There's the woman I did laundry with when I was first captured by the Resistance. She's holding a clipboard and checking off items. She's the one who adored her dog. I'm almost surprised to see she's still with the Resistance. I heard they let all the barking dogs go when they found out the angels had superhearing.

There's the clerk from the first aerie hotel. He's smiling tiredly as he talks with a woman. He looks much more relaxed than he ever did at the aerie, even though they're each carrying a bag full of guns. I wonder if he was a Resistance spy.

And there's the cook from the original camp in the woods. He was nice to me and gave me an extra scoop of stew when he found out I was new. He rolls a cart with packages of crackers and Fruit Roll-Ups down the hall.

Everyone looks exhausted. And everyone is armed to the teeth – handguns, rifles, knives, tire irons, and anything that might cut, smash, or rip. Everyone here carries at least two weapons.

Raffe pulls his cap lower onto his face. I can tell he's tense. He's in enemy territory. Now that I think about it, he's always in enemy territory no matter whose turf it is. Without his feathered wings, the angels won't accept him. And regardless of what kind of wings he has, humans won't accept him either.

Uriel or someone in his crew once said that angels were made to be part of a pack, but no matter where Raffe goes, he always seems to be the outsider.

Luckily, no one seems to be paying attention to him here. In this building, the name that I hear the most is Obi's.

'Obi wants us to—'

'But I thought Obi's plan was—'

'Yeah, that's what Obi said.'

'Need Obi's permission for—'

'Authorized by Obi.'

'Obi will deal with them.'

The two buildings definitely have their own personalities. One houses a refugee camp while the other holds a freedom-fighting army. Obi certainly has his hands full keeping the last dregs of humanity together during the worst crisis in history.

And I thought I had it bad trying to keep my family alive. I can't imagine how much pressure he must feel being responsible for all these lives.

A couple of guys with construction-worker tans and muscles turn to ogle me as we approach. Beside me, Raffe makes a low growl. The guys take one look at him and glance respectfully away.

I pause to talk to them. 'I'm looking for the twins – Dee and Dum. Do you know where they are?'

One of them points to a room down the hall. We walk over, and I push open the door without thinking about what might be inside.

'—hotels,' says Obi at the head of a conference table. 'How are we holding up on food and medical—' He glances up and notices me. He looks as tired as the rest of them, but his eyes are still bright and alert. He's not the biggest nor the loudest, but there's still something about him that commands attention. Maybe it's his straight posture or the confidence in his voice.

There are about a dozen people around him, sitting at a conference table. Everyone looks haggard and exhausted, with dark circles beneath their eyes and unwashed hair sticking out in various directions. It must have been a long night of saving Alcatraz refugees, then an even longer day of getting them settled in.

The room gets quiet, and everyone turns to look at me. So much for trying to be subtle.

17

'Sorry,' I say, trying to gracefully bow out.

Doc jumps up and knocks his chair back so hard that it clatters to the floor. 'Penryn.'

'You know her?' asks Obi.

'She's the sister of the child I was telling you about.'

'Penryn's sister is the great secret weapon?' asks Obi.

Uh-oh. I don't like the sound of this.

'Did you find her?' Doc skirts the table and heads my way. He still looks like a college boy with his brown hair and button-up shirt, but now he has a swollen black eye. 'Is she here?'

The twins sit beside Obi. Their matching hair is still bottle blond. I'd forgotten that they dyed their hair for kicks. They still look like skinny scarecrows to me whether they're redheads or blonds. A couple of the others look familiar, but I don't know any of them well.

Obi waves me in. I hesitate, not wanting to bring attention to me or Raffe. But I can't just run for it, so I go into the room with a wave of my hand behind my back, signaling Raffe to not follow.

'You've got to be joking,' says a guy I recognize. 'Her sister is a monstrous horror. You can't expect her to help us.' I realize where I've seen him before. He was one of the guys who lassoed Paige like a wild animal the last time she was here.

'Martin, not now,' says Obi.

The twins lean over in opposite directions to peer around me.

'Is that Raffe?' asks Dee.

'That is *so* Raffe,' says Dum.

I start to close the door.

'No, no, no,' says Dee. Both the twins get up and walk fast to the door.

'Raffe, you're alive,' says Dum as he pushes the door open.

Raffe has his head tilted down, his eyes in the shadow of his cap.

'Of course he's alive,' says Dee. 'He's a warrior. All you have to do is look at him to know that. Who's going to kill him? Godzilla?'

'Oh, Raffe versus Godzilla. Now that's a fight I'd love to take bets on,' says Dum.

'Don't be silly, man. Godzilla's all pumped up on nuclear waste. How's a mere mortal supposed to beat that?'

'He's not just a mere mortal,' says Dum. 'Look at him. He's probably got some super-strength badass juice in his pocket right now. One gulp and his muscles would have muscles.'

'Yeah, and we wouldn't need scary little girls if we had a few like him in our army,' says Dee.

'What, you think Penryn's sister can take on Godzilla instead?' asks Dum.

Dee thinks about it. 'Meh, probably not. Maybe her mom can, though.'

Dum's eyes get wide. 'Ooh.'

Dee sticks out his hand at Raffe. 'Tweedledee. This is my brother, Tweedledum.'

'Remember us?' asks Dum. 'We handle fights and manage betting.'

'Good to have you here,' Obi says to Raffe. 'We sure could use a man like you.'

'Oh, he's no ordinary man, Obi,' says Dee.

I try really hard not to look like a frightened rabbit, but I'm sure my eyes are wide and scared. We're deep in the building. I don't know how Raffe can escape.

'We can make you a star, Raffe,' says Dum, nodding. 'The women would be all over you.' He exaggeratedly mouths the words *all over* while he mimics rubbing his hands over his chest and body.

'He doesn't care about that,' says Dee. 'He's a guy who hangs with angels. There were tons of girls at the aerie in San Francisco.'

I try to remember to breathe. That's right. One of them saw him at the hotel room at the aerie.

'Never enough, bro,' says Dum. 'Never enough.'

'What do you mean he "hangs with angels"?' asks Obi as he gets up from the conference table.

My breath refuses to move out of my lungs.

'Remember?' says Dee. 'We told you that Penryn and this guy were in the hotel. Actually talking with angels.'

'Penryn's not the only one who knows stuff about them.' Dum nods.

I let out a deep breath. They remember Raffe, but only as a human.

Obi walks over and waves Raffe into the conference room. 'That's great news. We can use all the help and information we can get.' He puts his hand out for Raffe to shake. Raffe doesn't.

'Hello, Obi,' I say, waving to him.

'Penryn,' says Obi, looking over my way. 'If I wasn't so exhausted, I'm sure I'd remember whatever unfinished business we have. Instead, I'm just glad to see you alive and well.'

He steps over and hugs me.

I stand there, stiff and unsure. Raffe's face is expressionless as he watches us.

'Thanks.' I hover in front of the door. I remember our unfinished business. Obi locked me and my mother up in a police car, and we escaped in the middle of the night. But despite that, he's glad to see me.

I admit, after all I've been through, it's sort of good to see him and his gang too. Some people might call that messed up. I call it dealing with family. Not that he's family, but if things keep going the way they have been, I'll be glad to see any human being.

'Where's your sister?' asks Doc. He reaches for the door as if he suspects I'm hiding her just outside.

'Funny you should ask,' I say, lowering my voice. 'Can I talk to you for a minute? Outside?' I have a wild hope that Doc, Raffe, and I might be able to sneak away.

'No need for privacy,' says Obi. 'Doc told us all about his work on Alcatraz and his hopes for Paige. We'd all love to hear about your sister. Is she all right?'

I look at the faces around the table. All of them are older than me. Some of them look like grizzled veterans from previous wars. Others look like they're recently off the streets. What would they do if they knew they had an angel in the room?

'What do you want with her?' I ask. I can't help but sound suspicious.

'Doc tells us she might be our best hope.'

'Doc is an optimistic guy,' I say.

'There's no harm in seeing, right?'

'The last time you took a look at her, you had her tied in ropes like a rabid animal.' I can't help but glance at Martin. His hand still looks rope burned as he drums a pencil against the fingers of his open hand.

'That wasn't me,' says Obi. 'I came on the scene just before you did and was trying to figure out what happened. Look, people make mistakes. We're driven by fear and exhaustion and outright stupidity sometimes. We're not perfect like the angels. All we can do is rely on each other and do our best. I'm sorry for how your sister was treated. We need her, Penryn. She could turn this war around.'

'Not if she starves to death,' I say. 'Make Doc fix her, and we'll talk about what she can do for you.'

'Fix her?' asks Obi.

I glance at Doc.

'I'll see what I can do,' says Doc. 'I need to make sure she's all right first, which means I need to see her.' He gives me a pointed look.

'Can you bring her to us?' asks Obi.

I shake my head. 'I don't think that's a good idea.' I glance again at Martin, who is watching us with intense eyes.

'Fine,' says Doc before Obi can object. 'Take me to her.'

I turn, hoping for a quick escape, but Obi calls out my name.

'There's been a rumor about a teenage girl who killed an angel,' says Obi. 'They say she has a sword that might be disguised as a teddy bear.' He looks at Pooky Bear dangling off my hip. 'You wouldn't know anything about that, would you?'

I blink innocently at him, wondering if it's better to own it or deny it.

'I can see we need to rebuild some trust between us. Let me show you around so you can see what we're about. We could use fighters like the two of you.'

'I've seen the camp, Obi.' I fidget near the doorway. 'I know you rescued the people off Alcatraz. That was amazing. Really. You guys were fantastic. But I need to deal with my sister right now.'

Obi nods. 'All right. I'll go with you. We can talk while Doc looks over your sister.'

I try really hard not to exchange glances with Raffe. Unless we can get Doc alone, there's no chance of talking to him about sewing on Raffe's angel wings.

'I'll take you up on your offer for a tour,' says Raffe. 'It'd be interesting to see what you're putting together here.'

I freeze my expression in place, trying not to betray my thoughts. This is just getting worse by the second.

Obi's face breaks into a grin. 'Excellent. I'll introduce you to a few people. I think you'll be proud to call them your brothers in arms if you join us.'

'All right,' says Raffe.

'Great,' says Obi. 'I think you'll like what you see. This is the council. They're in charge of our strategic defense.'

I watch Obi and Raffe make their way around the table. Does Raffe think this is funny? Obi is about to give an angel a tour of the Resistance camp?

18

Doc slips his arm into mine and guides me out of the room. 'Is she hurt? What has she been eating?'

I look at the door closing on Obi talking to Raffe as we head out into the hallway. 'Um, my sister hasn't been eating . . .'

The twins follow us down the hallway. They glance out the windows and watch everyone around us as we walk, always alert.

'Hey, guys.' We push out of the building doors and into the night. 'What's Obi showing Raffe?'

'The usual stuff,' says Dum.

'Our refugees, our cutting-edge batteries, our amazing electric cars, and maybe some of our dried ramen noodle supply.' Dee shrugs.

I walk numbly in the cold, my mind mulling over whether any of that would be harmful. No big deal, right?

Right?

I must be moving too slowly as we talk, because Doc turns around and asks, 'Where are we going?'

'The grove across the street,' I say.

Doc takes off at a trot and disappears into the street. I'm about to chase after him when Dee puts his hand on my arm. 'Let him go. He'll wait for you at the grove anyway. He doesn't know where he's going.'

He's right, and it is good to see the twins again. I let go of my worries about Raffe. There's nothing I can do about it now anyway.

I turn to the twins. 'You guys are awesome. No one else would have gone out to save those poor people on Alcatraz.'

'Ain't no big thing,' says Dum, sauntering beside me.

'Yeah, we save hundreds of people all the time,' says Dee.

'All the time,' says Dum.

'We were born for it.'

'And sometimes we even turn down offers from women wanting to show us their gratitude.' Dum struts beside me.

'Once,' says Dee, looking humble.

'Yeah, okay, but if it happened once, that means it happened "sometimes," says Dum.

'Doesn't matter that she was an eighty-year-old lady who looked like our granny,' says Dee.

'A chick's a chick, man, regardless of her age. And an offer is an offer.' Dum nods.

Dee leans over and whispers to me. 'She offered to cook us Brussels sprouts, and we turned it down.'

'She was heartbroken. Probably needed to find some lucky dude to pour her affections on the rebound.'

'Rebound's a bitch.' Dee shakes his head.

'Not that we're ever going to know what that feels like.'

The twins bump fists like true champions.

'And was Obi totally on board with the Alcatraz recue?' I ask.

'Yeah, okay, maybe Obi might have had a little something to do with it.' Dee shrugs.

'Not that we wouldn't have gone ourselves to rescue those people barehanded, but you know, it was a teensy bit easier with Obi running the mission.'

'Good to know he's not a jerk to everyone.'

'Actually, you'd be surprised at what a good guy he is,' says Dee.

'I can tell he hasn't thrown you in jail and abused your sister like Frankenstein's monster.'

'He makes hard choices so the rest of us don't have to,' says Dum.

That shuts me up. Wasn't I wishing for someone else to make the hard choices for me?

'He's human,' says Dee. 'He has flaws.'

'That's why we're here,' says Dum. 'We make up for his imperfections.'

'Don't take it personally,' says Dee. 'He'd sell his first-born, his parents, his cookie-baking grandmother, his one true love, both his arms, legs, and his right nut for a chance to get the human race back on track.'

'He's the most dedicated guy we know.'

'And there's no sacrifice that he would ask of any of us that he wouldn't make himself.'

'Who else can you count on when you're chained up on an evil island like Alcatraz?'

They have a point. The Resistance was the only group that would even consider mounting a real rescue mission.

'He's a little like you, actually,' says Dee.

That almost stops me in my tracks. 'Like me? Obi and I don't have anything in common.'

'You'd be surprised,' says Dum.

'Stubborn, loyal, utterly driven to accomplish your mission.'

'Basically, you're both crazy heroes.'

'And everybody thinks you're both hot,' says Dee.

I scoff. 'Now I know you're full of it.'

'You're seriously going to tell us you haven't noticed the way guys look at you?'

'What guys? What are you talking about?'

They exchange glances. 'Girl,' says Dee, 'even before your latest stunt, you were becoming the most requested fighter of all our events. Butt-kicking girls have always been smokin' hot, but in the postapocalyptic world we live in, the hottest thing around is a sword-wielding, angel-slaying, foulmouthed—'

'I'm not foulmouthed.'

'Yeah, well, nobody's perfect,' says Dum.

'How did you hear about this hypothetical teen girl killing an angel? Not that I'm saying I believe in such a wacky story or anything.'

'The angels put a bounty on this hypothetical girl's head. Anyone who turns this angel slayer in to them will get safe passage from them. Even Obi didn't get that. His bounty is puny compared to this girl's.'

'Word is spreading like wildfire,' says Dum. 'There are crazy stories about her being able to control angel swords and even commanding demons. Everybody's excited. Half the people are looking for you – I mean, her – to turn you in for safe passage, and the other half are toasting you with their last beer. A lot of people are doing both.'

'So watch your back,' says Dee. 'Whether it was you or not, people think it was you, and that may be enough to get you killed.'

'What with your teddy bear sword and history with demons and all.' Dum raises his brows at me.

'It was you, wasn't it?' asks Dee, squinting at me.

'Just between us of course,' says Dum.

'We'd never tell.' They're freakishly identical when they say the same thing together.

A part of me is dying to talk about it. But the smarter part of me says, 'Oh, sure. Didn't I tell you I could kill angels and command demons? I can fly too, but don't tell anyone.'

'Uh-huh.' They look at me, watching my face for clues.

I scan my mind for a change of subject. 'You guys seem to be doing a good job here.'

They keep eyeing me as if not sure whether to let me get away from the topic.

'I mean, it must be hard to build a refugee camp while running a resistance army at the same time.'

'Obi's been trying to do it all, but we finally managed to get a council together to help him run some of the logistics. Oh, man, so many logistics.'

'And all because you had to go for a little joyride, and then give Obi an excuse to be the hero. Speaking of which, how was your bus ride?'

'Yeah, the last time we saw you, you were sending us love notes from your little bus jail.'

'We thought about busting you out, but Obi thought it was more important to get those people off Alcatraz.'

'We wouldn't have agreed if we'd known your mom was there.'

'Pain in the ass, let me tell ya.'

'You don't need to tell me,' I say. 'I know all about what a pain she can be.'

Dee laughs. 'She's like a weapons-grade pain in the ass. We figured out to sic her on the bad guys, and she became a huge asset.'

'Freaked out the human guards there until we came.'

'Did you know she can be truly frightening?'

I nod. 'Oh, yeah. I know that.'

'Most of us had no idea. Totally blindsided us all.'

'She's one of our captains now.'

'What?' It's hard to imagine my mother being in charge of anything.

'Yeah. For real. What kind of a scary world is that?'

I blink a couple of times, letting that settle in. I admit that if there's one thing I can expect from her, it's the unexpected.

'Your mom totally rocks.' The twins nod like little bobblehead dolls.

'Do you know where she is?' I ask.

'Yup,' says Dee. 'We should be able to find her for you.'

'Thanks. That would be great.'

We step onto El Camino Real, getting ready to hop from car to car when someone yells into the night. It sounds like a fight coming from the grove on the other side of the street.

Paige is in that grove.

I break into a sprint, running as fast as I can into the woods.

19

We race into the grove, chasing the noise. We're not the only ones running through the trees. But I can't see details, and everything looks like shifting shadows in the deepening night.

There are angry voices. I'm pretty sure hellions don't talk, at least, not in human voices. I hope this is not the day that I find out otherwise.

Beneath the canopy of trees, a group of shadows raise and drop their fists, kick, and yell at someone curled on the dirt. As we near, I catch a glimpse of the dried skins of the locust victims. Some of them are wearing ripped clothes covered in dirt as if they recently crawled out of graves.

Fists fly and pound into the victim, who is simply taking it, grunting with each impact.

'What's going on?' I ask as I run up. No one seems to hear me.

'Hey!' shouts Dee.

'What's going on?' asks Dum in a hushed but demanding voice.

Several of the locust stung glance at us. They don't stop their kicks, but one of them says, 'It's that bastard from Alcatraz. He did this to us. Created the monsters and fed us to them.' He viciously kicks at the man on the ground. I can't see any details, but it's obvious they're talking about Doc.

The twins must have reached the same conclusion. They jump into the crowd with their arms up. 'That's enough!'

'The council has already said to leave him alone,' says Dee, pulling a guy off Doc.

'The Resistance council has no power over us. We're not part of your camp, remember?'

'Yeah,' says another guy whose face is as withered as dried salami skin. 'You've all rejected us. And it's because of him.' Another vicious kick.

'The next person who kicks or hits him gets banned from all betting. You will be blackballed for the rest of your shriveled lives. Now back off.'

Amazingly, they all back off.

Everyone else might reject the locust victims, but I

guess the twins don't discriminate in their betting pools.

Dee looks just as surprised as I am. He glances over at his brother. 'Dude, we're the new HBO.' He flashes a grin.

Dum reaches down and pulls up a man who I barely recognize as Doc. He holds his arm awkwardly. His face, which was already bruised, is so swollen that he can barely open his eyes.

'Are you okay?' I ask. 'What's wrong with your arm?'

'They stomped all over it. They have no idea what they've done.'

'Is it broken?' It's starting to dawn on me what it means to have a surgeon with a broken arm.

'I don't know.' His conscious brain might not know, but his body sure thinks his arm's broken by the way he's cradling it. 'It's people like this that make me wonder why I bother to try to save them.'

Doc looks furious as he brushes past me. He only takes a couple of steps before he has to lean against a tree and take a break. Dum holds Doc to make sure he can walk steadily.

'We have another doctor,' says Dee to me. 'We'll see what she can do for him.'

'I'll go with you.' I see the locust stung with new eyes. Their shriveled chests and shoulders still heave with their anger and frustration. Several of them are crying with pent-up emotions that go far deeper than the ones stirred up by the fight.

I follow the twins as they help Doc across the street.

20

I lean against the wall in a room full of patients waiting to see the camp's doctor. Doc got high priority because he's the only other doctor in camp. They let one of the twins into the back with him while the other took off on an errand. I was told to wait with the others in the waiting room.

There is only one candle for the entire room even though the windows are blocked off by blankets. There's something particularly unnerving about being in a room that's more shadow than light and hearing people around you coughing and whispering.

The door opens, and Dee's bottle-blond head peeks in.

'What's the verdict?' I ask. 'Is it broken?'

'Badly,' says Dee as he walks in. 'It'll probably be six weeks before he can start to use his arm again.'

Six weeks. My stomach feels like I swallowed lead weights. 'Could he instruct the other doctor during surgery? You know, to work as his hands?'

'She's not a surgeon. Besides, no one wants to be known as Doc's minion. Bad for your health, you know.'

'Yeah, I noticed.' I chew on my lip as I think. I can't come up with anything to do except go back with the bad news. What are we going to do now? Doc was our one shining hope for both Paige and Raffe.

The entrance door opens, and Dum walks in. 'Hey, I saw your mom. Told her your sister was in the grove and that you'd be going there in a minute too.'

'Thanks. Does she seem all right?'

'She was pretty excited. Gave me a hug and a kiss,' says Dum.

'Really?' I ask. 'Do you know how long it's been since she's given me a hug and a kiss?'

'Well, yeah, a lot of women find that they can't resist my charms. They're all over me for any excuse they can find.' He takes a swig of pee-green Gatorade as if he thought that was sexy.

I walk to the door, trying to figure out if there's anything I can do other than head back to the grove with the bad news. When I put my hand on the door-knob, something strange happens that makes me pause.

The skin on the back of my neck prickles before my conscious mind knows that anything is wrong.

Running footsteps pound past the other side of the door.

Then the people in the waiting room huddle together like scared sheep, looking up with frightened eyes.

Someone screams outside.

'What now?' asks Dee. His voice is full of dread, like something is telling him to huddle up and hide too.

There's a part of me that doesn't want to open the door, but the twins pull it open to see what's going on.

Outside, everything looks quiet and still. Junk is all over the place – overturned desks, chairs every which way, clothes, blankets.

As my eyes adjust to the dark, though, I realize the piles of clothes strewn about the lawn are actually people. It's hard to tell with the bits missing.

Not bits as in bite marks, bits as in limbs. Some are missing heads too.

A woman runs from a car. A shadowy figure the size of a wolf chases her.

A couple standing in the shadows on a walkway jump and yelp in surprise as something else – or more accurately, several something elses – slink out of the darkness from the overhang above them and grab their hair.

Then, as if a signal has been given, shadows leap out of the night throughout the campus.

I catch a glimpse of one of them as someone lights it with a flashlight beam. It's a hellion.

They're smaller than the ones from the Pit, but still terrifying. Bat-faced, bat-winged, creepy little fiends with skeletal limbs and emaciated bodies.

Screams fill the school as hellions boil out of the night from all directions.

Two of them are especially large – spotted and beefy with red eyes. Cords of muscle flex along their elongated bones, making the other hellions look stunted. They're the two who chased me from Beliel's memory of hell.

They know I'm here. And they brought friends.

One of them lifts his mouth into the air and makes that same hyena call that I heard on Angel Island. If this is anything like the last time, we can expect a whole lot of company.

A guy jumps out of the shadows, writhing and screaming, with two hellions on his back. In his panic, he runs into a crowded building, bringing the two hellions with him.

A gunshot rings inside that building. I hope they shot the hellions and not the guy.

The hellions are after me, not them. I brought them here.

So it's up to me to lead them away.

Without thinking, I sprint out into the night.

21

I pump my legs as fast as they'll go. Screams shatter the air, interspersed by long gaps of silence. I imagine people holding their breath so they won't be heard by the monsters. My skin breaks out in goose bumps at the thought of what might be happening.

My plan, if you can call it that, is to run like hell away from the school and find a vehicle with keys.

There ought to be plenty right in the parking lot. Obi and his men have been working hard to make sure all the cars have their keys in the ignition and are fully gassed up for emergencies like this one. Well, maybe they didn't predict a situation just like this, but close enough.

Once in a car, I plan to honk that horn like nobody's

business and drive as far away as I can. Hopefully, the hellions will follow me.

I have no idea what I'll do if they don't. Or if I get caught on the way to the car. Or how to escape once they're swarming around me. But that's too much to think about in this panic.

And what about Paige and Mom and Raffe?

I shake my head. Focus.

A man starts screaming to my left.

If I keep running, the man will probably die. If I stop to help him, I'll lose my chance to draw hellions away from everyone else. No good choices left in the World After.

I hesitate but keep on racing into the parking lot. Pooky Bear bumps against my leg on her straps, as though demanding to be part of the action. But I need to get to a car as soon as possible and start drawing the hellions my way.

I throw open the door to the nearest car. I can't help but look behind me.

There are shadows already flying after me, getting closer with every heartbeat. Behind them, people are running every which way near the building.

I jump in the car and shut the door, hoping there's a key. Hellions slam into my door and windshield.

Thank everything left that's good in the world for Obi's paranoia and preparation. The keys are there.

The little red Hyundai starts immediately. The engine roars to life.

I screech out of my parking spot, dislodging the creatures on my car. More pile on, though, as soon as I stop.

I honk the horn.

The hellions who hadn't noticed me before stop chasing people to look my way. I'm tempted to run them over and smash their creepy bat faces under the tires.

But my job is to draw them away, not to waste time playing with them. I crack open the windows and scream, 'Hey, you! Dinnertime! I'm over here, you scabby rats! Come and get me!'

The Hyundai is rocking with hellions as they pile on. I'm about to screech out of the lot – or at least make donuts until all the hellions head my way and leave the rest of the people alone – when I feel a thump. The car drops on one side. Then I see the shredded rubber of a tire being flung over the hood.

That was the front tire.

I stare dumbly at the ripped-up tire as it flops and wobbles to a standstill in the parking lot.

Then so many hellions pile onto my car that I can't see the tire anymore.

I stroke the fur of my teddy bear. It's all I can think to do.

Pooky Bear can't help me in a vehicle. Not a lot of room to slice and dice.

That means I need to exit the car if I want a chance at getting out of this.

I sit in the car.

I wonder how long a person can stay in a vehicle.

But then, of course, the hellions begin pounding on the windshield.

Their bat faces and needle-sharp teeth scrape against the windows. How much force can a windshield take?

If they pound their way in, I'll be in close quarters and won't be able to use my sword or run. If I open the door, they'll be on me before I can get my foot on the ground.

One of the hellions hops onto the hood, shoving the others aside. It's one of the beefy ones who followed me from the Pit.

He's carrying a rock.

He heaves the rock above his ugly head and smashes it against the windshield. The glass cracks into a million lines webbing across my vision. I take a deep breath as he lifts his rock again. I put my hand on the door handle and get ready to sprint my way out of here.

As the rock smashes down on the windshield again, I slam my door open as hard as I can.

All the hellions' attention was on the rock, and I catch them by surprise. I manage to smack several creatures out of the way with my door. That gives me a sliver of room to run.

As soon as I get my foot on the asphalt, claws grab me. All teeth and spittle, it's the side of hellions I haven't seen in my sword dreams. They run from Raffe. With him, they are the victims. With me, they are the killers.

A hellion's teeth scrape my cheek. Hands grab my arm and then claw at my chest. I hear myself screaming.

I grab its chin, shoving the head and mouth as far back as I can. For such a skinny little thing, it's extremely strong. I'm twisted as far away from it as I can be while trying to snap its neck backward.

Its head is frantically moving back and forth, gnashing at me. It gets closer to my face, so close that I can smell its rotting-fish breath.

It gashes me with its claws, not even trying to save its own neck. It must be insane. I'm not going to win this battle.

My back is to the car. Out of the corner of my eye, I can see two others climbing past the door to get at me. I frantically look at one, then the other. No gun, I can't draw my sword, and I'm trapped in the wedge of the car door.

The best I can hope for is that people get a few minutes to run while the hellions are busy tearing me apart. It's a Penryn party.

Suddenly, they all stop.

Their bat-like faces lift into the air, their ugly nostrils sniffing madly. One of them shakes its head like a dog shaking off water.

The one that was about to reach my neck with its claws backs off, letting me go. The ones climbing over the door can't back off fast enough. All around me, I sense terror.

They all run away.

It takes me a second to realize that I'm free and still alive.

In the headlight beams, a pair of legs walk toward the rush of hellions who are running from the car. The beam of light creeps up the person's body as the legs move toward me until I can see who it is.

It's my mother.

The hellions run. Away from the school, away from the people, and especially away from my mother.

'What the hell?' I stare, dumbfounded.

Then the smell finally hits my awareness. It reeks here. The windshield is splattered with Mom's rotten eggs. Old yellow-and-black goo oozes across the windshield like a giant bird dropping.

The smell.

They're running from the smell. They're running with the same terror that the hellions did from the demon in the Pit when he hissed at them. Does the smell remind them of their evil bosses? Do they assume an angry demon lord is coming when they smell rotten eggs?

I stare at my mother as she walks toward me with eggs in each hand.

She may be insane, but she has seen and experienced things. Things that other people haven't understood.

By the time she reaches me, the hellions have all run off.

'Are you okay?' she asks.

I nod. 'How'd you do that?'

'It does stink something awful, doesn't it?' My mom wrinkles her nose at me.

I stare at her, speechless, before I let out a weak laugh.

22

I walk into the grove with my mother. Another woman follows us a few steps behind.

I turn to her and say, 'Hello.'

She bows her head slightly. She looks about the same age as my mom and wears a midlength coat with a hood that covers her head. Beneath the coat, a dress falls to her ankles and drapes over her slippers. There's something familiar about her dress, but the thought flitters through my mind and gets pushed out by bigger things.

'She's with me,' says my mom. I'm not sure what to make of her. My mother usually doesn't have friends, but it's a whole new world, and maybe I don't know as much about my mom as I thought.

The grove is quiet except for the crunching of our feet and the sound of someone running toward us. I look back and see Raffe fast approaching on foot. He's almost invisible with his dark trench coat and cap. He must have come running when he heard me scream during the hellion attack.

Both my mother and her friend freeze when they see his figure, but I put out my hand and nod to show that he's with me. They continue into the grove while I drop back to wait for Raffe.

My mom looks back to keep an eye on us and doesn't even try to be polite about it. She's fully vigilant, scanning the shadows. Good for her.

'You all right?' His voice is soft, almost apologetic. I wonder if he thought that it would be better for me if the hellions didn't see him fighting for me. There were too many for him to kill them all, so a lot of them would have escaped and told other hellions. Or maybe he couldn't afford to have Obi and the others see him fighting full force.

'Yeah, I'm fine. Those ugly bullies were more afraid of my mommy than any warrior angel anyway. She's far more scary.'

He nods, looking preoccupied and troubled.

'What did Obi show you?'

'He gave me a tour of the camp.'

'He showed you the ramen supplies?'

'He showed me their weapons stock. Their evacuation plan. Their surveillance system.'

I almost trip over a branch. 'Why would he do that?' The question comes out more forcefully than I intended. Alarm bells are going off in my head. 'He was Mr. Paranoid the last time he saw you.'

'He wants to recruit me by impressing me. And he's more desperate for fighters this time. He can sense I have military experience.'

'So are you joining the Resistance?'

'Not likely. I saw their dissection tables.'

'What dissection tables?'

'Where they dissect anything that isn't strictly human. They have a prime table reserved in case they ever catch an angel.'

'Oh.'

I want to remind him that we're at war with an enemy we don't understand. But it's pointless to argue. I'll never be okay with Uriel's experiments on humans regardless of what reasons he thinks he has, so why would Raffe understand any reason we might have to cut into his kind?

'They're also working on an angel plague that they hope will wipe out my entire species.'

'Really?'

'They raided the lab on Angel Island when they rescued their people and stole something they could tinker with. Apparently, Laylah is working on a human plague and generating various strains to optimize the damage. There's one strain that they hope might work against angels.'

'How close are they to creating this angelic plague?'

'Not very. Otherwise, I would have had to kill them.'

We walk in silence, the concept of kill or be killed heavy between us.

I'm relieved when we reach Paige, if only to interrupt the silence.

My sister is sitting beside her locusts. My mother and her friend stop at a respectful distance and stare at the beasts.

Paige gets up, sending the locusts flying to the branches above, and runs to Mom. Paige is the baby of the family, and she has a different relationship with our mother than I do. Mom strokes her hair while Paige snuggles into her hug.

'How did it go with Doc?' Raffe whispers.

I take a deep breath and give him the bad news about Doc's broken arm. He doesn't say anything, but I know the news hits him hard. His amputated wings are withering every second they're not on him, and I'm pretty sure they won't last as long as they did last time. And now, the only doctor who can reattach them won't be back in action for six weeks.

And then there's my starving sister . . .

I feel drained. There must be another answer, but I'm too emotionally beat up to think. I just want to crawl into the vault in my head and close the door on the world.

I lean toward Raffe and feel his muscles against my arm. I close my eyes and relax into him. He feels so solid. I'm not sure if I'm giving him comfort or the other way around.

When I open my eyes, my mom's friend is watching us. I quickly step away from Raffe and stand tall. It's a strange thing for her to do – watching us instead of the locusts or the cut-up little girl.

'Somebody is looking for you,' she says.

Oh, right. 'Yeah, I heard.' The angels, the hellions – who doesn't want a piece of me right now?

She nods toward Raffe. 'I meant him.'

Do they have a bounty on him too? He had a red mask over his face when we were fighting the angels, so they must have thought he was just some demon, right?

'I have a message for you,' says the woman to Raffe. 'The message is, freedom and gratitude. Trust, my brother.'

Raffe spends a couple of seconds taking that in. 'Where is he?' he asks.

'Waiting for you downtown at the church with the stained glass.'

'He's there now?'

'Yes.'

He turns to me. 'Do you know where that is?'

'Sort of,' I say, having a vague memory of a couple of different churches in Palo Alto. 'What's going on?'

He doesn't say anything.

I wonder if the twins got their message wrong. Maybe the angels are looking for Raffe and not me.

'Do you need anything more from me?' the woman asks. She's creeping me out a little with her calm and peaceful voice.

'No, thank you.' Raffe's thoughts are far away.

The woman takes off her hood. Her head is shaved, looking particularly pale.

She takes off her coat, letting it fall to the ground. A sheet is wrapped around her body, tied at one shoulder. Her dark eyes look huge in her bald head, and they gaze at me with peace and serenity. Her hands are together with her fingers interlocking in front of her. The only thing that mars her old-world look is the pair of white tennis shoes she wears beneath her sheet.

She gives us a little bow before turning toward my sister. She doesn't say any of the rehearsed recruiting statements that I would expect from someone so obviously part of an apocalypse cult. She just moves toward my sister quietly, then stops in front of her.

My mother bows to the lady. 'Thank you for your sacrifice. Thank you for volunteering.'

'Volunteering for what?' I ask, feeling uneasy.

'Don't worry about it, Penryn.' My mother waves me away. 'I'll take care of this.'

'Take care of what?' I'm not used to seeing my mom dealing with people, and I'm certainly not used to seeing her interacting with people the way she is with this woman. 'Take care of what, Mom?'

My mother turns to me with exasperation, as if I'm embarrassing her. 'I'll explain it to you when you're older.'

I stand under the trees and blink several times at her. It's all I can think to do. 'When I'm older? Seriously?'

'This is not for you. I know you, Penryn. You don't want to see this.' She shoos me away.

I take a few steps back and join Raffe to watch in the shadows. My mother gestures for us to move farther back, and we turn and walk away. I slip behind a tree to watch when Mom stops looking at us. Raffe stands beside me but doesn't bother to hide.

The cult woman bows her head and kneels humbly in front of Paige. A part of me wants to leave, never knowing what's about to happen. But another part of me wants to barge in between them and break it up.

Something is going on with my mother's full approval that definitely needs supervising. Are they trying to recruit Paige into a cult? I feel no guilt about spying right now. I'm normally big on privacy, but I just need to make sure that there's nothing . . . well, crazy going on.

'I am here to serve you, Great One,' says the woman.

'It's okay,' says Mom to Paige. 'She volunteered. We have a whole line of cult members who volunteered. They know how important you are. They're willing to make sacrifices.'

I don't like the word *sacrifices*. I rush over to them.

Paige sits on a fallen tree, looking down at the woman now kneeling in front of her. The woman loosens her sheet and tilts her head to the side to expose her vulnerable neck.

I stand frozen, taking in the scene. 'What are you doing?'

'Penryn, stay out of this,' says Mom. 'This is a private affair.'

'Are you offering her as meat?'

'This isn't like the other time,' says Mom. 'She volunteered. This is an honor for her.'

The cult member looks at me awkwardly with her head still tilted to the side. 'It's true. I have been chosen. I am honored to nourish the Great One who has resurrected the dead and will lead us to heaven.'

'Who wants to go to heaven anymore? There's nothing but angels there.' I look at her to see if she's joking. 'You actually volunteered to be eaten alive?'

'My spirit will be renewed as my flesh nourishes the Great One.'

'Are you kidding me?' I look back and forth between my mother, who is nodding seriously, and the woman, who must be on drugs or something. 'What makes you think she's the Great One anyway? The last time we were here, this camp tried to draw and quarter her.'

'The doctor from Alcatraz has told Obadiah and the council that she is the Great One, the chosen one who will be our savior. The rest of the camp doesn't believe, but we of the New Dawn know that she must be the Great One meant to save us from this holy tragedy.'

'She's just a little girl.' I want to say the word *normal*, but I can't.

'Please don't stop this,' says the woman, her eyes pleading. 'Please don't interfere. If you reject me, someone else will have the privilege, and I will be disgraced.' Her eyes actually fill with tears. 'Please allow my life to mean something in this world. This is the greatest contribution and the greatest honor I could have in this life.'

I stand there with my jaw slack, trying to think of something to say.

My baby sister, though, doesn't have any problems turning her down. She shyly shakes her head no and crosses her legs, sitting in her monk pose. We'd always called her our little Buddha since she decided to be a vegetarian when she was only three.

Tears stream down the woman's cheeks. 'I understand. You have different plans for me.' She looks like she's been personally rejected. She gets up slowly and ties her sheet firmly back into place, giving me a glare.

The woman bows and backs out, refusing to turn her back to Paige.

My mom sighs beside me in exasperation. 'This doesn't change anything, you know,' she says to me. 'I'll just have to go back and find the next one in line.'

'Mom, no.'

'They want to do this. It's an honor for them. Besides,' she turns to follow the woman, 'they come with their own sheet for easy cleanup.'

23

'You know where this church with the stained glass is?' asks Raffe.

'What?' I'm still thinking about the cult and the messiah belief swirling around Paige.

'The church?' Raffe looks like he wants to wave his hand in front of my eyes. 'With the stained glass?'

'There are a couple of churches downtown. We can just walk to there from here. What's this about?'

'Someone is apparently trying to meet with me.'

'Yeah, I got that. Who and why?'

'I'd like to find out.' I can tell by Raffe's shuttered expression and the tone of his voice that he probably already has a good guess.

'Is this an angel who knows where the Resistance camp is?'

'Probably not. Someone who can get the word out through humans but not likely to know about the camp. He was probably sent to the church by someone like her.' He nods in the direction that the cult woman went.

I'm probably better off bringing Raffe to this mysterious person than risking him finding the camp while looking for Raffe.

I glance at Paige, who is singing Mom's apology song to her locusts perched on the branches above her. I walk over to her. 'If I leave for a little while, are you going to be okay on your own?'

She nods. From the edge of the shadows, Mom walks back to us. I'm not entirely sure whether Paige is better off with or without her, but since Mom is walking back alone, we must have at least a little time before her next shenanigans.

I walk back to Raffe. 'I'm all yours. Let's go find that church.'

I'm not as familiar with downtown Palo Alto as I am with downtown Mountain View, so it takes us longer than I expect to find the churches. The first one only has a tiny strip of stained glass, and I'm guessing that's not the one they meant. When someone says 'the church with the stained glass,' I assume they mean a whole lot of stained glass.

Downtown Palo Alto used to be the hip spot to be. It was known for its waiting list restaurants and cutting-edge startup companies. My dad used to love coming here.

'Who's looking for you?' I ask.

'I'm not sure.'

'But you have guesses.'

'Maybe.'

We walk down a street lined with craftsman houses. The cute suburban neighborhood seems to have mostly survived, except for a few blocks where houses have been randomly destroyed.

'So is it a military secret? Why aren't you sharing your guesses?'

We turn a corner, and there's the church with the stained glass.

'Raphael,' says a male voice from above.

A ghostly shape floats down toward us from the church's roof. A painfully white angel lands in front of us.

It's Josiah the albino. His skin is as unnaturally white as I remember, and his eyes are freakishly blood red, even in this dim moonlight. He looks like pure evil. Backstabbing creepy bastard.

My lip twitches in a snarl, and I pull off the teddy bear, gripping the handle of my sword.

Raffe stays my hand.

'I'm glad to see you're well, Archangel,' says Josiah. 'That was quite the scene last night.'

Raffe arches his brow arrogantly.

'I know what you're thinking,' says Josiah. 'But it's not true. Look, give me two minutes to explain.' It's amazing how a guy who so blatantly betrayed Raffe could sound so sincere and friendly.

Raffe is scanning the area. Seeing him do this reminds me that this could be a trap and that I shouldn't get distracted by my anger toward this scum.

I glance around and see nothing but quiet shadows in what was once a sweet little neighborhood.

'I'm listening,' says Raffe. 'Talk fast.'

'I talked Laylah into agreeing to change back your wings,' says Josiah. 'For real this time. She swore to me.'

'Why should I believe her?'

'Or you,' I say. It was Josiah and Laylah who tricked Raffe into having demon wings in the first place. There's no reason to believe they'll do anything but trick him again.

Josiah turns his bloody eyes to me. 'Uriel blames Laylah for the locusts turning on us last night. He says no one else but the doctor who created them could have that kind of control over them. He has her locked in her laboratory. He would have killed her, except she's in the middle of creating some plagues for him. That, and she's the only one who can maintain his growing army of monsters.'

'Plagues?' I ask. 'Why is everybody trying to make plagues?'

'What's an apocalypse without pestilence?' asks Josiah.

'Great,' I say. 'So we're supposed to trust a known liar who's cooking up apocalyptic plagues? And why would we even care what happens to Laylah? Serves her right for transplanting demon wings onto Raffe and playing Dr. Frankenstein with human beings. We're not just biomass to be shaped into whatever dolls she wants to play with.'

Josiah looks at me, then back at Raffe. 'Does she need to be here?'

'Apparently, she does,' says Raffe. 'It turns out that she's the only one I can trust to watch my back.'

I stand a little taller when he says that.

'Laylah didn't know.' Josiah shifts his body to make it clear he's talking to Raffe. 'I warned her not to get involved, but you know how ambitious she is. Look, you can trust her this time because you're her only hope out of this mess. Uriel will kill her when he has everything he needs from her.'

'Kill her? You mean set her up for a fall?'

'No, I mean kill her. He was furious with her, wouldn't believe a word she said when she told him she had nothing to do with the locusts turning on us. He flew into a rage and told her he killed the Messenger and he could kill her too. The Messenger, Raffe. Uriel killed him.'

An image of the winged man who called himself Archangel Gabriel, the Messenger of God being shot down over the rubble of Jerusalem flashes through my mind. They looped it for days on TV.

Josiah shakes his head like he's still having trouble believing it. 'Uriel said Gabriel had gone insane, that he hadn't actually spoken to God in eons, that he'd made up all the rules that God had supposedly commanded him to make. He said there was no reason why Uriel couldn't be Messenger, that he could lie as well as Gabriel. So Uriel had him killed. Killed. He admitted it.'

They stare at each other, Raffe looking just as shocked as Josiah.

'So what's the big deal?' I ask. 'Our kings used to get murdered all the time.'

'We don't kill our own,' says Josiah. 'The last time that happened, Lucifer and his armies fell.' He tilts his head at me as if not sure the message got through. 'It was kind of a big deal.'

'Yeah, I've heard of him,' I say.

Raffe lets out a frustrated breath. 'I can't do anything about it from the outside.'

'I know,' says Josiah. 'That's why you have to let Laylah fix your wings. Somebody other than Uriel has to win the election. We've got word out to try to find Michael, but it's unlikely we'll find him in time.'

'Why does Laylah think they'd vote for me instead of Uriel?'

'You still have loyal followers. Rumors have been flying that you're back, and I've been careful to cultivate them in your favor. You have a shot.'

'No wonder Michael is staying away. Knowing him, becoming the Messenger is the last thing he wants to do. He can't lead armies in the field if he's smoothing feathers and buried under administration at home.'

'You're the only archangel who can challenge Uriel right now. Even if Michael wins in absentia, an archangel would need to stand in for him until he comes back. If you can do that, then Laylah can stand behind you. She now has every reason to want you to have your wings back.'

'Raffe, you can't trust him. Not after what he's done.'

'I know it looks bad,' says Josiah, 'but have I not made the oath? A life for a life. You gave me my freedom from eternal slavery and gave me the chance to earn a life worth living. And I pledged it to you.'

I push my face toward him. 'You didn't look so happy to see him back in San Francisco.'

'I thought he was dead. I thought I was free of my oath, free to make my own way. But I would never betray Raphael. Why do you think he came to me? I'm the only one guaranteed to be loyal. The only one without a clan, a lineage, or honor to protect that supersedes my allegiance to him. Do you understand?'

He looks at Raffe. 'I didn't know what they were going to do to you. I thought they were just going to reattach your wings. Laylah had every intention of following through, but Uriel found out you were here and she lost her nerve. But now she simply has no choice. She has no one to ally with but you. And she's the only one who can sew your wings back on.'

That last part hits home. With Doc's arm broken, who else can do the operation?

'You're running out of time, Archangel,' he says. 'The election is about to happen. And if you can't stop Uriel, we'll have a deranged murderer as our Messenger. His word will be law, and everyone who opposes him will fall. This could be the start of a civil war. We could end up having an all-out extermination of not only the humans, but all angels who oppose him.'

I can feel the tension radiating from Raffe. How can he say no? This is his chance at getting his wings back and setting things right. He can have everything he wants. He might even become Messenger and save everyone from this apocalyptic mess.

And then he would go home, never to return in my lifetime.

24

'Where would you operate?' asks Raffe.

'At the aerie,' says Josiah. 'Laylah is under guard. She can't get out. But I could sneak you in.'

'Go. I'll follow you with the wings in a minute,' he says, taking off the backpack that holds his blanket-rolled wings.

'I should go with you,' I say.

'You can't.' He takes off his coat and slides the backpack straps on backward so that he's wearing the pack against his chest. He fiddles with the waist strap, making sure it's in place. Wearing a backpack this way might not look great on someone else, but on him, it looks like a fitted piece of military gear strapped tight to his broad chest.

'You need someone to watch your back.'

He arches his back and spreads his wings the way I might stretch my legs after sitting too long. 'Josiah will have to do. It's too dangerous for you. Besides, you need to take care of your family.'

A thought occurs to me. 'Maybe Laylah could help Paige too?' I hate even saying it, but with Doc's arm broken, who else can we turn to?

'If things work out for me, I'll see if I can get her to help your sister.'

'Paige doesn't have any more time than you do.'

'It'll be safer for her if we know that we can trust Laylah first.'

He's right, but my mind keeps spinning. I nod. 'What about your sword?'

'I can't fly with her if she won't accept me. And that won't happen until I get my wings back. Take care of her until I return?'

I nod, warmth flooding my chest. 'So you'll be back?'

He looks at me with worry in his eyes.

I know we've gone our separate ways before, but this time, it feels permanent. He's about to reenter the angel world. And when he does, he'll forget all about that Daughter of Man he partnered up with for a few days. He's made it clear that he can't be with me.

'Is this goodbye?' I ask.

He nods.

We look into each other's eyes. As usual, I have no idea what he's thinking. I could make guesses, but they'd be fantasy.

He leans down, and his lips hover a hair's breadth from mine. I close my eyes, feeling the tingle of anticipation.

Then he presses his lips to mine. His warmth spreads out from my lips down into my chest and stomach. Time stops, and I forget about everything else – the apocalypse, my enemies, watching eyes, monsters in the night.

All I feel is the kiss.

All I am is Raffe's girl.

Then he pulls back.

He presses his forehead to mine, and I can feel the prickling of tears behind my lashes.

'You're going to get your wings back.' I swallow and talk fast before my voice can waver. 'You'll become Messenger, and they'll follow you as their leader. Then you'll take the angels home, away from here. Promise me that when you become the Messenger, you'll take them away from here, away from all of us.'

'Not much of a chance that I'll become Messenger, but yes, I'll do what I can to take them away.'

And he'll be the first one gone.

I swallow.

We stand there for a few moments, our breath mingling.

The wind picks up, and it feels like we're the only living beings in the world.

Then he straightens up, leaning away from me. 'It's not about what I want or need. My people, the entire fabric of my society is about to unravel. I can't let that happen.'

'I didn't ask you to.' I slowly wrap my arms around my middle. 'You're the best hope for *my* people too, you know. If you take control and take them back to where they came from, my world will be saved too.' *But you won't be with me.*

He shakes his head sadly at me. 'These are the rules we live by. We are soldiers, Penryn. Legendary warriors willing to make legendary sacrifices. We do not ask. We do not choose.' He says that like a motto, a pledge he's said a thousand times.

He slowly lets me go, firmly setting me aside.

He brushes my hair out of my face, strokes my cheek. He looks at every part of my face as if memorizing it. A half smile forms on his lips.

Then he drops his hand, turns around, and leaps into the air.

I put my hand over my mouth to keep from calling him back.

The October wind tugs at my hair. Dry leaves float by, lost and abandoned.

25

I should go.

Turn around and leave this place.

But my feet feel like they're rooted to the sidewalk. I stand there, worried. Worried that it's a trap, worried that I won't see him again, worried that he is yet again in the hands of his enemies.

I'm so lost in all the things that might happen that I don't hear the footsteps behind me until they're too close for me to run.

People step out from behind buildings. One, five, twenty. They're all dressed in sheets, and their heads are shaved.

'You missed them,' I say. 'They weren't much to look at anyway.'

They walk toward me from all sides.

'We're not here for them,' one of them says. The top of his head is more tanned than the others' like he's been shaving his for some time. 'The masters like to do their business in private. We understand that.'

'The masters?'

The group keeps closing in on me, and I start to feel trapped. But these are cult members, not street gangs. They don't exactly have a reputation for attacking people. Still, I put my hand on my teddy bear hanging at my hip.

'No, we're not here for them,' I hear a woman's voice say. 'No one has a bounty on your angel friend.' Then I see her – the woman who offered herself up to Paige.

'I guess I should have let her eat you.'

The woman glares at me as though I humiliated her by saving her life.

I pull off the bear and wrap my hand around the sword handle. It's cold and hard and ready for battle. But I'm hesitant to use it on them. We all have more than enough enemies trying to kill us already without going after each other.

I back away from Tan Head. The circle tightens. 'Are you really going to harm the sister of the Great One?' Hopefully, they believe in their own story.

'No, we mean you no harm,' says Tan Head. He reaches for me.

I step away and pull out my sword.

A hand holding a damp cloth reaches around me from behind and clamps down over my mouth and nose. The cloth reeks of something awful that shoots straight into my head and makes the world fuzzy.

I try to struggle.

I knew it was a trap. I just hadn't realized the trap was for me.

My thoughts turn into a jumbled mess.

The sharp scent of chemicals, the burning of the fumes going down my throat – these are the last things I remember as the world fades into darkness.

26

I wake up blinking in the sunlight in the back of a classic Rolls-Royce. Everything is sleek and shiny and polished. Big band music plays with glorious fidelity. The driver wears a black suit complete with a chauffeur's hat. He watches me through the rearview mirror as I groggily come to.

My head feels foggy, and my nose is still full of a chemical scent. What happened?

Oh, yeah, the cult . . . I put my hand up and touch my hair to make sure it's still there. You never know.

My hair is still on me, but my sword is not. Only my empty teddy bear hangs on my shoulder strap. I stroke the soft fur, wondering what they did with my sword. It's too valuable for them to have left it and too heavy for them to have taken it far. I can only hope they hefted it into the trunk or somewhere nearby as proof that they got the right girl for the bounty.

My car seems to be part of a matching caravan of classic cars – one in front of us and one behind.

'Where are we going?' My throat feels lined with sand.

The driver doesn't answer. His silence gives me the creeps.

'Hello?' I ask. 'You don't need to worry about anyone hearing us. Angels don't like Man's technology. They won't have a bug in here or anything.'

Silence.

'Can you hear me? Are you deaf?' The driver doesn't respond.

Maybe the angels have figured out that we are not as perfectly formed as they are. Maybe they've realized the value of some of our flaws and hired a deaf driver so that he can't hear me enough to be persuaded.

I lean forward to tap his shoulder. As I do, I glimpse the rest of his face in the rearview mirror.

The red meat of his gums and cheeks is clearly visible. It's like half of his face has been skinned off of him. His teeth sit exposed like he's a living skeleton. His eyes stare straight at me in the mirror. He's watching my reaction.

I freeze. I want to jerk back, but he's watching me. His eyes are not those of a monster. They are the eyes of a man who expects yet another person to cringe and pull away from him.

I bite my lip to keep from making a sound. My hand still hovers above his shoulder. I hesitate for two breaths, then gently put my hand on his shoulder to tap him.

'Excuse me,' I say. 'Can you hear me?' I continue to look at him in the mirror to let him know that I saw his face.

His shoulder feels solid, the way a shoulder should feel. That's a relief, both for me and for him. He's probably not some new ghoul that the angels have created, but a regular man they injured.

At first, I think he'll continue to ignore me. But then he nods, slightly.

I hesitate, wondering if I should ignore the elephant in the car or if I should ask him what happened to his face. From spending time with my sister's friends, I know that people with disabilities sometimes wish others would simply ask and get it over with, while other times, they want to be treated normally and not have their disability define them. I choose to get on with business.

'Where are we going?' I keep my voice as friendly and casual as I can.

He says nothing.

'You've got the wrong girl, you know. Lots of people have weapons. Just because I had a sword doesn't mean I'm the girl the angels are looking for.'

He continues to drive.

'Okay, I get it. But do you really believe the angels will give you safe passage? Even if they don't kill you today, how will you know they won't kill you next week? It's not like every angel will get a notification with your picture that says you've captured the girl they wanted.'

The big band music continues to fill the car, and he keeps on driving.

'What's your name?'

No response.

'Do you think you could slow down a little? Maybe a lot? Maybe even stop for just a teensy second and let me out? There's been a mistake. I don't belong here. Come to think of it, neither do you.'

'Where do I belong then?' His voice is harsh and full of anger.

It's hard to understand him. I guess it's not easy to talk when your lips have been ripped off. It takes me a minute to translate what I heard.

I have more experience than most in figuring out what someone with a speech impediment is saying. Paige had a couple of friends with disabilities that kept them from communicating easily. It was her patience with her friends and her translations that finally allowed me to start understanding them. Now it's second nature.

'You belong with us,' I say. 'The human race.'

Isn't this what Raffe's been saying all along? That I belong with the human race and he doesn't? I push that thought away.

The driver glances up at the mirror in surprise. He didn't expect me to understand him. He probably spoke just to scare me off with his otherness. His eyes narrow as though he's wondering if I'm playing a trick on him.

'The human race doesn't want me anymore.' He watches me as if suspecting that I just got lucky in understanding him last time.

He eerily says the things that Raffe won't say about himself and his own situation. Does Raffe think of himself as this deformed in the eyes of angels?

'You look human to me.'

'Then you must be blind,' he says angrily. 'Everyone else screams when they see me. If I drove off, where would I go? Who would I call my own? Even my own mother would run from me now.' There's a world of sadness behind his angry voice.

'No, she wouldn't.' Mine wouldn't. 'Besides, if you think you're the ugliest thing I've seen this week, boy, do you have a lot to learn about what's going on out there.'

He gives me a glance in the mirror.

'Sorry. You're not even in the league, frankly. You'll just have to settle for being classified as perfectly human like the rest of us.'

'You've seen people more horrible than me?'

'Oh, heck yeah. I've seen people that would make *you* run and scream. And one of them is a friend of mine. She's sweet and kind, and I miss her. But Clara's back with her family, and that's the best I can wish for her these days.'

'Her people took her back in?' There's disbelief in his voice but hope in his eyes.

'It took a little coaxing, but not much. They love her, and that goes beyond what's on the outside. Anyway, where are we going?'

'Why should I tell you? You're just pretending to be friendly to get me to do what you want. Then you'll run off to your friends and tell them what a freak I was. That I actually believed you might not be repulsed by me.'

'Get over yourself. We're all in danger. We all need to work together and help each other if we can.' That sounded a little too much like Obi. Maybe the twins are right and we do have something in common. 'Besides, I haven't asked you to do anything yet. I'm only asking for information.'

He assesses me through the mirror. 'We're going to the new aerie in Half Moon Bay.'

'And then what?'

'And then we hand you over to the angels. The New Dawn members can collect their bounty – assuming the angels are in a generous mood – and I get to continue living.'

'All at the mercy of our invaders.'

'Do you want to know what happened to my face?'

I don't. It doesn't seem like a story I want to hear.

'They ripped it off for fun. Half my face. Skinned alive, I guess. It was the most excruciating thing I could ever have imagined. In fact, I couldn't even imagine it before. You know what it's like to have your life changed like that? One moment, you're normal, the next, you're a monster freak? Do you know that I used to be an actor?' He snorts. 'Yeah, I made my living off my charming smile. Now I don't even have lips to smile with.'

'I'm sorry.' I can't think of anything else to say. 'Look, I know it's been hard.'

'You have no idea.'

'You'd be surprised. Just because I don't have a problem on the outside visible for the world to see doesn't mean I'm not messed up on the inside. That can be just as hard to deal with.'

'Spare me your self-centered teen angst. What you feel is nothing compared to what I feel.'

'Gee, okay,' I say. 'You're not at all wallowing in self-centeredness. I see that now.'

'Listen, kid. I haven't talked to anyone in weeks. I thought I missed it, but now you've reminded me that I really don't.'

The music fills the car with old-world style before he speaks again. 'Why should I help you when no one bothers to help me?'

'Because you're a decent human being.'

'Yeah, one that wants to live. If I let you go, they'll come down and kill me.'

'If you don't let me go, you won't feel quite so human anymore. Being human isn't about whether you fit in or look like the rest of us. It's about who you are and what you're willing to do or not do.'

'Humans kill all the time.'

'Not decent ones.'

Outside, the deserted world slides by. I guess no one wants to go near the new aerie. Word must have gotten around about that apocalypse party.

'Did you really kill an angel?' he asks.

'Yeah.' I've killed two.

'You're the only one I've met who has. What happens if I let you go?'

'I return to my family and try to keep us all alive.'

'Everybody? You'd try to keep all of us alive?'

'I meant my family. That's hard enough. How would I even begin to keep *everyone* alive?'

'If the only one who can kill an angel can't do it, then who can?'

It's a good question, one that takes me a minute to come up with an answer. 'Obadiah West can. Him and his freedom fighters. I'm just a teenager.'

'History is filled with teenagers who lead the fight. Joan of Arc. Okita Soji, the samurai. Alexander the Great. They were all teenagers when they began leading their armies. I think we're back to those times again, kid.'

27

We weave sedately through the abandoned cars on the road. Occasionally, I see people scurrying away when they spot our car. It must be a strange sight, seeing a luxury caravan cruising down the road. Not that everybody hasn't already picked an expensive car to try out, but that phase mostly ended in the first couple of weeks. After that, it was all about keeping a low profile.

The miles pass as I try to figure out how and when my escape should happen. We're moving too fast for me to jump out of the car. Just as I decide that I won't be able to make a run for it, we slow to a stop.

There's a roadblock of cars up ahead.

At first glance, it looks like a mutated, multi-angled scarab grown to fill the entire road. The cars are artfully laid out to make it seem as if it were happenstance, but my intuition tells me it's probably tactical.

My driver reaches down and pulls up a pistol. I don't have my sword on me, so I'm on my own.

I casually check the back door to see if I could make a run for it. But before I can make a move, men with guns emerge from behind the cars. Homemade tattoos are scrawled across their necks, faces, and hands. A street gang.

They come at us with bats and tire irons. One of them swings a tire iron into the windshield with a thunderous slam that makes me jump in my seat.

The glass turns white with a million cracks around the impact area but leaves the rest intact.

Baseball bats pound on the hood and doors. The gang spreads out to attack the other cars. The shiny perfection of our antique Rolls-Royce is turning into a demolition derby car.

The passenger window of the car in front of us rolls down before the men can reach it. The black barrel of an Uzi submachine gun sticks out of it.

I duck my head just as the gunfire begins. The rat-tat-tat of the Uzi is deafening even with my palms against my ears.

When it stops a few seconds later, all I can hear is the ringing in my ears. A train could be rolling by outside my window and I wouldn't know it right now.

I peek my head up to see what's going on. Two cult members with shaved heads and sheet dresses – one man, one woman – stand beside our car, holding matching Uzis and scanning the area.

Three men lie bleeding on the road. One fell beside a spontaneous roadside memorial. These street shrines have cropped up all over since the Great Attack. Photos of lost loved ones, dried flowers, stuffed animals, handwritten notes pouring out words of love and loss.

Fresh blood glistens on a framed photo of a smiling girl with a missing front tooth.

I had always assumed the roadside memorials were for people who died because of angels. Now I wonder how many of them died because of other people.

The other attackers are nowhere to be seen.

After a few seconds, the cult members hop into the two largest cars in the roadblock. They drive slowly into the dead cars, shoving them out of the way like tanks to create a path for us. When they finish, they jump back into their classic cars, and we keep driving.

By the time we arrive at the aerie, I can feel the fear rolling off the driver. He's more afraid than I am, which is saying a lot.

We pull up to the side of the hotel's main building. It looks more like a country estate than a hotel, with its

sprawling mansion, golf course, and large circular driveway. There are guards posted there, looking official.

My stomach turns icy at the thought of being in this
place again. The last two times I was here, I barely got
out alive.

The cars stop, and the cult members get out. One of
them opens my door like a chauffeur, as if he expects me
to step out like a lady attending a party. I slide to the far
side of the car and crouch in the corner. It's pointless to
run with so many angels, but I don't have to make it easy
for them.

I kick the guy who leans in to pull me out. Now
they're starting to look embarrassed as well as scared.
Eventually, though, they open the door I'm leaning
against and drag me out kicking and screaming.

It takes four of them to do it, and I'm glad to see that
my driver is not one of them. The guy holding me is
trembling, and I don't think it's because he's afraid of
me. Whatever it is their new religion tells them about
the angels, they must know that they're violent and
merciless.

'We've brought the girl to be exchanged for your
promise of safety,' says Tan Head.

The guards assess me. Their eyes look like they were
chiseled out of stone – emotionless and alien. The feathers on their wings ruffle in the breeze.

One of them motions for us to follow him to the main entrance.

'You can either walk or we can drug you and drag you there,' says Tan Head.

I put my hands up in defeat. They let me go but stand only an inch away, blocking my path in every direction but toward the aerie. We walk along the circular driveway to the main entrance, with every angel posted on the rooftop and balconies watching us.

We stop in front of the double glass doors. One of the guards goes inside. We wait in silence under the predatory gaze of far too many warriors. The cult people rush to the trunk of one of the cars and heft the sword out. It takes two of them to drag it across the driveway toward us.

Then the glass doors open, and several angels come outside. One of the newcomers is Uriel's footman, the one who helped him get ready for the last party.

The men bow deeply to the angels. 'We've brought the girl as promised, masters.'

The angel lackey nods at the guards who then grab my arms.

When they lay the sword in front of Uriel's footman, he says, 'Kneel.'

The men kneel in front of him like prisoners awaiting execution. The angel marks their foreheads with a black smear.

'This will ensure your safety from angels. None of us shall harm you so long as you have this mark.'

'And the rest of our loyal group?' asks Tan Head, looking up at the angel.

'Bring them to us. We'll mark the rest of you. Let it be known that we can be generous to those who serve us.'

'Let it be known that they tore apart their last set of servants,' I say to the cult members.

The men glance at me fearfully, looking worried. I wonder if they knew about the massacre that happened here.

The angels ignore me. 'Continue the good work, and perhaps we'll allow you to serve us in heaven.'

The men try to bow deeper, pressing themselves onto the ground. 'It is our honor to serve the masters.'

I would make a gagging noise if I wasn't so scared.

They shove me into the building. My sword scrapes the pavement as an angel drags it behind us.

28

Inside, the lobby is crowded and roaring with noise, every inch of standing space bursting with angels. Either they've all come indoors or their numbers have swelled overnight.

They must be gathered for the election. That would explain the angel host we'd seen flying this way.

The crowd parts to let me through.

It must be the sound of the sword dragging behind me that catches everyone's attention. They all stare as we pass. I feel like a witch being paraded through town. I guess I'm lucky they're not throwing rotten tomatoes at me.

Instead of going into a room, they take me through the building and out onto the lawn where the massacre happened. They're putting me on display for all angels to see.

There are still patches of dried blood on the terrace. Apparently, there's no one left to clean up after them anymore. The place is a mess. Confetti and costumes litter the ground, and for some reason, the grass is churned up like an army had randomly gone through it with shovels.

Signs have sprouted up over the lawn. The last time I was here, there was only one booth, but now there are booths everywhere. They seem to be grouped in threes – red, blue, and green. I can't read the symbols on the colored banners, but I recognize Uriel's from when Raffe pointed it out to me. His is the red banner.

The other two banners in each booth cluster are azure blue with symbols that are curved lines and dots and misty green with dashed lines that flow both thick and thin. Even though I can't read them, I like them better than Uriel's, which is all angles and screaming in red.

Angels fly all over the sky and walk over the lawn that used to be a golf course. They begin gathering around the colored banners, looking like distinct teams. Many of the angels are chanting, 'Uriel! Uriel! Uriel!' near the red-bannered booths like they're at a football game.

The second largest group gathers around the misty green booths and shouts, 'Michael! Michael! Michael!'

And a few others collect around the azure blue booths and begin shouting, 'Raphael! Raphael! Raphael!'

Most of the angels mill around in the sky or between the booths, as if they're still deciding. But as Raffe's supporters keep chanting, more soldiers join them and begin shouting his name.

I'm so surprised that I stumble to a stop in the middle of the lawn. My guards have to shove me to get me to go again.

'Raphael! Raphael! Raphael!'

I hope he's somewhere nearby, hearing his people shouting his name.

He belongs here.

That thought echoes through my mind because I still have a hard time believing it. Angels are not meant to be alone, and he's been alone for far too long.

Does he dream about this? To have his wings again and be welcomed back into the host? To lead his soldiers and be part of his tribe again?

'Raphael! Raphael! Raphael!'

Of course he does. Isn't that what he's been telling me all this time? He belongs with them and not with me.

I wonder if he has his angel wings back yet. Is he just on the verge of getting everything he wants? On the verge of going back to his world?

I throw the rest of my thoughts into the vault in my head and lean as hard as I can to close the door. I don't quite succeed. That's been happening a lot lately.

A brawl breaks out at the cluster of booths to my right. Some take to the air. Others grapple on the ground. Angels who had been meandering on the lawn fly over to watch the fight.

Four warriors battle against a dozen while spectators cheer. No one uses his sword. This is apparently more of a contest than an angry fight.

The smaller group tosses the other angels around like rag dolls. The brawl is over in seconds.

When the last one is pinned to the ground with another warrior sitting on top of him, the winner shouts, 'Raphael! First vote goes to Archangel Raphael!'

The four winning warriors jump up with their arms raised in victory and scream into the air. And I realize something. Despite Raffe's supporters being outnumbered, they are the toughest, fiercest, most skilled fighters.

Then, almost immediately, the spectator angels congregate at another cluster of booths. Another fight is beginning there.

Within seconds, the next round is determined as someone shouts, 'Michael! Second vote goes to Archangel Michael!' The crowd cheers.

It's pure chaos, but somehow everyone seems to know the rules. I'm guessing the winning team of each fight wins a vote for their favorite candidate. The archangel with the most number of winning fights must win the election. So their election isn't just about the number of people behind you, it's a matter of having the best fighters behind you.

My guards shove me forward, but they're not even looking at me. They're watching the crazed winged warriors as they perform their version of an election.

Some of the angels have what looks like blood smeared across their faces like war paint. Others snarl as they fly past each other over broken plates and crushed champagne glasses. Those who are still wearing dinner jackets from the last party rip them off their shoulders, tearing the seams along the fabric.

They've stopped pretending to be civilized and are letting their inner barbarians out.

No wonder Uriel has to go to such extreme sliminess. Raffe and Michael are warriors with armies of fighters loyal to them. Uriel is just a politician and probably wouldn't stand a chance unless he offered something like a legendary apocalypse as a treat for crazed, bloodthirsty warriors.

Being the only human in the center of all this violence makes me feel like my fate is sealed. I probably have until the end of the voting before they kill me. I wonder how long that will be.

By the time my guards shove me through the chaos and up onto the raised stage, my insides are trembling and I'm fighting to keep my legs moving. I'm surrounded by a sea of frenzied angels, and I can't see a way out.

29

So far, it's a surprisingly close election. Surprising in that Uriel has been campaigning for so long, and Raffe and Michael haven't even been here.

'I hate to interrupt the festivities,' shouts Uriel from up in the air, 'but this is something worth seeing.' He floats down to the stage at the edge of the lawn.

My guards drag me up the steps to meet him. Angels climb the steps on the other side, dragging two huge cages crammed full of thumping and screeching hellions.

Another group of angels climbs up with a third cage between them. In among the ugly hellions thrashing behind the bars is Beliel.

I haven't seen him since Angel Island. It looks like partnering up with the hellions hasn't worked out for him. The dried-up demon holds on to the bars with his shriveled hands. He looks around, assessing the assembled host.

Uriel faces the crowd. 'Before you decide which candidate to fight for, I have two pieces of crucial information you may want to consider.' He sounds as though he's impartial to this whole affair. 'First, we have found hellions skulking about far too close to the aerie,' says Uriel. 'Certainly we can expect them in a hellhole like earth, but I'd like you to take a close look at these two in particular.'

Two angels step forward, each holding a spotted hellion they've extracted from a cage. They are considerably larger, and they fight and thrash more fiercely than the others.

'These are not one of the local breeds,' says Uriel. 'Take a good look at them. These hellions emerged straight from the Pit.'

And so they did. I recognize them as the ones who followed me from Beliel's hell. The angels fall silent.

'You may remember that we exterminated this cunning species – wiped them out from every known world to be rid of their intense ferocity and their nasty habit of organizing the others,' says Uriel. 'The only place they could still exist is in the Pit.'

His eyes sweep the crowd. 'We all know that nothing leaves the Pit without being let out. The hellions who infest this world have become puny and stupid. These, however, are fresh from their hellish homeland and are being led by this demon.' He points to Beliel.

Beliel is still not healed, although he has patches of pink skin beginning to grow on his face. He looks horrible, like he's been ravaged by a designer disease. His skin is still crusty and withered, but now it's split by fresh pink strips of new skin. His back is bleeding, as if his body is having particular trouble healing from the severed wings.

'Somewhere, gates have been opened to the Pit,' says Uriel. 'Somewhere, the beast lurks and is letting out his creatures. Somewhere, the apocalypse is starting without us.' He pauses.

'As I have promised in the past – and I continue to promise today – elect me now, and by morning, you will be a legendary warrior for the apocalypse. Raphael is absent. Michael is absent. If you elect one of them as Messenger, the glory of the apocalypse might be over by the time they lead you into battle. You might already be dead by then, or worse, perhaps you'll be saggy, out of shape, and unprepared. You never know. It could happen.'

A dutiful chuckle goes through the crowd.

'The second thing I'd like to present,' says Uriel, 'is the girl.'

My guards shove me onto center stage.

'If you've just arrived, I thank you for traveling such a great distance to participate in the election. Many of you were not present during the fight on the beach when one of ours was slain by this Daughter of Man. But I know you've all heard the story by now. I'm here to tell you that it's all true. This human girl – as puny as she seems – somehow managed to convince an angel sword to allow her to wield it.' Uriel pauses for effect. 'Even more astonishingly, she used the sword to kill one of our own.'

He lets that sink in. I notice that he doesn't say anything about my sword commanding theirs to stand down. If only they knew that the sword that dominated their weapons is called Pooky Bear.

'I captured her with utmost speed and have brought her to justice. It's time we avenge our fallen brother.'

The crowd cheers.

30

'Uriel murdered Archangel Gabriel!' I point my finger at Uriel. 'He's making up a false apocalypse so he can become the new Messenger!'

The crowd quiets down. I don't for a second think that they believe me. But I'm guessing that I'm entertaining enough for them to listen to, for now anyway. 'At least investigate if you don't believe me.'

Uriel chuckles. 'The Pit is too good a punishment for her. She should be torn apart by hellions. How convenient that we have some.'

'I don't even get a sham trial? What kind of justice is that?' I know this won't get me very far, but right now, I'm too amped to keep my mouth shut.

Uriel raises his eyebrows. 'That's an idea. Shall we give her a trial?'

To my surprise, the angels take up the chant. 'Trial! Trial! Trial!'

The way they're saying it makes it sound like Romans at a stadium, demanding the death of a gladiator.

Uriel puts out his hands to quiet the crowd. 'A trial it is.'

I'm suddenly not so excited about getting a trial.

My guards shove me. I stumble forward and climb down from the stage. They push me until I'm in the middle of what used to be the golf course.

I rotate around, realizing that I am at the center of a large circle of angels. The circle quickly becomes a dome as angel bodies fill in the space all around and above me.

The sun becomes blotted out by layers of bodies and wings. I'm in a living dome with no way out.

A breach opens up in the wall of bodies. Through it, the hellions get tossed my way. They flap around, trying to find a way out, but there are no gaps in the dome.

Everyone is chanting. 'Trial! Trial! Trial!'

Somehow I don't think their idea of a trial and my idea of a trial are the same.

The last hellion cage that gets poured into the domed arena is Beliel's. As he spills onto the ground, he looks up at Uriel, snarling.

For a second, he looks angry and betrayed. Fear peeks through before he puts on his sneer again. His declaration of always being alone and unwanted seems to be proven over and over again. For an instant, I forget what a horrible being he is and I feel a flash of sympathy for him.

He walks into the center of the dome, at first stumbling and unsure, then with more confidence and even outright defiance. The angels cheer like he's their favorite football player in a championship game. I suspect hardly any of them even know who he is. I know who he is and what happened to him, and I barely even recognize him.

The hellions are scrambling in a mad panic. They bounce from one edge of the dome to the other, frantically trying to find a gap between bodies.

'What kind of a trial is this?' I ask, suspecting the answer.

'A warrior's trial,' says Uriel as he flies above me. 'It's more than you deserve. The rule is simple. The last one alive goes free.'

The crowd cheers again, roaring their approval.

'Try to make this entertaining,' says Uriel. 'Because if it's not, the crowd will decide whether the last one standing lives or dies.'

The angels chant, 'Die! Die! Die!'

I guess that answers the question.

I have no idea if the hellions understand the rules, but they screech and try to attack the wall of warriors. The angels grab one and throw it down onto the ground where it lies dazed and shaking its head. The other angels roar at the hellions as they approach. The beasts pause in midair and back away.

'Hellions,' says Uriel. 'One of you gets to live.' He puts up an index finger for emphasis. 'You must kill the others.' He points to everyone else. He speaks slowly and loudly, as if speaking to a befuddled dog. 'Kill!' He points to me.

The hellions all look my way.

I step back without thinking. What am I supposed to do?

I back into the hard body of an angel who is part of the living arena. He bends down and growls into my ear. I look around frantically for an escape as the hellions begin flying toward me.

Amazingly, I see my sword lying on the ground between me and the oncoming hellions. I'm sure that was no accident. They want to see the Daughter of Man slaughter hellions with an angel sword.

I race for the sword as fast as I can. I grab it off the ground, roll to manage my momentum, and begin swinging my blade even as I jump to my feet again.

I slice just as the first hellion reaches me. It screeches as blood gushes out of its belly.

Without thinking, I swing at the second one that comes at me.

It's so close I can smell its rotting-flesh breath. It swerves, and I miss by an inch.

I steady myself and take a solid stance. During the next couple of swings, I calm down and let the sword take over. This is easy for her. Pooky Bear has killed thousands of these things. Walk in the park.

Only the things aren't behaving the way the sword is used to. The two from the Pit make their hyena noises, calling to the others. The others pause, listening, then they start circling me.

They hover, just out of reach of my blade. I spin around, trying to see them all, unsure of what's happening.

In the meantime, Beliel is backing away – I can see him out of the corner of my eye. He grabs a hellion and snaps the neck as if it were a chicken.

He silently drops the body and grabs the next one nearest him. The others are all focused on me. All except the spotted hellions from the Pit. They look smarter, craftier, and they watch him with intelligent eyes.

Beliel isn't trying to save me, I know that. He's just killing off as many as he can while they have me as a distraction. Then, by the time they're finished with me, he'll only have a few to contend with.

That's okay. I don't need him to be my friend, so long as he's killing off my enemies.

The spotted hellions make their hyena calls again, and the others fly to include Beliel in the circle. Then they tighten their flight pattern, corralling us.

Beliel and I are forced to back up until we're as close to each other as we can stand. Obviously, neither of us likes it, but for now, the bigger threat to both of us is the hellions, and we have to make a choice to either stand alone or fight together.

We decide simultaneously and step back-to-back against our enemies. Together, we can now see all of the hellions coming at us.

I have to count on Beliel needing me to survive for as long as possible. We both know that if we succeed in killing off the hellions, it'll be me against him, but for now, it's us against them.

The hellions hesitate like none of them wants to go first. Then one dives in at us.

Beliel catches it.

Another dives in while Beliel is occupied snapping the neck of the first hellion.

I shift and slice through it.

Two more come at us.

Then four.

Then six.

I swing my blade as fast as I can and am surprised at how fast that is. Pooky Bear is working overtime. She's almost a blur. She's wielding me, not the other way around. My job is to keep a steady stance and point her in the right direction.

If even one of them gets past the sword, it's game over.

That thought puts a little zest in my swing, slicing three of them in one completion of a figure eight. One across the throat, another across the chest, the third across the belly. The best part is that two of the injured are thrashing in midair, blocking the others from getting too close.

My back prickles with vulnerability, but I just have to trust that Beliel is holding up his end of the fight. Our biggest advantage right now is that the hellions are getting in each other's way. There's not enough room for all of them to rush us.

Since I have a weapon and Beliel does not, I take more than half our circle. I swing from side to side, taking on as many hellions as I can. But I can't cover my back. If Beliel goes down, I'll be following him soon thereafter.

He holds his own, though, even without a weapon. His strength is fierce, his fury fiercer as he snaps, kicks, and punches at the hellions.

Beliel and I kill off the last two local hellions while

the two from the Pit hover and watch. We deliver our final blows at the same time – I slice through one, and he snaps the neck of the other.

Beliel then backs off, stepping away from me, leaving a clear opening for the remaining two hellions from the Pit.

But there are only two of them left, and although they're clever, they can't surround me. They don't even try. Instead, they fly to Beliel – slow and unthreatening. They chirp at him. They point their monkey fingers at me, look at Beliel, and nod.

They're offering to ally with him to take me out.

I take a couple of steps back with my sword raised. I want as much time as possible to react to whatever is about to go down.

Beliel may have been my fighting partner for a few minutes, but these hellions freed him from our chains on Angel Island.

He nods to the hellions. There's no glee in it, just a grim determination to survive. At least I can take some pride in knowing that he assessed me as the greater threat over these Pit hellions.

The two bat-faced uglies circle around – one above me and one to the side – while Beliel walks forward to stand just out of reach. Perfect position to charge me head-on as soon as I'm distracted.

If both the hellions had stayed at my level, I could have swung in a circle and kept all three of them at bay. But with one above, I can only cover two directions and be vulnerable to the third.

Before I can work out a strategy, teeth and claws come at me from above and to my right. Beliel holds back, forcing my move.

I swing my blade up first at the one diving on me, then circle it around for the one attacking me from my side. At the same time, I'm sure that Beliel will leap on me.

But he doesn't.

He feints as if he's going to dive on me, but he holds back.

At the same time, the hellions pull back just as they get into my cutting range. I still manage to slice one across the torso and the other across the face, but neither is a killing blow.

Beliel chuckles as I go back to my ready stance. They all had tried to double-cross each other.

If they all had dived on me, I would be dead. But if one had betrayed the others by feinting an attack, then I would have probably killed one and maybe injured the other. The one who betrayed the others would have had the best chance of being the only survivor.

But now they all know that no one can be trusted. Their alliance is over.

The two Pit hellions fly up in opposite directions as far as the angel dome will let them. They've figured out that if they stay up there, Beliel and I will have to fight it out on the ground. One of us will die, and the other will be tired and easier to kill.

Beliel curls his lip in distaste. 'Outmaneuvered by hellions and threatened by a scrawny Daughter of Man. Insult upon insult.'

We get ready to face off, Beliel and I.

31

'Stop!'

Everyone turns to see who shouted that command. The tone is almost irresistible.

I keep one eye on Beliel while trying to see what's going on. Blood drips down into my eye, and I have to blink several times before I see what everyone else sees.

There's now a gap in the dome letting the light in. A pair of large snowy wings glides through, blocking out the sun.

Raffe's perfect form comes into view.

He is both the Raffe I know and a terrifying stranger. He looks like a pissed-off demigod. I've only glimpsed him once in this perfect angel form.

His wings are magnificent as they sweep the air behind him – white against blue.

The angels all stare at Raffe. They hover, silent and still except for the slow beating of wings. A whisper echoes through the winged crowd: *Archangel Raphael.*

'I hear there's an unsanctioned election going on,' says Raffe.

'There's nothing unsanctioned about it,' says Uriel. 'And if you had been here, you'd know that. In fact, you are one of the candidates.'

'Really? And how am I doing?'

A couple of angels yell out in support of Raffe.

'You've been away too long, Raphael.' Uriel raises his voice to address the rest of the angels. 'He's too out of touch to lead the greatest battle in history. Does he even know that the legendary apocalypse is about to begin?'

'You mean the one you artificially created out of your lies and parlor tricks?' Raffe addresses the angels too. 'He's been lying to you all. Fabricating monsters and manufacturing events to pressure you into a quick and dirty election.'

'He's the one lying,' says Uriel. 'I can prove that I was meant to be the chosen archangel.' He raises his arms to the crowd. 'God spoke to me.'

The crowd bursts into a low roar as everyone begins talking at once.

'That's right,' says Uriel. 'I am already the Messenger in His eyes. God spoke to me and told me He has chosen me to lead the great apocalypse. I waited to tell you because I know that it's shocking. But I have no choice now that Raphael has come back, trying to challenge God's will.

'How many signs do we need before you're convinced that the End of Days is happening without us? How much of it are you willing to miss because we don't have an elected Messenger to lead you into battle? Do not allow Raphael to keep you from the glory that is rightfully yours!'

The angels closest to Uriel open their mouths wide and begin what I can only call singing. But it's not a song with words, just a melody. It's a gorgeous, holy sound that's so unexpected from these bloodthirsty warriors.

The beautiful sound ripples through parts of the crowd as a dozen heavenly voices join the chorus throughout the dome. Then a group of angels shifts out of the way, letting in a beam of sunlight.

The light hits a spot just beside Uriel. He subtly shifts into it so that he glows. His face splits into a genuine grin. If nothing else, Uriel is certainly a good showman.

Then he lowers his arms and bows humbly. There's something about the ray of light shining off his head and shoulders, the way he bows, the way he quietly holds himself that implies that he's communing with God. It makes me hold my breath. Everyone else must feel it too, because there's a hushed expectancy.

When he lifts his head, he says, 'God just spoke to me. He says the End of Days begins *now*.'

He sweeps his arms like a conductor.

A crash hits the cliff at the end of the golf course. I assume it's a huge wave, but I can't see it with all the angels blocking my way. Then they all turn to look, and I can see the beach through the spaces between their bodies.

The water is boiling near the shore. Something is rising up out of the sea. At first, I think it's a cluster of animals, but as the heads clear the water, I see that it's a single monstrosity. The waves crash around it as if the ocean itself were raging against this unnatural thing.

The beast shakes off the water with a scream, and races toward us.

It's shockingly fast. In almost no time, it's close enough for me to get a good look at it.

Laylah has outdone herself on this one. It has seven heads clustered around the shoulders, but one of the heads appears dead. The one that looks dead is the head of a man. The face is split and trickling blood, as though he was recently killed with an ax.

The rest of the heads are alive with each one looking like a mix of human and animal – a leopard, an eel, a hyena, a lion, a giant fly, and a dead-eyed shark. The torso of the beast looks vaguely bearlike.

'And a beast shall rise up out of the sea,' says Uriel in a prophetic tone. 'And upon his heads is the name of blasphemy. Let us count the number of the beast, for it is the number of man. And his number is six hundred threescore and six.'

Each of the monster's heads has numbers tattooed in a puckering scar on its forehead.

666.

32

They're just numbers, I tell myself.

Just numbers.

I know the beast was concocted by Laylah according to Uriel's instructions. I know that Uriel copied his monsters from descriptions out of the apocalyptic prophesies. I know this is a fake – a *fake*.

Then why is my skin prickling with goose bumps?

The numbers are not subtle, and it'll scare the bejesus out of anyone who sees it. I'm guessing that tattooing the number on the foreheads was Uriel's idea.

The dripping beast roars and screams and yelps through all its faces except the dead one. It pauses near us before racing by and disappearing into the broken landscape.

Uriel raises his arms again, as if in a trance.

The ground shifts and puckers beneath my feet. It's like worms frantically boiling in the ground.

Fingers burst out of the soil.

A hand reaches for the sky like a newborn zombie.

A head pushes its way through the dirt.

All over the old golf course, dirt-covered bodies claw their way out of the ground and climb onto the lawn. Thousands of them.

The angels on the ground spread their wings and take to the air. Raffe looks at me, but I understand that he can't lift me up without betraying weakness. A hand claws the air near my leg, grasping. I jump, trying to get away from the hands, wishing I could fly too.

When the bodies climb out of the soil, they're so dirty that I can only tell they're human by their shapes. That and their gasping sobs.

'And the dead shall rise,' says Uriel, his voice carrying over the wind.

Some of the bodies lie on the lawn, gasping for breath. Others scramble away from the hole they crawled from, clearly afraid something will drag them back in. Still others just huddle on the churned-up lawn, sobbing.

What I thought at first was all dirt turns out to be dirt on dried, shriveled flesh. These are locust victims. They look traumatized and terrified, staring down at their arms and legs as though seeing their jerkylike flesh for the first time. Maybe they are.

Uriel must have had them buried alive while they were paralyzed. He was prepared to impress the gathering even before Raffe came. If anyone could have timed something like this, it was him. His team knew just how much venom to use to keep the victims paralyzed until showtime.

I wonder if the locust stung know what happened to them. I wonder if they think that they *are* the rising dead.

'Resurrected!' Uriel looks eerie. His bowed head and his open wings glow in the beam of light. 'I am the Messenger of God.'

Many of the angels glance uneasily at each other when Uriel declares himself the Messenger.

'You have been chosen to share the glory of the apocalypse. Punish the blasphemy that is mankind, and you will be received in heaven. Shirk your duties, and you will be dragged back into hell where you came from.' He points east. 'Go. Find the humans and kill them all. Cleanse the earth, and make it righteous once again.'

The locust stung stare at him, stunned. Then they gaze around at each other, looking frightened and disoriented.

One person turns to move east.

Someone follows him. Then another. And another, until the entire group is migrating.

Wave after wave of resurrected claw their way out of the dirt. As soon as they can stand on their feet, they follow the crowd heading east.

East, toward the Resistance camp.

33

'That was an impressive show,' says Raffe, hovering in the air among the angels. He doesn't look at all impressed at the army of resurrected or the multiheaded monster. 'But you'd all be making a huge mistake to believe him. Anyone who follows Uriel will fall when the truth comes out.'

'Your scare tactics won't work here,' says Uriel.

'If Uriel is lying, then he alone should fall,' says a warrior. 'The rest of us are just following orders.'

'You think Lucifer's angels got leniency just because they were following orders when they revolted against heaven?' asks Raffe. 'You think they understood the archangel politics behind the revolt and knew what was really happening? They were just wing soldiers, like you.

Many of them probably thought they were doing the right thing. Some of them even thought that they were fighting to defend the Messenger. But that didn't help them when the smoke cleared. Every one of them fell.'

The angels look at each other. A low mutter rumbles through the crowd. Their wings flutter in agitation.

'If Gabriel is still alive and out there somewhere,' says Raffe, 'he won't have any mercy for the angels who lost faith in him. If Michael comes back and realizes what happened, he might not have a choice but to declare you all fallen to nullify the election. And if the angels back home catch wind of what's been happening down here . . . my brothers, this could be the start of a bloody civil war. The angels here won't have a choice but to stand behind Uriel as your chosen Messenger.'

'How are we supposed to know who to believe?' asks an angel.

'There is no way to know,' says another.

'Trial by contest,' declares one.

'Trial by contest,' says another. Others murmur in agreement.

I don't like it when angels murmur in agreement. Nothing good ever comes of that.

'God has spoken to me. I am your Messenger, and I have given you a command.' Uriel's voice is thunderous and filled with the promise of retribution.

'So you claim,' says Raffe. 'But the election isn't complete.' He turns to the angels. 'It's quite a string of coincidences, isn't it? Messenger Gabriel being killed without telling anyone why we're here. Uriel being the only archangel available for the election. Every time there's any doubt, another apocalyptic monster appears as a sign.'

Raffe looks at Uriel. 'How convenient for you, Uri. Yes. I agree to a trial by contest.'

Angels nod and echo. 'Trial by contest.'

As in winner takes all and is declared to be telling the truth? What are we, living in the Middle Ages?

Uriel sweeps his gaze over the crowd.

'Fine,' says Uriel. 'So be it. I call Sacriel as my second.'

Everyone looks to the largest angel in the group and his enormous wings. 'I accept,' he says.

Raffe looks at the angels, gauging them. Who is loyal enough to back him as his second? There were angels who voted for him, but voting for him and dying for him are two very different things.

'I'm flattered that you need the biggest, meanest warrior on your side to best me, Uri. Let's see, how big a warrior do I need as a second to beat you and Sacriel? Hmm . . . I'll take . . . the Daughter of Man. She should even out the odds.'

Angels laugh.

I stand on the churned-up ground, stunned.

Uriel's lips purse. 'You still think everything is a joke, don't you?' Uriel spits out his words. He definitely doesn't like being laughed at. 'Have your fun now, Raphael, because she'll be the only one to follow you when you fall. Perhaps you've forgotten that you don't have your Watchers anymore.'

Uriel gives me a knowing look. I can tell that he knows Raffe didn't just pick me as a joke. 'You have until sunrise to collect your team before we meet to decide on the contest.'

He flies out of the crowd with his usual entourage following in a burst of fluttering wings. The angels buzz with excitement as the crowd dissolves toward the main building of the aerie.

A few of Uriel's guards corral the two remaining hellions and stuff them back into their cage. They also lock Beliel in with them.

But they leave me alone on the field. It must be because I'm Raffe's second, whatever that means. I roll my shoulders, trying to ease the tension.

Raffe glides down to me. His snowy wings are wide and frame his statuesque body perfectly. The edges of his feathers are downy, giving him a soft glow in the light.

I still can't believe he has his wings back. They look amazing on him. Perfect in every way, except for the notch that I cut out of his wing when I first met him. I assume the feathers will grow back in over time, and all traces of me will disappear off him.

I want to say something about his wings and thank him for keeping me alive, but I don't want to be over-heard. I can tell that he sees it all in my eyes anyway, just as I can see him wondering how the heck I got here. I suppose I have a special talent for showing up where I shouldn't be.

As the last of the angels fly away, Josiah lands beside Raffe. His unnaturally white skin matches Raffe's feathers.

'Well, that was an unexpected choice for a second,' says Josiah, watching Raffe with his red eyes.

Raffe gives him a grim expression. 'What are the chances that we can recruit a decent team?'

'Very low,' says Josiah. 'Whether they back him or not, too many are convinced Uriel will win. If he does, he'll make sure that anyone who opposes him will fall, and no one wants to risk that.'

Raffe's shoulders slump. He must be exhausted after the operation.

'How are you feeling?' I ask.

'Like I flew on my wings a month before I should have.' He takes a deep breath and lets it out. 'Nothing I haven't done before.'

'How many will Uriel have on his team?' I ask.

'A hundred maybe?' says Josiah.

'A hundred?' I ask. 'Against the two of us?'

'You're not actually going to be fighting,' says Raffe. 'No one expects it.'

'Oh, so a hundred against just you. Why do you have a second if you're supposed to have a team with you?'

'It's traditionally meant to make sure that no one stands alone,' says Josiah.

He glances at Raffe with sympathy. 'No one declines the honor of being second, but it's completely optional as to whether someone joins a team for a trial by contest.'

Seeing pity in Josiah's eyes makes me want to kick something. Raffe helped me, but now I can't help him. A girl who can't fly can't play in angel games.

I look at the cages on the field. The two remaining hellions are attacking each other and fighting around Beliel. They probably would have shoved me in there too if Raffe hadn't named me his second. How long would I last in there?

'Uriel's right,' says Raffe. 'I don't have my Watchers anymore. I can't count on anyone stepping into their duties.'

'The warriors still talk about them, you know,' says Josiah. 'No group has come close to being the elite fighting team that the Watchers were. They've become legend.' He shakes his head. 'What a waste. And all because of—' He looks at me with some hostility in his eyes and bites off whatever insult he was going to call Daughters of Men.

'Don't blame the women for the angels breaking your own stupid rules. Their women didn't even break any rules, but they got punished anyway.'

'The Watchers would still be here if it weren't for the Daughters of Men,' says Josiah. 'We lost our most elite group of warriors because they married your kind. The least you can do is have the decency to—'

'Enough,' says Raffe. 'The Watchers are gone and arguing about whose fault it is won't bring them back. The only question left is, can we find a substitute?'

'Where are they now?' I suspect they're still in the Pit, but who knows? I think what I saw in Beliel's memory was from a long time ago.

They both glance at Beliel. He's swatting at the hellions who are squabbling near his shoulder. They fly away from him to hang on to the bars and stare at us.

No, not at us.

At my sword.

The Pit hellions want to go home. However bad it was there, it had to have been better than being caged, waiting to be killed.

Home.

'What if we could go into the Pit and get the Watchers?' I ask.

It's an insane thought, one I wouldn't consider if the entire human race didn't depend on it. If Raffe could dethrone Uriel, then no more war, right?

The guys glance at each other as if wondering whether I've lost my mind. 'No one voluntarily goes into the Pit,' says Raffe, scowling at me.

'And once you're in, you don't get out without being let out by the Pit lords,' says Josiah. 'That's the problem with the Pit. Otherwise, newly Fallen angels would be rescued left and right.'

'Besides,' says Raffe, looking at Beliel. 'The Watchers aren't what they used to be.'

'What if we could get the Watchers you remember?' I ask. I nod toward Beliel. 'The Watchers he remembers?'

Raffe looks back at me, and I see a spark of interest.

34

We half drag, half fly Beliel's cage off the torn grass toward an outer building that's out of sight of the main hotel.

'Do we have any reason to believe it'll work both ways?' asks Josiah.

'I was hoping you guys would know,' I say.

'There are ancient stories of hellions jumping out through very powerful swords,' says Raffe. 'But there's never been a reason to jump *into* the Pit.'

'You mean to tell me that I discovered a talent of your beloved swords that even you guys didn't know about?' I pull as hard as I can on the cage bars.

'You seem to bring out new and unimagined dimensions from both me and Kooky Bear.'

'Pooky Bear.'

'Right.'

I step over a hole that someone must have crawled out of.

'Come on. Say it, Raffe.' I give him a half smile. 'I love it when you say Pooky Bear. It's just so perfect when it comes out of your mouth.'

'She might kill you in your sleep one of these days just so she can get rid of that name.'

'Can't she have a new name now that she can be with you again?'

'You were her last solo wielder, so she's stuck with the name until she gets a new solo wielder.'

I keep expecting him to ask for his sword now that he has his angel wings back, but he hasn't. I wonder if he's still annoyed with her for showing me his private moments. I can feel Pooky Bear's yearning to be held by him, but I don't say anything. This is one fight I should stay out of.

We set the cage down behind the outer building. It's quiet and deserted here.

Josiah shakes his head but is no longer arguing against the idea. He's right. We all agree that it's a terrible plan. But when Raffe asked him to come up with a less terrible idea, he didn't have one.

Now that it's time, my hands tremble as I pull out the sword.

My mind searches frantically for a better plan, but I can't think of one. We could run away now that Raffe has his wings. But he's on trial as much as I am. They won't just let us fly out of here.

If Raffe loses this trial, I die. I'm not sure what will happen to him, but it's clear what will happen to me. But if Raffe could win this trial by contest and take control of the angels, he'll take them away. And it'll all end.

Is it worth the risk of losing Raffe to the Pit and having him trapped there?

I bite my lip, not willing to answer that question. I'll probably pace a ten-foot-deep trench in front of this cage while waiting for him to come back.

'Do it,' says Raffe. His wings are closed tightly along his back, and he stands rigid, ready for the worst.

Before I can get sappy, I nod to Josiah. He unlocks the cage door, and it swings open with a creak. The two hellions from the Pit back as far away from Josiah as they can.

Hopefully, they know how to use the sword to get back to their world. We just need to catch one for Raffe to ride on.

Beliel also backs away to the far end of the cage, looking like a shriveled zombie. 'What are you doing?' He watches us suspiciously.

'Come on, creepy hellions. You want to go home, don't you?' I croon, sticking my sword into the cage.

The Pit hellions creep slowly toward me. They watch the sword greedily, sniffing as if trying to sense a trap.

As soon as Raffe moves toward them, though, they bolt back into the farthest corners of the cage, hissing. I don't know how to make the creatures travel through the sword if they don't want to.

'They're afraid of you.' I put out my free arm in front of him. 'Get behind me.'

I step into the cage. I raise my voice and make myself sound like I'm talking to puppies. 'Come on, ugly squat-faced things. You want to go home, don't you? Mmm, home.'

They creep cautiously toward me, watching Raffe carefully.

'I'll open the doorway to your home as soon as you let me hold your hand.' I have to keep myself from cringing away at that thought.

'No!' says Beliel. His eyes are fierce, like he's just realized he's in a nightmare that he can't wake up from. 'Get away—'

I grab the nearest hellion.

It grabs my forearm back, sinking its claws in. Pain pierces through my arm, but I hang on.

At the same time, Raffe jumps in and grabs the other hellion.

Then total chaos breaks out.

With an intensity bordering on panic, Beliel shoves Josiah out of the way and tries to leap out of the cage. Raffe's hellion freaks and tries to rush the cage door, flapping madly.

I instinctively swing my blade to stop Beliel's escape and end up skewering Beliel's side.

As he roars, Raffe's hellion leaps onto my sword.

It slides down the blade with Raffe gripping its leg. It disappears into Beliel.

And Raffe, still hanging on to its leg, disappears right after it.

Before I can blink, the hellion I'm holding dives down the sword as well, dragging me with it.

At first, I try to let go – Raffe's the only one who's supposed to go into the Pit – but the hellion still has a grip on my arm. In the split second before the hellion lets go of me, my hand slips into Beliel, and I'm falling.

I clench so tightly that I almost pull the hellion's arm off.

We slam through Beliel's body, and the breath gets knocked out of me. For a painful split second, the shock of going through the barrier almost tears me off my ride. But I hang on, tortured by the idea that if I'm jarred loose, I could end up in an even worse place than I might be going.

We fall through a darkness that seems endless.

I turn to see Josiah's stunned face staring down at me through a fast-closing tunnel.

I shut my eyes, convinced that there are some things we humans aren't meant to see. Josiah's shocked face burns out of my mind as only one thought begins to dominate.

We are going into hell.

35

This isn't the same as the last time I went into Beliel's memory. This time, it hurts.

Every cell in my body cries from the pain of it. Hopefully, it's because my physical body is actually going on the trip along with my mind.

Just when I think my eyes are going to pop from squeezing them shut so tightly, we slam onto the ground.

My stomach clenches, and my chin and chest sting where they hit the ground.

No wonder the hellions were so disoriented when they landed on Angel Island. I feel like I just got rolled as flat as pizza dough and slapped onto the ground.

I also feel like I'm baking in an oven. A very stinky oven cooking rotten eggs.

I force myself to roll over and open my eyes. There's really no time for recovery when you've just landed in hell.

The sky – if it is a sky – is a cracked purple black with darker blotches. The weak light throws a purple cast over the hulking shadows above me.

Edging my vision, there are faces looking down at me.

I'm not really sure what I'm looking at. They remind me of angels, but I don't think they are. They also remind me of demons, but I don't think they're those either.

Their open wings look mangy, and what's left of their feathers look like dried leaves on a dead tree. The exposed parts of the wings look cracked and leathery. The wing bones are splintered, sticking out painfully through the edges of the wings. Many of the bone splinters have curled into a sickle shape, not entirely unlike Raffe's demon wing blades.

The thing that shocks me the most, even though it probably shouldn't, is that one of these guys is Beliel. It shouldn't surprise me since I did jump into his memory – or a world in which he has a memory – or whatever. So of course, Beliel would be here.

But he looks different. For one thing, his wings are neither the demon wings I'm familiar with nor his original feathered wings. They're half dark and half still covered with tufts of sunset feathers.

I guess since I'm physically here, I might have jumped in time and space, but that's too much for my brain to handle without exploding. Besides, I don't have time to think about it.

When my eyes adjust to the purple light, I see that Beliel stares in my direction with empty sockets.

Beliel is blind.

It takes me a second to convince myself that it really is him. He has deep lash marks across his cheeks and nose. He's been whipped in the face. He also has gouge marks around his eye sockets.

The others don't look much better. One of them has half a perfect Greek-god face and another half that looks like it's been chewed off. Without their injuries, I can tell that they would have been perfect specimens, just like any other angel.

Between their damaged bodies, I can see we're in a war zone or, at least, what's left of one. The buildings are burned out, the broken trees are charred, and the vehicles are smashed and gutted. At least, I'm assuming these were buildings, trees, and vehicles. They don't look like ours, but the hulking shapes look like they used to be inhabited a long time ago. Like a village of some kind. Something that looks like stunted cacti that have been stomped and twisted sits rooted into the ground. And there is debris strewn around that looks vaguely like wagon wheels.

A nonangel with canary-yellow feathers reaches for me. His skin has been ripped right off his arm, leaving only the glistening muscles beneath. I cringe, but he grabs me by the hair and yanks me up to my feet.

'What is it?' asks Beliel. 'Can we eat it?' I don't know if I've ever seen anything more disturbing than empty eye sockets, especially on someone I know, even if it's Beliel.

He puts a pointy ear in his mouth and chews on it. It looks a lot like a hellion's ear. I wonder what happened to the hellion I rode.

Then I see what's left of it on the ground, all smashed and torn apart. It's hardly recognizable anymore.

Where's Raffe?

'It's a Daughter of Man,' says my captor. His voice is ominous, like those words have some deep meaning.

There's a long silence as everyone stares at me.

'Which one?' Beliel finally asks.

The one holding me looks around at the others. He doesn't ease up on my hair. 'Is this one of yours? She's not mine.'

'There's no reason to believe she would be one of ours, Cyclone,' says Beliel. His voice is raspy as if he'd either been screaming himself raw or someone had choked him.

'I'm through with them,' says one. 'The thought of them makes me ill.'

'Yeah, maybe Big B's right,' says another. 'Maybe we're better off eating her. We could use some meat to help us heal.'

I squirm trying to get out of the nonangel's grip. Where is Raffe?

'Let her go,' says another. This one has blue-tinged feathers.

'Thermo, if we let her go, she'll wish we had cooked her up and eaten her. Setting her free here is not a mercy.'

That's not what I wanted to hear.

'And is that a sword?' Several of them lean down to look at my sword, which lies on the ground just out of reach.

One of them tries to lift it and grunts at the weight. He lets it go.

They all stare at me, scrutinizing.

'What are you?' asks Cyclone.

'She's a Daughter of Man, can't you see that?' says Thermo.

'If she's a Daughter of Man, where's her pack of hellions?' says a guy with black feathers and sharp eyes.

'Where are her chains? Why does she look so healthy and whole?'

'And how does she have an angel sword?' asks one who has brown wings streaked with yellow.

'It can't be hers. Somehow, it got here. And somehow, she got here. But that doesn't mean it's her sword. We haven't been here long enough to believe things that are that crazy.' They all look at Pooky Bear with longing, but none of them tries to pick her up.

'So whose is it?' They all look at me.

I shrug. 'I'm just a Daughter of Man. I don't know anything.'

No one argues with that.

'Where am I?' I ask. The pull on my hair is becoming unbearable. Two of them have their scalps partly torn off, and I'm beginning to wonder if this is why.

'In the Pit,' says Thermo. 'Welcome to the hunting district.'

'Is this the same as hell?' I ask.

The one with black feathers shrugs. 'Does it matter? It's hellish. Why do you care if it matches your primitive myth?'

'What do you hunt here?' I ask.

The angel with the brown-and-yellow wings snorts. 'We don't. We're the prey.'

That doesn't sound good. 'What are you?' I ask. I'm

assuming they're Raffe's Watchers, but better to be sure. 'You don't look like angels, and you don't look like . . .' What do I really know about what demons look like?

'Oh, do excuse us for not introducing ourselves,' says the one with the brown-and-yellow wings. He emphasizes his sarcasm by bowing to me. 'We are the newly Fallen. The Watchers, to be precise. And probably your executioners. Not that it'll take more than one of us to do the deed. But you get the point. I'm Howler.'

Howler points to the one with black feathers and brown skin. 'That's Hawk.' He points to the one with blue-tinged feathers, then to several others. 'Thermo. Flyer. Big B. Little B. And the one holding you is Cyclone.' He looks around at the others. There are too many to introduce them all, not that I'd remember their names. 'Do we care who she is?'

'Sure,' says Flyer. 'Maybe it'll give us something to think about when we're bored out of our minds for the next millennium. Who are you?'

'I'm . . .' I'm hesitant to give them my name. Raffe said names have power. 'I'm the angel slayer.'

It sounds kind of ridiculous now that I've said it. It sounded better in my head, but whatever.

For a moment, they all stare at me.

Then, as if on cue, they burst out laughing.

Howler curls over his left ribs with his hands protectively covering them like they're broken. 'Oh, don't make me laugh. That hurts.'

Cyclone chuckles behind me. He finally lets go of my hair, leaving my scalp tender. 'Holy Mother of God, I didn't realize I could laugh anymore.'

'Yeah, it's been a long, long time,' says Little B.

'The angel slayer, huh?' asks Howler.

'Well, that was great,' says Beliel, who apparently is Big B. 'Can we eat her now?'

'He's got a point,' says Little B. 'I can't remember the last time we had a full meal. She's scrawny, but I'm desperate for food to manage all this healing—'

Something grabs him – a tentacle? – and yanks him back. He yells and thrashes, kicking and twisting, but he can't get loose.

It drags him behind a pile of rubble, bashing his head and shoulders on jagged fragments along the way.

The Watchers all become fully alert and ready for battle, but they're practically hyperventilating. These guys have not fared well here.

I stand frozen. If these legendary warriors are afraid, what should I be feeling? I'm beginning to wish I had just kept my mouth shut about coming here. Being killed in a gladiator arena is starting to sound merciful now.

They all fly after Little B even though there's more than a little stress on their faces. They kick and yank and try to pull him out of the tentacle's grip.

Then another one of them gets sucked backward. As far as I can tell, the thing that took him was the scorching wind.

He gets yanked back through a window of a half-demolished building. Within seconds, screams erupt from inside.

The nearest Watchers rush to the window and look inside. They look away like they wish they hadn't seen what they just saw.

Somewhere, another kind of screaming heads our way. It's a mad shriek in the distance that sets my nerves on edge.

The Watchers back away with Little B who is kicking off the last of the tentacle that had him. They turn and begin rushing away from the building and the direction of the mad screams.

Someone grabs my arm and pulls me with him. To my surprise, it's Beliel. 'Stick with us. We're your best chance.'

I notice he doesn't say best chance at what. I bend to grab my sword off the ground, not caring if any of them see me do it. They're too busy getting in formation and scanning for danger to pay any attention to me.

We scatter, half running with our backs to each other. These guys have worked together before. Too bad it doesn't seem to help them much here.

Where's Raffe?

What have I gotten myself into?

36

We run through the district, zigzagging this way and that like a pack of wolves escaping from a hunter. The place is full of broken bricks and old bones. Charred and twisted chunks of wood lie alongside rusted pieces of metal among the debris.

I try to keep up with the Watchers, some who run and some who fly low to the ground as though worried they could be seen higher up. Beliel flies with his hand on a Watcher's ankle to guide him. It must take a lot of trust to fly blind. The Beliel I know would have a lot of trouble doing that.

They'll probably kill me as soon as they get the chance, but I'll deal with that after we escape from whatever it is that's trying to kill us now. I make the mistake of turning around to see what we're running from.

There are three pumped-up demons like the one I saw the last time I was in the Pit. They're all enormous, with huge muscles encased in leather straps crisscrossing their bodies. Their torsos are otherwise naked, and that's as far down as I can see.

They probably don't have cows here in the Pit. I try not to think about what animal hide they use for their leather.

They ride on chariots pulled by a dozen newly Fallen harnessed in bloody chains. The Fallen frantically sweep their wings as their demon lords whip them. I can tell they're newly Fallen because they still have most of their feathers, although they're crushed and twisted. I don't have to look to know the chariots probably have broken angels strapped to the wheels as well, just like Beliel was in my last visit.

The demons use multiheaded sticks like the one I saw back then to whip and bite the angel slaves pulling the chariots. These sticks are topped by circles of shriveled heads all with the same shade of red hair and green eyes. The hair floats as if underwater just like the ones I'd seen before. And like the others I'd seen, these are also screaming soundlessly.

When their masters whip the stick, they come

shrieking toward the Fallen, biting and ripping strips of skin and feathers off them when they land.

One of the demons looks at me. I can't help but think that it's the same one who saw me the last time I visited the Pit. His wings are on fire, and his glistening body glows red from the reflection. He snaps his multiheaded whip at me as all the chariots charge closer.

The matching heads scream as they come at me with an intensity that's beyond insane. All balls of teeth and eyes and writhing hair.

All I know is that I do not want one of those latching onto me. I pump my legs as fast as I can. I do a sharp turn around a corner and run behind a broken building.

There's a hatchway in a crumbling wall. I throw it open.

I'm about to race down the stone steps into the darkness below when one of the Watchers crash-lands on the ground in front of me.

It's Beliel. He has a whip head chewing its way into his back.

Two more of the screaming heads land on him. One latches on and rips a strip of flesh off his arm. The other catches itself on Beliel's hair and begins whipping around, pulling part of Beliel's scalp with it.

Beliel grabs the one off his scalp and crushes it.

I jump in and viciously kick the head off his back. Beliel is my ticket out of here, and I can't let him get killed. My head hurts just trying to understand what it would mean if he dies here.

The last head is chewing its way up the strip of torn skin on his arm. I yank the head and rip the skin all the way off, ignoring Beliel's bellow of pain. I stomp on it until it stops moving.

Beliel staggers up onto his feet. I shove him down the dark stairs and slam the hatch behind me.

I try not to pant too loudly as I latch the door shut.

We seem to be in a basement below a crumbled building. The only light is from the cracks of the hatch door, and it's too dark to see whether there's another exit.

The ground vibrates. Large, heavy chunks of debris thunk down against the hatch.

I stiffen and get ready, gripping my sword with both hands. A sense of doom vibrates off Beliel as he stands with his ear cocked toward the hatch, as though he's been here a thousand times before and lost the battle each time. Looking at how torn and trashed he and the other Watchers are, that doesn't seem far-fetched.

The hatch rattles and jiggles as the heads attack it with their teeth. The gnawing and bumping against the hatch goes on forever before it finally stops.

Then a great rattling and the sound of whipping moves past outside. The demons must not have seen where we disappeared to, even if their whip heads did.

The chariot rattle fades into the distance.

I cautiously let my breath out and look around. We're in an underground hovel of some kind. Trashed bedding lies in the shadows, a raised seat made of mud, charred remains of a long-ago fireplace.

'Do you know what they would have done to you?' asks Beliel in a raspy whisper beside me.

I jump. I hadn't realized he was so close.

'Those heads,' he says. 'Do you know what they scream for?'

I shake my head, then remember he can't see me.

'A new body. They're desperate for it.' He leans against the wall of the hovel with his empty sockets turned to me. 'Welcome to the Pit. Like it or not, you've just joined the initiations for the newly Fallen.'

'How long do the initiations go on?'

'Until you become Consumed or something equally horrible. Or it's possible the Pit lords might feel like promoting you out of maggot status. I've heard it only happens sometime after your wings fully turn. Then the real fun begins.'

'It gets worse after you're promoted?'

'That's what I heard.'

Something thuds on the hatch outside. I stay silent until whatever it was that hit the hatch goes away.

'What about those screaming whip heads? Are they being initiated too?'

'They're the Consumed. They're the ones who didn't make it through initiation. There's a legendary feast that goes on with the Pit lords. The Consumed are the ones who were sacrificed for the feast.' He shakes his head. 'We can grow back a lot of things, but not a whole body or even major parts.'

He rubs his empty eye sockets. 'But when you're in the Pit, there are infinite opportunities for more misery. The Consumed cry out by the thousands to be included in a head whip for the chance to claim a new body.'

I've never seen Beliel so chatty. This earlier version of him is going to take some getting used to.

'If they get their teeth into you, they'll burrow before you can blink. They'll work their way up to your head where they gnaw until your head falls off. Then they plant themselves in your neck. Sometimes, they fight, and two or three of them plant themselves before it's all done. That's a sight that makes you wish your eyes had been gouged out.'

I look at him to see if he just told a joke, but there's no change in his expression.

'A Fallen body is a prize, but they'll take anything with limbs. They'll even take rat bodies with the hope that they can move up the food chain so long as they can find the next victim. So watch your feet.'

He slides down the wall, sitting against it. 'Rumor has it that some of the most powerful Pit lords were once Consumed. Of course, by the time they reach Pit-lord status, they're beyond insane.'

I like to think I can handle insanity, but this is taking it to a whole new level.

'So always be on guard,' he says. 'You could lose more here than you could possibly imagine.'

Is Beliel really looking out for me? There must be an ulterior motive, but I can't think of one right now. 'Why are you telling me all this?' Maybe he's not Beliel but just someone who looks like him. He sure doesn't sound like him.

'You saved me out there,' he says. 'I pay what's owed, good or bad. Besides, I have a soft spot for Daughters of Men. My wife used to be one.' His voice trails off, and I can barely hear his last sentence.

'You're offering to protect me?' The disbelief clearly comes through in my voice.

'No one can protect you, little girl, certainly not a

newly Fallen whose eyes haven't grown back yet. Anyone who says they can protect you is lying. It's just a question of friend or foe. That's all.'

'And you're telling me you're my friend?'

'I'm not your enemy.'

'What the hell kind of bizarro world am I in?' I whisper to myself.

I don't expect Beliel to answer, but he does. 'You're in the ruins of the hellion world.'

I think about that for a minute. The hellion world? Not the Fallen world? The hellions and the Fallen do look very different. 'They're not the same species, are they?'

'The Fallen and the hellions?' He snorts. 'Don't let anyone hear you even suggest that. Both sides would tear you to pieces and feed your bits to the Consumed.'

'This was the hellions' world before the Fallen angels came? The hellions are the natives of the Pit?'

'I doubt they were much of anything before the Fallen came. All they're good for is causing torture and pain. Disgusting little rats. They're even beneath the Consumed, who won't eat them because even without a body, a Fallen refuses to drop that low.'

I remember how the hellions tortured both Beliel and his wife, and I can see why he hates them. But there might be two sides to this story.

I look around again at the dim basement.

There are remnants of shattered pottery, bits of faded cloth, broken metal and wood. Someone used to live here. A family of someones, maybe. A very long time ago.

37

Beliel tilts his head, listening. 'Open the hatch. The other Watchers are coming.'

I'm not keen on letting the others know where we are. I don't want them to kill me before Raffe can recruit them.

Raffe. He should have landed near Beliel, just like me. What does it mean that he's not around?

'Do it, girl. They're our best hope for survival.'

I hesitate a moment longer. He might be right. Or he might be setting me up for a trap.

Beliel takes the choice out of my hands. 'We're in here!'

I quietly slide my blade back into her sheath and put the teddy bear on top. I can't fight my way through that many Watchers anyway, so I might as well try to keep Pooky hidden for now.

Someone bangs on the hatch. 'We knew you'd be alive, Big B. Open up. Don't be shy.'

The wood rattles.

'You want to live, little angel slayer?' Beliel nods toward the hatchway. 'They're your best chance.'

I could be stubborn and wait until they force it open. But what's the point? I reluctantly walk up the stone steps and open the hatch.

The Watchers pour in, filling the small hovel.

'Nice find,' says Thermo, looking around.

'Maybe we can relax here for a few seconds,' says Little B.

'Oops, time's up,' says Howler, slapping his hand on Little B's shoulder. 'Back to being tense and hunted.'

The rest just scan the room, silently taking everything in as they walk into the hovel.

More than a dozen Watchers crowd into the space. Some of them sit down on the dirt while others lean against the wall, closing their eyes like they haven't rested in years. No one talks. No one fidgets. They just rest as if they're sure they won't get another chance for several more years.

A loud *thunk* on the hatch interrupts the quiet.

Everyone tenses, turning toward the opening.

A flapping hellion crashes and tumbles just outside the open hatch. An angel skids after it in a jumble of white feathers and curses.

'Raffe!' I rush up the stairs to him. 'Where have you been?'

He looks up at me from the ground with disorientation in his eyes. The spotted hellion flies out of his grasp. It flitters in a panic into the hovel, and the Watchers swat and kick at it until it frantically flies back out of the hatch.

Raffe blinks at me a couple of times as he slowly gets up.

'Are you okay?' I've never seen him so disoriented. He looks like I must have when I first arrived here.

And then it hits me that maybe he did just arrive. At first, I think what a great coincidence that he landed near me, but of course, I'm not the connection – it's Beliel. We went through him, so we arrive near him on the other side.

'Did you just get here?' I ask.

But he's not looking at me. He and the Watchers are staring at each other as each Watcher comes out of the hovel. They position themselves in a circle around him, as though in a dream.

'Yeah,' I say. 'I guess you guys know each other.' I awkwardly step back.

'It can't be,' says Flyer.

'Commander?' asks Hawk with doubt in his voice. 'Is that you?'

'What do you mean *Commander?*' asks Beliel as he turns his empty eye sockets to Raffe.

'It's Archangel Raphael,' says Thermo.

'What the hell did you do to get yourself down here?' asks Cyclone.

'Your wings . . .' says Howler. 'How are they pristine?'

It's ironic now that Raffe finally has his angel wings back that he's in the land of demons.

'Are you on a mission with Uriel?' asks Thermo, sounding skeptical. 'I thought he was the only archangel who could come down here. You haven't turned into a diplomat, have you?'

'Maybe it's a trick,' says Hawk. 'Maybe it's not really him.'

'What was the biggest kill you ever made?' asks Cyclone.

'A foot taller and wider than the biggest kill you ever made, Cyclone.' Raffe brushes dust off himself.

'It really is you,' says Cyclone.

'What happened?' asks Flyer. 'How are you here?'

'Long story,' says Raffe. 'We have much to catch up on.'

'Betrayer!' Beliel looks furious. He slams his body against Raffe. They hit the ground and grapple as Beliel tries to pummel Raffe.

The others grab him and pull him off.

'You swore!' yells Beliel as he struggles against his buddies. 'I left her in your care! Do you know what they did to her? Do you?'

The Watchers subdue Beliel, putting a hand over his mouth and whispering in his ear to calm down.

'We should talk,' says Raffe, getting up. 'Is this a good place?'

'There are no good places in the Pit,' says Hawk.

'We should go someplace where we have easy escape routes,' says Thermo. 'Anything that might be looking for a meal just heard its dinner bell.'

In the distance, something screams. It's hard to tell how close it is.

Beliel stops struggling, but he's breathing hard and fast. He may be blind, but there's nothing wrong with his ears.

'Let's get out of here,' says Cyclone. He takes the lead. The rest of us follow.

Even though Beliel is obviously furious with Raffe, he still walks with his back to him like they weren't archenemies. He also follows the group as if it never occurred to him to not cooperate. His bulging muscles start to unclench, and the tension in his shoulders softens as he walks.

The hate-filled edge I'm used to seeing in Beliel is not

there, even in this horrid place. Whatever happened to him to make him that way hasn't happened yet.

We follow the Watchers away from the hovel just as the screaming of those Consumed whip heads fills the air again.

Raffe pulls me into his arms and takes flight.

38

'Stay low,' says one of the Watchers, 'where they can't see you.'

Raffe swoops down and flies at almost ground level along with the Watchers. We swing side to side, barely avoiding broken wheels, piles of rubble, and burned-out husks of something unrecognizable.

Behind us, the Pit lord with the flaming wings comes roaring after us. He whips his screaming heads at his set of newly Fallen who strain to fly as fast as they can. The spotted hellion that came with Raffe flies beside the Pit lord like a giant winged rat, pointing at us.

We glide along the broken street until we turn a corner and come face-to-face with a set of screaming heads.

Raffe shifts me so that he's holding me from behind. Without speaking, I know what he wants me to do. He can't carry me and fight at the same time. I pull out my sword.

Raffe swoops left, and I cut a swath through the Consumed. Their teeth and hair fall to the ground as the blade slices through them.

Behind us, the Watchers fan out in a wedge formation with us in the lead. I'm the only one with a weapon, so it becomes my job to cut through whatever gets in our way. The Watchers punch and kick their way behind us.

I've never fought on a real team before other than with Raffe, but we all fall into a rhythm that doesn't require words for us to coordinate.

Someone yells behind us.

We all turn to look. The Pit lord has caught Flyer, who was at the end of our formation. Flyer is bent over on his back over the edge of the chariot with the Pit lord pressing on either side of him so that his back is about to snap in half.

Everyone exchanges a quick look, then the entire formation veers, returning to rescue Flyer.

The air is filled with the screaming Consumed looking for bodies.

Hawk and Cyclone lead the charge back to Flyer with a fierce war cry. They are the first hit with the screaming heads. Instead of trying to avoid them, they charge right into them, getting hit with half a dozen each.

As soon as they land on Hawk and Cyclone, they begin chewing and burrowing into their flesh.

Hawk and Cyclone grab the hair of a couple of heads per hand and yank them off their skin. They swing the heads by the hair and use them to bat away the others. Their hands drip with blood as the Consumed hair cuts into them, but they don't seem to care.

The other Consumed converge on Hawk and Cyclone.

Four other Watchers zip in and pluck and smash the chewing heads off the two kamikaze Watchers, acting as their support to keep them alive. Meanwhile, the rest of us fly in toward the Pit lord while Hawk and Cyclone distract the Consumed.

Instead of waiting, the Pit lord lets go of Flyer and leaps at us.

His blazing wings sweep the air with flames, looking like he's shooting toward us in a ball of fire.

His fiery wings make it impossible to come at him from any direction other than head-on. And Raffe and I are directly in front of him.

As the Pit lord swipes his blazing wing at us, a Watcher charges between us, protecting us with his body as he punches the Pit lord. Instead of punching back, the Pit lord grabs him by the throat and closes his wings. For a moment, we can't see anything but a giant ball of fire as his wings encase the Pit lord and the Watcher.

When he opens his wings again, the Watcher is in flames. His remaining feathers along with every scrap of hair on his body are on fire.

The Pit lord drops him, and the Watcher roars as he falls, landing hard and rolling on the ground, trying to smash the flames out.

The Pit lord comes back for us. Raffe holds his air space while the other Watchers rescue Flyer.

Raffe nods to one of the Watchers who then takes position below us. I'm guessing he's there to catch me if I fall.

'Don't you dare let me go,' I say.

'I'm not letting you get burned,' he says.

The Pit lord charges us in a halo of flames.

Raffe veers down, avoiding the burn.

The Pit lord turns and chases us. I realize that Raffe is reluctant to turn and face him, because that puts me in the flame's line of fire.

'Take the sword,' I say. We haven't tested out whether Pooky would take him back. But as he zigzags, avoiding the Pit lord's charge, I decide this isn't the best time to test it.

Raffe spins in midair. A wall of fire comes at us as the Pit lord sweeps his enormous wings toward us.

I swing my blade as hard as I can. I can feel the surge of excitement coming through the blade as Pooky gets a chance to cut into a Pit lord.

The blade slices through the fire. A piece of the flames cleaves off and tumbles down.

The Pit lord bellows as he watches a part of his wing crash onto the ground, spraying embers everywhere.

He whips his wings frantically, trying to stay up, but his wings are now uneven, and he begins spiraling. Raffe presses our advantage and flies up to him.

I slice at the first thing I can reach. Another piece of the Pit lord's wing blazes down.

And he tumbles from the sky.

39

As soon as we land, I start sweating from the heat. I can't help but cover my nose even though it does nothing against the rotten-egg stench.

The Pit lord has landed and rolled. The fire in his wings has sputtered out, leaving dead-looking wings that are burned to leathery husks. He's bleeding from both wings.

He yells a command, and the hellions and Consumed gather near him. The hellions watch their master fearfully, looking ready to bolt any minute, while the Consumed seem insanely excited at the prospect of bodies.

Watchers land all around us, forming a protective circle.

They have no weapons, and most of them have ugly wounds, some of them severe, but that doesn't stop them from looking fierce. To my surprise, Beliel is one of them. He stares blindly ahead, ready to battle for Raffe.

I look at our crew and compare them to the Pit lord's gang. I give us a good chance of beating the Pit lord, assuming none of his friends are heading our way to join the fight.

'Oh, I miss my blade,' says Cyclone, looking at mine with longing. 'The damage we could do here if we'd only been able to keep our swords.'

'That's exactly why the swords have to reject us, my brother,' says Howler. 'Nobody wants Pit lords wreaking havoc with an army of Fallen armed with their swords.'

'You may think you're stronger, Archangel,' says the Pit lord. 'But my Pit lord brethren are on their way right now. They all saw us fighting in the sky.'

'They won't be here in time to save you,' says Cyclone.

The Pit lord makes a noise like a thousand snakes slithering over dead leaves. 'But if you take the time to fight me instead of flying away, the other lords will kill you,' says the Pit lord. 'So we have a deadlock.'

He sweeps his burned and sputtering wings forward, then back, as if trying them out. The cut sections bleed all over the ground. 'I find that I'm in need of a new pair of wings.'

He looks over at Raffe's wings, which are magnificent beside the Watchers' mangy ones. 'Yours are quite nice. A Pit lord with a set of archangel wings would be both respected and feared. There would be much speculation about how he came to possess them. Care to make a deal?'

Raffe laughs.

'Think on it. No angel becomes an archangel without ambition. Ambition sometimes requires deceit. Sometimes, it requires an army. I can offer both.'

'Deceit can be found everywhere,' says Raffe. 'And it's freely given.'

'But an army – now that's worth something. I have several for rent. For the right price. Interested?'

'Not for my wings. No one's ever taking those from me.' He doesn't say *again*.

'Perhaps you'll have something else I might want one day.' The Pit lord looks pointedly at me. 'If you're ever interested in something I can provide in exchange for . . .' – he shrugs – 'something I want, just bite into this.'

He tosses a small, round item strung on a thong. Raffe doesn't bother to catch it, and it lands at his feet. It looks like a strung-up dried apple. Dark and wrinkly. I'm not sure I'd eat it if I were dying of starvation.

'When you bite into it, it'll bring me to wherever you are so we can talk details,' says the Pit lord as he climbs onto his chariot.

Cyclone takes a step toward the chariot. The Pit lord's hellions and Consumed bare their teeth at him.

Raffe puts out a hand to stop him. 'We're not here to fight.'

'He's only offering a bargain to save face,' says Cyclone. 'He won't win this, and he knows it.'

'Neither will we.' Raffe nods to the sky. Three chariots fly toward us. Behind them is a cloud of hellions.

The Pit lord in front of us cracks his whip at the angels harnessed to his chariot. The Consumed whip heads cut into the angels, who are drenched with bloody sweat trickling down their hard bodies. They take off into the air.

As soon as the chariot is on its way, the Watchers circle Flyer, who is lying on the ground. His back is clearly broken, by the look of the unnatural bend of his body.

His head shifts back and forth on the ground, so I assume he's alive. But as we lean over him, the shifting motion of his head becomes more and more wrong.

His neck tears, bubbling blood.

I jump back.

Teeth gnaw out from the inside of Flyer's neck, quickly chewing through. A Consumed whip head covered in blood emerges from Flyer's neck.

I look away, wishing I could wipe out what I just saw. From the edge of my vision, I see Cyclone grab a rock and hoist it above his head. Then I hear a wet *crunch*.

Everyone's shoulders seem to slump at the same time.

'You have to get us out of here, Commander,' says Hawk with heavy sadness in his voice. 'This isn't how we were meant to die.'

40

We move out of the area before the other Pit lords arrive. Some of us walk, while some of us fly low and scout ahead.

I keep expecting someone to ask about my sword, but no one does. The Watchers seem a little shell-shocked after seeing Flyer die. It's like tragedy happens too often yet they still can't accept it.

The broken street we're on ends abruptly as the town ruins disintegrate into a rocky desert. I keep an eye out for hellions to catch along the way, but I don't see any. They must have either run off or been recruited to fight for the Pit lords when they were gathering to come at us.

The sky is changing into what I guess is the equivalent of daylight here. Instead of the purple black I'd seen earlier, there's now a red glow casting a fiendish tint over the desert – not quite night, not quite day.

One of the Watchers sighs beside me. 'Most of us made it through another night.'

'Let's go back into that street tonight,' says another. 'Safer there.'

I throw them a sidelong glance. They have fresh gashes across their faces and arms. One of them is limping and bleeding from a missing chunk out of his leg.

'How long have you guys been here?' I ask.

The guys give me weary looks as if to say forever.

'No idea,' says one. 'Since before I was born, I think.'

We walk onto an outcropping of rocks. The desert is full of weird rock towers spiraling up to the red sky, twisted and tortured. In the distance, there are ruins of cities. One of them is on fire, with black smoke rising to the sky.

'What are those?' I ask. 'Are they cities?'

'Once,' says Thermo. 'They're just death traps now. They used to be hellion cities.'

I turn to Beliel. 'I thought you said the hellions weren't much of anything before the Fallen came?'

Beliel sneers. 'You think it excuses their torture of innocent people just because they used to have cities?'

'They must have had a nice little primitive society here,' says Thermo. 'Lucifer and his army put them in their place quickly enough though.'

Things begin to come together in my head. 'Is that why they love torturing the newly Fallen?'

'Who knows why they do the things they do,' says Beliel. 'They should be exterminated, not analyzed.'

'Whatever they used to be, they've devolved into lower-class animals,' says Thermo. 'I doubt they have any motive other than instinct.'

'But the newly Fallen are the only angels or demons that they can torment, right?' I ask. 'They're afraid of the seasoned Fallen, aren't they?'

'They'd be afraid of us too if the Pit lords weren't using them to torture us. If there's one pleasure the Pit lords give them, it's the job of tormenting us during initiation.'

I nod. Maybe the hellions were so gleeful in hurting Beliel because torturing the newly Fallen is the only revenge they can get for the destruction of their world.

If this keeps up, I'm going to end up like Paige and start talking crazy about having respect for all living things, even for things as hideous as hellions.

The old Paige, I mean.

I watch the smoke rising above the ruined hellion city and wonder how she's doing. Is Mom okay? Is the Resistance still holding it together? Will I ever get back to them?

The Watchers look each other over in the brighten-
ing light, assessing themselves for injuries. They look
the most carefully at Raffe, but not to see if he's hurt.
They seem to just be assessing him.

Raffe is the only one of them who is whole, uninjured, and fully winged with healthy feathers. He stands
tall and muscular, with no scars or scabs on his powerful
body.

The only thing marring his appearance is the dried-
fruit necklace that the Pit lord gave him. One of the
Watchers had picked it up off the ground, telling Raffe
that it could be used to show that a Pit lord favored
him. I think it looks like a dead mouse dangling off
his neck.

'We thought we'd never see you again, Commander,'
says Thermo. 'We thought we were forsaken.'

'We always knew we were meant to be forsaken,' says
Howler, 'but it's a different thing when it actually
happens.'

'What's happening topside?' asks Thermo.

Raffe tells them about Messenger Gabriel dying, Uriel
expediting an election by creating a false apocalypse,
the invasion on our world, and what happened with his
wings.

While he's talking to them, I watch Beliel. Like the
others, he's handsome, masculine, and torn up. But

unlike the others, he looks toward Raffe with a conflicting mix of hope and anger.

'You're here to take us back with you, right?' asks Beliel. 'We're not fully Fallen yet. We still have some of our feathers even.' Some of the others chuckle like that's a joke.

Beliel strokes the remaining patches of sunset feathers on his wing. 'They'll grow back once they can see real sunlight again. Won't they?'

'Let us help,' says Hawk. 'Give us a mission.'

'Let us earn our way back, Commander,' says Cyclone. 'We're wasted down here.'

Raffe takes a good look at them. He looks at their tufts of feathers and splintered wing bones sticking out at odd angles. He looks at their skinned limbs and gnarled wounds. I can see in his eyes that it hurts to see his loyal soldiers like this.

'What happened to the others?' asks Raffe. He looks at the dozen or so Watchers around us.

'They have their own journeys to travel now.' Thermo's voice holds a world of sadness.

So if we brought them back, it'd be a dozen Watchers against a hundred of Uriel's angels.

'Where are the hellions?' I ask.

'They're the least of our worries,' says Beliel.

I look around at the barren landscape. No hellions in

sight. 'I need them. I might be able to use them to get out of here.'

They all stare at me.

'Have you even been here long enough to be this crazy?' asks Little B.

'That's how we got here,' I say. 'The hellions can jump in and out through my sword, and I grabbed one to hitch a ride.' I shrug. 'I guess you guys never held a sword on a demon long enough to do this before.'

'It only takes a second to kill one,' says Raffe. 'No reason to pause before skewering him.'

There's a moment of silence as they stare at me, then they look at each other.

I brace for the barrage of questions, but all they ask is, 'Can we catch a ride too?'

I glance at Raffe. He nods. It wouldn't surprise me if this has now turned into a rescue mission for Raffe as much as a mission to save the angel host back in our world.

'You don't really believe her, do you?' asks Little B.

'You got something better to do than listen to her?' asks Howler.

'I don't know if it'll work,' I say. 'But if you could help me find hellions and convince them to jump back into my world, then we can all try to leave here together.'

'She's as crazy as the rest of them,' says Little B. 'No one has ever escaped the Pit without permission from the higher-ups. Ever.'

'She's telling the truth,' says Raffe. 'We come from a different time, and we came through . . . one of you.'

They all look at each other.

Raffe nods at me, and I tell them my story. I tell them a version of it that I hope is a diplomatic one – one where I don't mention which of them was the gateway and what condition he was in when we came through. When I'm done telling them about how we got here, everyone is silent.

'If one of us is the gateway,' says Beliel. 'Then that must mean that the gateway Watcher can't leave, right?'

I drop my gaze. If we manage to get out of here, he'll be left behind for however long it takes him to claw and connive his way out of the Pit and onto earth. I have no idea how long that will be. But it'll obviously be long enough to kill off all decency in him.

41

You'd think since we're in the natural habitat of hellions, the place would be crawling with them. But most of them must be hiding, because we can't find any. I've seen more hellions in Palo Alto than here.

Black smoke rises on hell's horizon above one of the city ruins. I take a step onto the desert rocks near the sand, wondering how far it is to the nearest city. I have a strange urge to see the ruins. It might be an indication of what my world could be like one day.

'Stop!' one of the Watchers calls out just as I'm about to step onto the sand.

A hand whips out of the sand and grabs my ankle.

I scream, trying to yank my foot back. I kick the hand, but it pulls me off balance.

More hands burst out of the sand, reaching for me.

I try to scramble back, but the hand pulls me down.

I get my sword out and frantically slice.

Strong arms wrap around my waist, and a boot kicks the severed hand off my ankle, leaving maggots on my leg.

I shut my eyes and try not to squeal. 'Get the maggots off me!'

Raffe brushes them off, but it feels like they're still crawling on my skin.

'So you do scream like a little girl,' says Raffe with some satisfaction in his voice. I open my eyes a second too soon, because I catch him tossing the severed hand into the sand.

A forest of hands sprout up from the sand to grab it and tear it to pieces, fighting for the scraps.

I scoot away from squirming maggots. Raffe sees my distress and flicks them off the rock.

'Maggots are freaky hideous,' I say, getting up. I try to salvage some dignity, but I can't help but shiver and shake my hands in the air. It's an instinctive impulse, one I'm not up for resisting right now.

'You've fought off a gang of men twice your size, killed an angel warrior, stood up to an archangel, and wielded an angel sword.' Raffe cocks his head. 'But you scream like a little girl when you see a maggot?'

'It's not just a maggot,' I say. 'A hand burst out of the ground and grabbed my ankle. And maggots crawled out of it and tried to burrow into me. You would scream like a little girl too if that happened to you.'

'They didn't try to burrow into you. They were just crawling. It's what maggots do. They crawl.'

'You don't know anything.'

'Hard to argue with that, Commander,' says Howler with a laugh in his voice.

'That's the Sea of Killing Hands,' says Thermo. 'You don't want to get near it.'

I can see why they call it a sea. The sand shifts like waves. I'm assuming it's because of the hands or whatever moving beneath it. I can't help but see the similarities between the Pit and my world now that Uriel and his false apocalypse are creating things like the resurrected crawling out of the ground.

'Oh, she could have handled the killing hands like the truest warrior,' says Raffe proudly. 'It's the little naked worms that make her tremble.'

'Maybe we should call her maggot slayer,' says Howler. The others chuckle.

I sigh. I probably deserve this, but that doesn't make it any easier. Now I know how Pooky Bear feels.

I see a small hellion over the desert, and I point to it, excited. But it flies too close to the sand, and three hands shoot out and grab it. The arms are not the length of a regular arm. They reach up at least six feet to grab the hellion. It screeches all the way down until it gets dragged beneath the sand.

One of the guys points to an outcropping of rocks.

The small hellion that was caught by the hands must have been a scout, because a group of hellions flies toward us.

My sword is up, ready for a fight. 'Don't kill them. We need them alive.'

The flying creepies come at us all teeth and claws. They're as big or bigger than the ones that came after me out of the Pit. There are four of them.

Beside me, Raffe opens his wings and takes to the air over the Sea of Killing Hands. The others do the same. Beliel and I are the only ones left on the ground.

They corral the hellions toward Hawk and Cyclone who catch them.

When they come down, they've caught all four. They tie the hellions down with leather thongs that some of them had wrapped around their wrists. Apparently, Raffe had trained them to collect bits of useful items from the local environment whenever they were on a mission.

'You're smarter than you look,' I say to Raffe.

'But not as smart as he thinks,' says Howler.

'I can see discipline has broken down during your vacation,' says Raffe.

'Yeah, it's all that lounging on the beach with nothing to do but drink and watch women.'

At the word *women*, the Watchers become awkward and self-conscious.

'I have to ask,' says Thermo. 'I know the others are wondering this too. Is she your Daughter of Man?' He nods toward me.

I glance at Raffe.

Am I?

Raffe thinks about that for a second before answering. 'She is *a* Daughter of Man. And she is traveling with me. But she's not *my* Daughter of Man.'

What kind of answer is that?

'Oh. So she's available?' asks Howler.

Raffe gives him an icy look.

'We're all single now, you know,' says Hawk.

'They can't punish us twice for the same crime,' says Cyclone.

'And now that we know you're out of the race, Commander, that makes me the next best-looking in line,' says Howler.

'Enough.' Raffe doesn't look amused. 'You're not her type.'

The Watchers smile knowingly.

'How do you know?' I ask.

Raffe turns to me. 'Because angels aren't your type. You hate them, remember?'

'But these guys aren't angels anymore.'

Raffe arches his brow at me. 'You should be with a nice human boy. One who takes your orders and puts up with your demands. Someone who dedicates his life to keeping you safe and well fed. Someone who can make you happy. Someone you can be proud of.' He waves his hand at the Watchers. 'There's nobody like that in this lot.'

I glare at him. 'I'll be sure to pass him by you first before I' – *settle for* – 'choose him.'

'You do that. I'll let him know what's expected of him.'

'Assuming he survives your interrogation,' says Howler.

'Big assumption,' says Cyclone.

'I'd like to be there to watch,' says Hawk. 'Should be interesting.'

'Don't worry, Commander,' says Howler. 'We've all come to our own conclusions. We've all been there.'

Then a somber mood comes over them. Thermo clears his throat. 'Speaking of . . .'

'Some of them survived,' says Raffe.

'Which ones?'

'It won't help to know,' says Raffe. 'Just know that I managed to rescue some of them, and they lived.'

'And the children?' There's no hope in Thermo's voice when he asks this.

Raffe sighs. 'You were right. I left to hunt "the nephilim monsters" only to find they were just children. Gabriel said the spawn of an angel and a Daughter of Man would grow into a monster. I didn't want to kill them while they were still harmless, so I waited. And waited. Generation after generation, to root out the evil that I'd been warned about.'

He shakes his head. 'But none came. I searched everywhere for nephilim monsters, but they were just people. Some of them were particularly large people, and they had fewer children than most. The children they had were sometimes especially talented and beautiful, but nothing monstrous. And eventually, the bloodlines thinned among the humans to the point where it wasn't uncommon to have at least a drop or two of angelic blood in a population.'

'I knew it was a lie,' says Cyclone.

'Thank you, Archangel,' says a Watcher with a tuft of spotted feathers on his wing. 'Thank you for sparing them.'

'My orders were to kill the nephilim *monsters*,' says Raffe. 'Gabriel's words exactly. I found the nephilim. I can't do anything about it if none of them were monsters. I did my duty.'

'But you stayed a long time, didn't you?' I ask.

Raffe nods. 'If I went back too early to report on my mission, Gabriel could have clarified his order to just kill the nephilim and sent me back.'

Now I understand. 'You were waiting until the nephilim blood thinned, until no one could identify one.'

Raffe shrugs. 'Or until one of them turned monstrous. Preferably two. Then I could have come back and said that I killed the nephilim monsters as ordered.'

'But that didn't happen,' I say.

He shakes his head.

The Watchers look like they need a moment. Some of them find a rock to sit on, while others just look away or close their eyes for a minute.

'Why would Gabriel lie and make a rule that an angel who married a Daughter of Man would fall?' asks one of the Watchers.

'Maybe he didn't want to taint the angelic bloodline with our human blood,' I say. 'Most angels think of us as animals.' I shrug.

'How long have we been here?' asks Thermo. 'Our children have great-great-grandchildren?'

'From your perspective, I don't think it's been long

since you fell,' says Raffe. 'But we're from a different time. In our world, your fall is ancient history.'

The Watchers exchange looks with each other.

'You have to get us out of here,' says the Watcher with the spotted tuft. 'Please, Commander. Who knows when Judgment Day will come.' His voice cracks at the end.

There's desperation on their faces.

'It's one thing to die in battle,' says Beliel, 'but to die in the Pit, or worse – to live eternally in the Pit . . .' He shakes his head. 'It's incomprehensible. We're being punished for nothing.'

'Uriel says that Gabriel went insane,' says Raffe. 'That he hasn't actually spoken to God in eons. Maybe never.'

Most of the Watchers stare at him openmouthed. A couple of them, though, nod as if they had been suspecting this for some time.

'I have no idea if it's true,' says Raffe. 'Nobody does, except for Gabriel. But it does seem like he was wrong about the nephilim. I'd been telling myself that it was a mistake. But now . . . who knows what else he was *wrong* about?' He glances at me.

'In the end, it doesn't really matter,' says Hawk. 'Our loyalties are to you, whatever happens.'

'Do you have a plan, Commander?' asks Thermo.

'Sure,' says Raffe. 'The plan is to bust you out, then you'll help me take down Uriel.'

Everyone's face changes. I'm not sure if it's awe or disbelief. Maybe a little of both.

'Don't get excited,' says Raffe. 'We don't know if we can all get out. And even if we can, we don't know what's waiting on the other side.'

He glances at Beliel, who looks excited at the thought of getting out. 'Sacrifices will need to be made.'

42

The Watchers are sure there are more hellions in the direction where the first ones came from. We decide to split up to increase our chances of finding them.

'Howler and Cyclone, come with me,' says Raffe. 'The rest of you, split into small groups and each take a direction. We'll meet back here.' He looks at the sky. 'How do you tell time here?'

'It'll get hotter,' says Thermo. 'We can meet when we feel like we're baking.'

'That'd be now,' says Howler.

'We'll meet when Howler feels like he's burning and the rest of us feel like we're baking,' says Raffe. 'Ready?'

'Uh, can I go with Thermo?' asks Howler.

'Thermo?' asks Raffe. 'The last time I assigned you with him, you said it was dangerous to pair up with him because you were afraid you'd fall asleep on the mission.'

'Yeah, that's why he'll be the odd man out, and if I go with him, I won't have to go with you and your Daughter of Man.'

'Good point,' says Cyclone. 'Can I go with Howler and Thermo? They're helpless without me.'

Howler snorts.

'What's wrong with going with me?' I ask.

'No one wants to be stuck with love birds.' Howler shakes his head.

'Awkward,' says Cyclone, already walking toward Thermo.

'You think I'd do something to risk a fall?' asks Raffe.

'You can't fall for anything you do here, Commander,' says Thermo. 'You're already in the Pit, so technically, it's equivalent to being in a Fallen state during the time you're here.'

The heat intensifies in my cheeks, and I want to crawl behind a rock.

Raffe looks like he wants to be stubborn but then says, 'Fine, but you'd better bring back a bunch of hellions, Howler.'

'You can count on it, boss.' Howler throws us a broad wink, and takes off into the air. Cyclone and Thermo fly after him.

The rest of the Watchers take off in small groups, each taking different directions. It's a wonder that they can still fly on their mangy wings. I guess there's nothing functionally wrong with the wings since they fly expertly. It's just that they're not pretty to look at.

Raffe watches them go, then looks at me. 'Shall we go for a ride and see what the place looks like?'

I nod, trying not to look embarrassed.

I step closer to Raffe. I'll never get used to stepping into his arms.

Instead of putting his arm under my knees, he holds me up with his arms around my waist, with us facing each other in a hug. With a couple of sweeps of his wings, we take off.

I have my arms around his neck, but my legs are dangling. I don't feel as secure as I normally do when he holds me with his arms behind my back and below my knees. I instinctively slide my knees around his middle and squeeze for a better hold.

But that's not enough. As we go higher, I can feel myself sliding just a little. His arms around my waist are firm, but as we rise above the Sea of Killing Hands, I feel an equal mix of excitement and fear.

'Don't drop me.' I cling tighter and press myself up against him a little more.

'Never.' There's so much confidence and assurance in his voice. 'I have you. You're as secure as can be.'

Oh, what the hell. I wrap my legs completely around his hips and hook my feet across his butt.

He tilts his body forward a little with a smile spreading across his face. My cheeks flame.

Now I'm hanging on like a monkey as we glide over the Pit. I can't see as well as I'd be able to if he had been holding me the other way. Instead of looking over his shoulder at his sweeping wings, I turn my head to see the landscape below. That puts my face almost lip to lip with his.

I try to focus on the smoldering city ahead of us, but my head is filled with the warmth of his breath and the electric tingle of his cheek against mine.

Flying is not as smooth a glide as it might look from below. There's a subtle shifting of our bodies as his wings push against the air. I'm hanging on to him so tightly that I begin to notice that he's rubbing against me with every whoosh of his wings.

The heat in the Pit is becoming more intense. The Sea of Hands below shifts and moves like currents of lava flowing over each other.

The rubbing is causing a warm, tingly sensation, as if all my blood is rushing to the parts of my body that are pressed against him. My head begins to feel light. My breathing comes faster.

His breath speeds up to match mine, or maybe it's the other way around. Before I know it, he's nuzzling his head against my cheek. A low moan escapes his lips.

I shift without thinking, tightening my legs around his hips, pressing myself against him. He strokes the curve of my back, pressing me even closer to his warmth. I marvel at the sensation as he subtly shifts his body against mine.

He lowers his head while we're flying and touches his lips to mine. His kiss is hot and wet as it intensifies.

My head seems to be rumbling. Then I realize it's the sky. It's thunder. Suddenly, warm raindrops fall on us, spraying us until we're completely wet.

Raffe ignores it and continues to kiss me. We hold each other, pressing tighter and harder together.

We fly in each other's arms in the rain over a smoldering hell.

43

By the time we get back to the group, the Watchers have caught the rest of the hellions that we'll need. A dozen hellions are tied up on the ground, flapping around and trying to gnaw through the thongs that tie them.

The Watchers eye us like they know what we've been up to. As soon as we land, I hop off and step away from Raffe. I'm glad it's so hot that I won't have to explain why my face is so red.

Raffe immediately gets down to business. He explains what needs to be done to ride a hellion out of the Pit and what we might find on the other side. He doesn't seem at all embarrassed that they assume we made out.

He then talks to the hellions. 'Take us to the other

side.' He motions along Pooky's blade and uses his hand to show a sliding motion into the sky.

A hellion hisses at him, all sharp teeth and hate.

Cyclone steps forward. 'They need a firm hand, Commander.' He looms over the hellions. 'Do what we tell you, or you die.' He makes a tearing motion with his hands.

A hellion pisses at him, squirting a yellow-green stream of foul-smelling liquid that Cyclone barely avoids.

The other hellions seem to snicker. Cyclone leans in, looking like he's going to strangle them, but Raffe stops him.

I step forward. Let's see how they respond if they're treated like I would want to be in their place.

'Freedom,' I say.

The hellions look sideways at me.

'Escape.' I crouch down to look at them at their level. They watch me with distrust, but they're listening. 'No more Pit lords. No more masters. Be free.' I do the sliding motion along my sword the way Raffe did earlier.

The hellions begin chattering among themselves, as if arguing.

'Take us with you.' I point to me and the others. 'Be free.' I motion along my sword into the sky again. 'With you.' I point to them.

More chatter.

Then they quiet down.

The one in the center nods at us.

My eyes open wide. It worked. One by one, the Watchers nod in my direction with respect in their eyes.

Raffe doesn't go into the details of Beliel's involvement with Uriel or with his wings. In fact, he doesn't even say who the gateway Watcher is. He just says that it's one of them.

'Think long and hard about this,' says Raffe. 'We've always taken pride in never leaving one of us behind. You can stay here together and I'll find another way to beat Uriel. Or you can come with us, but one of you must stay behind. Isolation is the worst thing that can happen to an angel. You think it's bad now? It'll be a hundred times worse when you're alone, knowing that all your fellow soldiers made it out and left you here. You'll become twisted, angry, vindictive, vengeful. You'll become someone you wouldn't recognize.'

He stares at the squirming hellions tied on the ground. 'And for that, I'm sorry. I see now my role in it.'

He looks at every Watcher around him. 'For the rest of you, remember that your families won't be there anymore. Your Daughter of Man, your children – they'll all be gone. If this is successful, we're going to a different time, a different place. We'll land in the middle of a war. But it'll be a war where some of the fighters might have your blood in their veins.'

The Watchers look at each other as though trying to process that. I'm having trouble with it myself. Some of us could be their descendants.

They all look at each other, understanding that the gateway Watcher could be any of them.

Beliel is the first to nod. There's naked hope in his face. 'I'd do anything – risk anything – for a chance to have the yellow sun on our faces again.'

I clamp down hard on the sympathy that's blooming for him. I run through the litany of his crimes – my sister, the murders, Raffe's wings, his part in turning humans into monsters – I list all the names and faces that I knew at Alcatraz.

One by one, the Watchers nod grimly. Each prepared to take the risk.

We don't tell Beliel that he's the one until the very last second.

When Beliel finds out it's him, his face freezes. It's disturbing to think of someone gazing out into nothing when he has no eyes. The only sign of life from him is his chest pumping in and out as his breathing gets heavier.

The Watchers are somber. Each of them touches

Beliel's shoulder until he flings Thermo's hand off him. After that, everyone quietly grabs a hellion.

Beliel stands alone in a circle of the only friends he had in his life. He jerks when I prick him with my sword.

Raffe gives the command to the hellions to jump through.

The Watcher-ridden hellions leap at Beliel. He stands frozen, as if electrified, while the hellions fly into him.

Raffe is the first to go so he can usher the Watchers who are sure to be disoriented when they arrive on the other side. I am the last to go so that I can hold the sword and keep the gateway open until we're all through.

By the end, Beliel is on his knees, his empty eye sockets shut tight and his teeth clenched. There's shock, but there's anguish too, even though he volunteered. They all volunteered.

But I'm sure that's little comfort. Everyone else is making it out of the Pit and leaving him behind. To suffer alone for what will seem like eternity to him.

Alone and unwanted.

Probably for the first time in his life.

I run through the litany of his crimes again as I ride my hellion into the gate that is Beliel.

44

Going into the Pit was like falling. Getting out of the Pit is like being dragged through a vat of Vaseline. It's as if the air itself is trying to push me back. I cling to my hellion as tightly as I can. I don't even want to think about what happens if I can't hold on.

I pop out into cramped quarters, feeling covered in goop even though there's nothing physically on me. I should be back in my world, my time if everything went as planned. Raffe made it clear to the hellions that they would be free only if they brought us to our own where and when, but you never know.

Instead of jumping out through the portal and onto firm ground, I end up smashing against something hard.

There's enough light to see that I'm shoved against the dashboard of a truck.

The truck swerves, and I'm so disoriented that I might as well be upside down in a fish bowl. All I can see is the hellion I rode on bouncing in panic inside the truck cab. Luckily, it's a large truck cab, but there are still far too many people and creatures crammed into it.

My disorientation settles enough for me to realize that I'm sitting on Beliel's lap.

It's not the same Beliel we left behind. He's more weathered, beaten, and weary. Not to mention dried up, wingless, and bleeding. He breathes in a slow, painful rasp.

I see my surroundings in a way that my mind can't quite comprehend right now. A white hand pushes through the open rear window. It grabs the flapping hellion and yanks it awkwardly through the window.

Behind us is an open truck bed full of confused and disoriented Watchers. Several of them look queasy as we bounce and swerve around debris.

Beyond the truck bed, a group of angels chases us through our plume of dust that spreads into the dawn sky. And is that my sister and her three scorpions flying beside us?

Shrinking in the distance is the dark shadow of the new aerie and its outer buildings. Before I can comprehend what I'm seeing, the windows of one of the outer buildings explode in a burst of fire and shattered glass.

The angels who had been chasing us stop, watching the fire. Then they circle back to the aerie to defend their home base from whatever is attacking.

The truck swerves left, then right, like the driver is drunk.

Beside me, I hear a cackling full of genuine joy. My mother is behind the wheel. She has a triumphant grin on her face as she glances over at me.

She looks back at the road just barely in time to swerve around an abandoned car. She must be going sixty miles per hour. That's suicidal on these roads.

I push myself away from Beliel. I'd gotten used to seeing him with a fresh, hopeful face. Now he's bleeding through his chest, ears, mouth, and nose. It's hard to look at him, much less sit on his lap.

It's awkward and dangerous holding my sword in such cramped quarters. I have to be careful in the swerving cab while putting the blade back into my scabbard.

'Be careful, Mom,' I say as she swerves again.

I crawl through the rear window and land in the standing-room-only open truck bed. There's barely enough room for me, but I'm small enough that I can slip between two large warriors.

When I see their disoriented and drained faces, I don't need to wonder why they're not all airborne. Even the few who are flying hold on to the truck's roll bar, looking like they need a little guidance. These guys clearly need a minute to adjust.

At this speed, the aerie is fast disappearing behind us.

'Are you ready to go back and fight?' It's Josiah, the albino.

The Watchers answer with a general groan. It vaguely sounds like 'yeah, okay' if I'm being optimistic, 'hell no' if I'm not.

The overall impression is that they're completely sick and in no condition to fight. I'm disoriented too but not sick to my stomach. They've probably never ridden with Mom before. Okay, maybe they've never even ridden in a car before.

'You'll feel better once we stop.' I bang on the window. 'Mom, slow down. You can stop the truck.'

She speeds up.

I bang on the window again and stick my head through to the cab. 'Mom, it'll be all right.'

The truck slows down and comes to a halt. Paige and her locusts fly past us, then swoop back to where we're stopped.

The Watchers climb out of the truck, looking shaky on their legs. They unravel their wings and stretch them out, as though testing them. The rest land around us, looking not much better.

The dust settles behind us and over the Watchers. They're quite a sight. Their partially feathered wings with their curling, splintered edges and their half-skinned bodies must be monstrous even in my mother's imagination. I glance at Mom through the window, wondering what she thinks of all this.

My sister and her locusts do happy loop-de-loops in the air. Paige waves to me.

'Report, Josiah.' Raffe turns to Josiah.

Josiah stares at the Watchers with wide eyes. 'After you left, a guard saw me, and we got into an argument about whether to put Beliel back in his cage. I couldn't let that happen. If things went according to plan – and I can't believe that they actually did – you would have all come out into a cage and been crushed to death.'

'Penryn!' The door of the truck opens, and my mother runs toward me. She enfolds me in a hug that's too tight.

'Hi, Mom.'

'This ghost angel told me that you were inside that demon over there.' She points to Beliel who seems on the verge of losing consciousness in the passenger seat. 'He said that you might come out any minute. I didn't believe him of course. That's crazy talk. But still, you never know.' She shrugs. 'And look what happened.' She squints at me suspiciously. 'It is you, isn't it?'

'Yes, it's me, Mom.'

'How did you get us out?' asks Raffe.

Josiah rubs his face. 'After my little *argument* with the guard, I took Beliel. But Beliel is big and heavy even in his shriveled state. I couldn't fly with him, but I had to get him somewhere safe until you came back. I wouldn't have been able to do it without her.' He points to my mother. 'Or her.' He nods to my sister, who lands in the trees with her locusts.

'And how did you end up with them?' I ask.

'Your mother found out the cult sold you out,' says Josiah. 'And she and your sister trekked here to rescue you.'

I look at my mother, who is nodding as if to say, of course we did. Wiry gray now streaks her dark hair. When did that happen? For a second, I see her through the eyes of a stranger and see a frail and vulnerable woman who looks tiny next to the brawny angels.

I look at my sister up in a tree. She's being carried by a locust the way I used to carry her from her wheelchair only a couple of months ago.

'You went to the aerie?' My voice wavers a little as I look back and forth between my mom and sister. 'You risked your lives to rescue *me*?'

My mother gives me another too-tight hug. My sister twitches the corners of her lips up despite the pain it must cost her to move the stitches on her cheeks.

My eyes sting at the thought of the danger they faced to rescue me.

'Paige has three large pets with scorpion stingers who can fly her out at any time,' says my mom. 'I told them they'd be in big trouble if anything happened to her.'

'Oh.' I look at Raffe with a watery smile. 'Even the locusts are afraid of my mother.'

'I can see why,' says Josiah. 'She came with a group of shaved-headed humans who were requesting safe passage marks on their foreheads.'

'Amnesty?' asks Raffe. 'Uriel's giving some of the humans amnesty?'

'Just the ones who gave her up.' Josiah nods toward me.

The muscles in Raffe's jaw dance as he clenches his teeth.

Josiah shrugs. 'Your mother somehow convinced those people to wander into the aerie after they received their amnesty marks. Uriel had to drive them out like rats. Your sister also distracted the angels by doing flybys with her three locusts. We all kept looking to see where the rest of the swarm was. While everyone was distracted, your mother set the place on fire. She is one fierce woman.'

'Fire?'

'What do you think caused that explosion?' Josiah nods in appreciation. 'I never would have gotten Beliel out if it wasn't for all the distractions your family caused.'

Josiah gestures to the truck. 'Once I convinced your mother that you were inside Beliel, she convinced me we needed to ride in this vehicle. It got us out, but I'm never going to ride in one of those metal coffins again.'

'Amen,' says Thermo, who still looks queasy.

Mom has a smudge on her forehead. It looks like ashes, but I know that it's the amnesty mark. It looks just like the smudges that Uriel's soldier gave to the cult members who sold me out.

'You're not in a cult, are you, Mom?'

'Of course not.' She looks at me like I just insulted her. 'Those people are all nuts. They'll regret having sold you out. I made sure of that. If Paige eats someone, it'll be someone outside their cult. It's the worst punishment they can imagine.'

45

A groan reaches us from the passenger seat of the truck. We walk back toward Beliel and open the passenger door.

He's in bad shape. There's blood everywhere.

He opens his eyes sluggishly and looks at me. It's a relief to see him with eyes in his sockets. I wonder how long it took to grow them back?

'I knew I recognized your voice from somewhere.' He coughs. Blood bubbles out of his mouth. 'Been a long time. So long I thought it was a torture dream.'

How long did he spend down in the Pit, taking the punishment for an entire squad of newly Fallen?

'I actually thought . . . I actually thought, once, that there might be hope,' says Beliel. 'That you might come back and figure out a way to take me with you too.'

Watchers gather around behind me.

Beliel's eyes lift to look at them. 'You're all just like I remember. You haven't changed at all. As if it just happened this morning.' He coughs again, and his face scrunches in pain. 'I should have made you all wait with me in the Pit.'

His eyes drift closed.

He takes a shuddering breath and lets it out. He doesn't take another.

I look up at Raffe, then at Josiah.

Josiah shakes his head at me. 'It was too much for him. He wasn't doing well after you guys went through him. His healing slowed down, almost stopped. He was in no condition to handle so many coming through. I don't think biological beings were really meant to be gateways.'

Josiah sighs. 'But if it had to happen to someone, it might as well have been Beliel.' He turns and walks away from Beliel's ravaged body. 'No one will miss him. He didn't have a friend in the world.'

46

The Watchers decide to do a proper ceremony for Beliel. We drive until the aerie is long out of sight before we stop to bury him.

'Do we even have shovels?' I ask.

'He's not an animal,' says Hawk. 'We won't bury him.'

There's an uncomfortable silence as the Watchers gently pull Beliel's body out from the car. None of the guys will look at each other, as though stubbornly and silently insisting on something that each thinks the other might object to.

Finally, Cyclone speaks up. 'I'll be a bearer.'

'Me too,' says Howler.

The floodgates open, and all the other Watchers speak out, volunteering to be bearers.

They all look at Raffe, waiting for his approval. Raffe nods.

'What?' asks Josiah, looking baffled. 'After all he's done, you're going to bestow an honorable—'

'We know what he's done for us,' says Hawk. 'Whatever else he's done since then, it looks like he's paid the price. He's one of us. We should give him the proper send-off that we couldn't give our other brothers in the Pit.'

Josiah looks at them, then at Raffe, who nods.

'What do we have that will burn?' asks Thermo.

'We have gas, but he said I couldn't use any more,' says my mother, pointing to Josiah.

'And you can't,' says Josiah. 'But they need some for the ceremony.' He walks back to the truck and climbs into the bed.

'You brought gas?' I ask.

'To burn down the angels' nest,' says Mom. 'I figured that once I got you out, we might as well burn it all down. But he wouldn't let me.'

Josiah comes back with a gas can. 'She did enough damage. She would have been caught if she had tried to burn the whole aerie down.' He shakes his head as he puts the can down. 'I still don't know how she got away with doing as much damage as she did. Or how I convinced her about you being inside Beliel. I'm not even sure I believed it.'

'Why not?' asks my mother. 'Did you think she was hiding inside someone else?'

'Never mind, Mom.' I hold her hand and pull her away from the Watchers. 'Let them do their burial.'

Josiah splashes the gas over Beliel's body. 'You're sure you want to do this?'

'He's earned this,' says Howler.

Josiah nods and steps back.

My mom steps forward with a lighter and lights a strip of cloth on fire.

Thermo takes it and drops the flaming cloth onto Beliel's soaked body.

Beliel ignites.

His hair fizzles like quick sparklers, lighting up, then disappearing. His shriveled skin and pants light up as the flames spread all over his body. Waves of heat distort the road beyond him and warm my exposed neck and face. The air fills with the smell of burning gasoline mixed with the faint scent of meat beginning to char.

Five of the Watchers step forward and grab his burning arms, legs, and shoulders.

I move to stop them, but Raffe puts out his arm to block me.

'What are they doing?' I ask. 'They're going to burn themselves.'

'It'll be painful. But they'll heal,' he says.

All the Watchers take to the air. Their wings spread and beat in unison against the sunrise.

Just as I think that the flaming body between them must be burning them to a crisp, a new set of Watchers relieve them and take over the flaming burden. The others fly, crisscrossing each other like a net far below the body. Bits of burning debris fall, much of it burning out before reaching the other Watchers. The bits that continue to fall, the Watchers catch, one by one.

'They won't let any part of him fall to the ground,' says Raffe in a quiet voice. 'His brothers will keep him from falling.'

In the distance, the Watchers weave a beautiful dance in the dawn sky beneath Beliel's shower of fire.

47

I stand by a tree on the side of the road and scan the sky above us. The Watchers are done with their ceremony and are flying back to us.

'We need to get back,' says Josiah. 'The contest announcement should be happening soon. And then the big scramble for recruits will start in earnest.' He glances at the Watchers, and I know what he's thinking. It's going to be a tough sell to get angels to join with the half-feathered, half-skinned Watchers.

'We have to try to convince some to join us,' says Raffe. 'And we'll work with whatever we have. We can't let everyone fall, and we can't allow a civil war to start.'

I won't be shedding tears for Uriel's angels if they fall. They've earned it as far as I can see.

He looks at me. 'Earth would be the battle ground if there's a civil war among the angels. Everything in this world will be scorched to the ground, regardless of who wins.'

Just like the Pit. We would be like the hellions – half starved and insane, cowering in the shadows, constantly in fear of our angel masters.

I have to clear my throat before getting my question out. 'Isn't that what they're doing now?'

'Your civilization was destroyed, but your people would survive, at least in pockets around the world. The apocalypse was never meant to annihilate an entire race. It was just the big event before Judgment Day. But the direction Uriel is taking everybody in . . .' He shakes his head. 'If anyone survives that, I'm not sure you'd recognize them as human anymore.'

What did the hellions look like before their invasion?

I've tried not to think much about the future, but in the small moments when I've let myself do it, I assumed that there would be a time after the angels were done with their rampage. Our world would need to be rebuilt, but there still would have been people somewhere, wouldn't there?

Locusts, the resurrected, the low demons. We've already been pushed beyond the limits of humanity. If this continues, earth will be the new Pit.

'You should go,' Raffe says to me. 'This is no place for a human.'

'What about me being your second for the contest?'

'Nobody will remember that once they see the Watchers.'

'Are you sure you're not just trying to avoid getting back into the truck with me and my mom?'

He almost smiles.

He walks me back to the truck. 'Where will you go?' he asks.

'I don't know.' Every step feels like a goodbye. 'There are no safe places. The only place that might come close to that is the Resistance camp.'

A small frown mars his expression. 'From what Obi showed me, those people are full of fear and anger. That's an ugly combination, Penryn. They'd kill every one of us if they could.' By *us*, it's clear he means angels. 'They wouldn't care if they killed us by plague or on the dissection tables.'

'They're as good as it gets right now,' I say. 'And you know where it is so you can find me there and let me know how things went. If you want.'

His eyes look over my face and hair. Then he nods.

'You're going to win this trial by contest, right?'

'Absolutely.' He squeezes my hand. His grip is firm and warm.

Then he lets go.

'You better. And remember your promise. Get the angels out of our world when you win.'

I reluctantly lift the sword strap over my head. I hold the scabbard for a moment and feel the weight of it.

Of course, he should have it now that he has his wings back. I'm surprised he hasn't taken it already. They missed each other so much. Besides, he can't be part of a trial by contest without his sword.

But Pooky Bear made me special. I was more than just a girl with it. I was an angel killer.

'She missed you,' I say.

He hesitates, just looking at the sword. He hasn't touched her since he got his wings back.

When he takes her, his hands are gentle. He holds her out in his palms for a heartbeat. We both wait to see if the sword will accept him back.

When she doesn't drop to the ground, he closes his eyes in relief. His unguarded expression makes me understand that he hadn't made a move to take her back because he wasn't sure if she would accept him.

All those years when he was alone, he had nothing but his sword for company. I hadn't fully understood how hard it must have been for him to lose her.

It's good to see him happy, but it's bittersweet. 'Good-bye, Pooky Bear.' I stroke my fingers along the sheath.

Raffe pulls off the stuffed bear with its wedding-veil dress. 'I'm sure she wants you to have this.' He smiles.

I take it and hug the bear to my side. The fur is soft but doesn't feel right without its steel core beneath my hands.

We reach the truck, and I slide into the driver's seat. Raffe looks into my open window as if he has something more to say. The dried fruit the Pit lord gave him swings back and forth below that vulnerable spot between his collar bones as he leans toward me.

He gives me a kiss.

It's slow and silky, and it makes me melt all over. He caresses my face, and I tilt my head into his touch.

Then he steps away.

He opens his beautiful snowy wings and takes off into the air to meet his Watchers.

48

I watch Raffe and his soldiers head toward the aerie along the blue sky and wonder what will happen there. A part of me wants to see this contest, while another part wants to run and hide. It's bound to be violent. And I'm not sure I could handle watching, knowing Raffe's team is the underdog.

I take the wheel, still preoccupied. Before I can start the engine, Mom curls up on the seat like a girl and lays her head on my lap. She rubs my leg as if reassuring herself that I'm really here.

Her breathing becomes deep and steady as she falls asleep. How long has it been since she slept? Between worrying over Paige and me, she hasn't had much chance to rest. I've been so obsessed with finding

Paige and keeping her safe that I haven't had much room for Mom.

I put my hand on her coarse hair and stroke it. I hum her apology song. It's haunting and brings up all kinds of complicated feelings, but it's the only lullaby I know.

My mother hasn't asked the questions that a normal person would ask, and I'm grateful for it. It's like the world has become so crazy that it makes sense to her now.

I turn on the engine and drive us out.

'Thanks, Mom. For coming to rescue me.' My voice comes out reedy and a little wobbly. I clear my throat. 'Not every mom would do that in a world like this.'

I don't know if she hears me or not.

She has seen me in the arms of a demon, or what she thinks is a demon. She has seen me pop out of Beliel, riding a creature from hell. She has seen me in the company of a group of tortured, half-skinned Fallen. And she just saw me kiss an angel.

I couldn't blame even a rational person for believing I was now deeply involved with the devil, or at least the enemy. I can't even fathom what goes on in her head. This is a scenario she's always feared, always warned me about. And here we are.

'Thanks, Mom,' I say again. There's more to be said.

And in a healthy mother–daughter relationship, more probably would be said.

But I don't know how to begin. So I just keep humming that haunting lullaby that she used to sing to us when she was coming out of a particularly bad spell.

49

The road is empty of life. As we drive, I see nothing more than a deserted world of abandoned cars, earth-quake-damaged landscape, and fire-gutted buildings.

The similarities between our landscape and the Pit are becoming disturbing.

We're halfway to the Resistance camp when I see a growing speck in the sky behind us. It's a single angel.

I debate whether to speed up or stop. I pull over and hide among the dead cars on the road. My mom and I slide down in our seats. Paige has already moved ahead of us.

I watch through the rearview mirror as the angel nears. He has bright white wings with a torso to match. It's Josiah.

I make sure he's alone before I get out and wave him down.

'Raphael sent me to tell you not to go to the Resistance camp,' says Josiah as he lands. He sounds out of breath.

'Why? What's going on?'

'You need to stay away from any concentration of people. The trial by contest is going to be a blood hunt.'

'What's a blood hunt?' Just saying those words makes me want to run and hide.

'Two teams hunt as much game as possible,' says Josiah. 'It starts at dusk and ends at dawn. At the end, whoever has the most kills wins.'

'What kind of game?' My lips are numb, and I'm vaguely surprised the words come out.

He has the decency to look uncomfortable. 'Uriel insists there's only one prey worth hunting. The only one that's attacked back.'

'No.' I shake my head. 'Raffe wouldn't do that.'

'He has no choice. No one backs out of a blood hunt.'

I have to lean against the truck.

'So Raffe is going to slaughter as many humans as he can? You too?'

'Whoever wins the contest wins the trial. If Raphael wins, he'll be in charge, and everyone who survives the blood hunt will be better off.'

My stomach feels like an acid volcano, and I swallow hard to keep it down.

'But it's a long flight to victory,' he says. 'A blood hunt includes everyone who wants to join. All of Uriel's angels will join him. A Watcher can kill three times the game that a regular soldier can, but we'll still need to go to the most populated area if we have any shot at beating Uriel's team.'

'You do know that you're talking about killing my kind, right? We're not prey, and we're not game.' I can't get away from the thought that I helped Raffe get his team together.

Josiah's look softens. 'Your orders are to survive. Run as far away from populated areas as possible. Then hide in the most buried, most secure place you can find. You'll have until sunset.'

There's only one place that's densely populated now. The Resistance camp.

And Raffe knows where it is.

Because I showed it to him.

It feels like the acid in my stomach is boiling and bubbling up to my throat. I can't seem to get enough air into my lungs.

'He wouldn't do that.' My voice comes out choked and wobbly. 'He's not like that.'

Josiah just gives me a look filled with pity. 'Raphael

wants you to run as far away as you can. You and your family. Go. Survive.'

Then he leaps into the air and flies back toward the aerie.

I take a deep breath to try to calm myself.

Raffe wouldn't do it.

He won't hunt people. Slaughter them like they're wild pigs. He wouldn't do it.

But no matter what I tell myself, I can't blot out the image of him watching angels fly in formation without him. All I hear in my head is someone saying that angels weren't meant to be alone. The main reason he so desperately needed his wings back was so he could return to the angels, right? Be one of them? Take his rightful place in their ranks as an archangel?

He wants to be accepted back into the angel world as much as I want to keep my family safe. If I had to kill a few angels to keep my family safe, wouldn't I do that?

Absolutely. No-brainer.

Then I remember the look of distaste on his face as he talked about the dissection tables at the Resistance camp. He wouldn't *want* to wipe out the camp or kill anyone. I'm sure of that. But if he *had* to? If it was the only way to take his rightful place as an archangel and save his angels from falling?

I slide down the side of the truck and hug my knees.

I took Raffe to the Resistance camp. Knowing he was an angel, I showed him where the largest surviving group of humans was hiding.

A memory of the ruins of the Pit runs through my mind. Did the original hellions have some lovesick teenager who betrayed them too? The thought of a perfectly chiseled ex-angel falling in love with a hellion is laughable. But I'll bet the teenage hellion didn't think so.

I shut my eyes.

I feel sick.

Beliel's words after he showed me what happened to his wife echo in my head. 'I once thought of him as my friend too . . . Now you know what becomes of people who trust him.'

I climb back into the truck and sit there with my hands gripping the steering wheel. I take a deep breath and try to think things through.

My mother watches me with trusting eyes. I don't know how much she heard, but she wouldn't believe anything he said anyway. Even if she worked with him to rescue me, she would never trust him. Maybe I should be more like her.

Ahead of us, down the road, my sister perches on a tree branch, ready to follow my lead.

My family is here with me, and all we have to do is

drive away. North or south – either way, we could be far away from the fight if we drive all day. We are about as safe in this moment as can be expected during the End of Days.

It makes perfect sense for us to head away from where the angels will be.

Perfect sense.

I start the engine. We head east. Toward the Resistance camp.

50

We see smoke in the distance long before we reach Palo Alto. Paige flies ahead with her locusts while we continue to weave through dead traffic.

The angels shouldn't be attacking until dusk. People should still be safe. But by the time we reach the Resistance camp, I know I'm only telling myself fairy tales.

I park the truck on El Camino and get out of the cab. The buildings are intact except for one, which is on fire.

There are bodies strewn across the street. The cars and walls of the school are splashed with blood. I hope it's not people blood, but I'm not confident about that.

'Stay here, Mom. I'll see what's going on.' I check the sky as I get out of the truck to make sure Paige hid in the trees like I told her to. She and her locusts are nowhere in sight. The Resistance probably would have seen her coming if they weren't so preoccupied.

I walk toward the school, trying to see if anyone is alive. I only take a few steps toward the carnage before I stop. I'm afraid I might see someone I know among the bodies.

The wind blows leaves and bits of garbage. People's hair flows in the wind, thankfully covering some of their faces. A piece of paper tumbles by and lands on a body that is staring at the smoke-filled sky.

The paper plasters itself against the body's shoulder, right beside the pale, dead face staring blankly into the sky. It's a flyer for Dee and Dum's talent show.

Come one, come all
To the greatest show of all!

A talent show. Those guys actually thought we could have something as silly and frivolous as a talent show.

I scan the faces of the bodies draped across the hoods of cars, the road, the schoolyard, hoping I won't see Dee or Dum. I walk slowly through the parking lot. A few people are whimpering, curled and crying on the asphalt.

In the school, the windows are smashed, the doors are unhinged and broken, the desks and chairs are thrown all over the yellow grass. There's more life and motion here, though. People cry over bodies, hug each other, walk dazed and in shock.

I stop to help a girl who is trying to stop the blood flow from a man's severed arm.

'What happened?' I ask, bracing myself to hear a horror story of angels and monsters.

'Dead people,' she says, crying. 'They came shambling in after a bunch of our fighters left for a mission. We just had a skeleton crew to defend the rest of us. Everyone freaked. It was a bloodbath. We thought it was over. But word must have got out that we've been attacked and defenseless, because then the gangs came.'

People did this? Not monsters, not angels, not Pit lords. People attacking people.

I shut my eyes. I could blame the angels for turning us into this, but we were doing stuff like this long before they came, weren't we?

'What did the gangs want?' I ask, reluctantly opening my eyes to face the world again.

'Whatever they could get.' She wraps a ripped shirt around the unconscious guy's severed arm. 'Some of them kept yelling that they wanted their food back. The stuff we took from them when we took over their store.'

The memory of the bloody handprint smeared across

the nearby grocery store's door comes back to me. I had guessed the Resistance had taken it from a gang.

When an older guy comes over to help, I drift off into another group carrying the wounded into the main building.

I came here to say a quick warning and then head north or south with my family. But we end up helping out while I look for Obi. No one knows where he is.

My mom rushes to our old classroom for her stockpile of rotten eggs. Not surprisingly, they're still there. I guess no one wanted to clear out that mess. She hands out cartons of them just in case hellions come. People gather around her to take them.

'They're coming back!' someone yells.

On the edge of the grove, shadows lurch toward us.

Everyone who is mobile stampedes toward the nearest building. A few stand by the injured, pointing guns or lifting shovels or knives as they get ready to defend their loved ones.

It's the locust victims who were dubbed the resurrected by Uriel. Their shriveled bodies shuffle toward us in a strange, zombielike fashion. It's as if they're so convinced that they're dead and resurrected that they play the part. It's as if being treated like monsters convinced them that they're supposed to behave like monsters.

But before they get close enough to begin a fight, my

sister circles overhead with her locusts. There are only three of them, but if there's one thing the locust victims fear, it's the locusts.

As soon as the resurrected see them, they scatter back into the grove across the street and disappear, no longer shuffling like zombies.

The Resistance people stare at the fleeing attackers, then at Paige and her pets as they fly low overhead. Some of the people give up on their injured and take cover, apparently more afraid of the locusts than of the resurrected.

The rest, though, stand firm and point their guns at Paige.

One of them is the guy who was in the council room with Obi the last time I was here. The one who lassoed Paige like an angry villager chasing after Frankenstein's monster. I think Obi called him Martin.

'She's here to help.' I put my arms out to try to calm everyone. 'It's all right. She's on our side. Look, she scared the attackers.'

No one lowers their gun, but no one shoots either. That probably has more to do with not wanting to attract angels with the noise than believing anything I said.

'Martin,' I say. 'Remember what Obi said? That my sister could be humanity's hope.' I point to Paige. 'That's her. You remember her?'

'Yeah, I remember her,' says Martin. His gun is firmly aimed at Paige. There are two others near him who look familiar. They were part of the group that held Paige down with ropes when they caught her. 'I remember she has a taste for humans.'

'She's on our side,' I say. 'She came out into the open to protect you. Obi believes in her. You heard him.'

Everyone watches Martin to see what he'll do. If he shoots, they'll all shoot.

He maintains his aim on Paige as if fantasizing about shooting her.

'Hey!' he yells to Paige. 'The gangs who hit us went that way.' He swings his rifle to point north up El Camino Real. 'I shot several of them. They should be easy pickin's for you and your pets.'

He lowers his rifle and slings it over his torn shirt. 'Never let it be said that we didn't feed our honored guests.'

There's a moment when everyone watches Martin. Then one by one, the Resistance people lower their guns.

Paige looks down at me from the sky as her locusts circle low above us like vultures. She looks both eager and confused, like she's not sure what she's supposed to do.

She's looking to me for answers, but I don't know what to do either.

'Yes!' says my mother as she runs toward Paige, waving her arms in the direction that Martin pointed. 'Go, baby girl. It's lunchtime!'

That's all the permission they need. The locusts fly north along the road with my sister.

'Be careful,' I call out.

I'm horrified. Relieved. Scared. Confused.

Nothing is as it's supposed to be.

51

I keep expecting Obi to show up and take charge, but I still don't see him. Not knowing what else to do, I continue to help carry the wounded while looking for Obi.

The injured sometimes scream and are sometimes too silent as we carry them into the main building. I have no idea if there's even a doctor there, but we carry injured people in as though there were a full hospital in there.

We act as if this Spanish-style high school building is full of doctors and equipment. We tell the patients they'll be okay, that the doctor will be with them soon. I suspect that some of them die while they wait, but I don't stop to confirm as we lay down the wounded and head out for more.

There's a rhythm to it, this task of carrying the injured. It gives us all something to do, something that feels organized and proper. I shut my brain off and just move like a robot, one wounded after another.

Surprisingly, everyone else behaves as though there's order as well. Some bring water to people who need it, others gather crying children and reassure them, while others put out the fire still lingering in one of the buildings. There are people who stand guard with their rifles pointed at the sky, protecting the rest of us.

Everyone steps into a role to help without being told what to do.

That sense of organization falls apart, though, as soon as we find Obi.

He's in bad shape. His breathing is shallow, and his hands are freezing. He has a wound in his chest that has soaked his entire shirt in blood.

I rush over and press my hands to his wound. 'We got you, Obi. You're going to be just fine.' He doesn't look at all like he's going to be fine. His eyes tell me that he knows I'm lying.

He coughs and struggles to breathe.

He's been lying here, watching the whole drama unfold with my sister, and patiently waiting for us to find him while we carried the other wounded.

'Help them,' he says, staring into my eyes.

'I'm doing my best, Obi.' I can't press hard enough to stop his bleeding.

'You know the angels better than anyone.' He takes a labored breath. 'You know their strengths, their weaknesses. You know how to kill them.'

'We'll talk later.' No matter how hard I press, the blood seeps between my fingers and out of the sides of my hands. 'Rest now.'

'Get your sister to help with her monsters.' He closes his eyes and opens them again sluggishly. 'She listens to you.' Breath. 'People will follow you.' Breath. 'Lead them.'

I shake my head. 'I can't. My family needs me—'

'We're your family too.' His breathing slows. His eyelids droop. 'We need you.' He puffs out his words between breaths. 'Humanity. Needs. You.' His words are barely a whisper now. 'Don't let them die.' Breath. 'Please . . .' Breath. 'Please don't let them die . . .'

He lies still and stares blankly into my eyes.

'Obi?'

I listen and feel for another breath, but there's no sign of life.

I pull back my trembling hands. They're covered in blood.

He wasn't even my friend, but my eyes sting with tears anyway.

It feels like the last linchpin of civilization just broke.

I look around, noticing for the first time that everyone around me has stopped to watch Obi. Everyone has tears shining in their eyes. Not everyone may have liked him, but everyone respected him.

No one had realized he was lying there among the other injured until we found him. Now the people carrying the injured, the ones giving water to the thirsty, the ones handing out armfuls of blankets – all are frozen and staring at Obi, who lies on the blood-stained grass with his empty eyes staring at the sky.

A woman drops her pile of blankets. She turns, her face crumpling, and walks away, stooped and shuffling like a broken person.

A man gently puts down an injured woman on the main building steps. He turns and walks dazedly away from the battle scene.

A boy my age pulls his water back from an injured man propped against a building wall. He screws on the top of his water bottle while looking thoughtfully at the next injured man beside the first. He walks away as the second man reaches out to him.

As soon as the first few stop helping, the others stop doing their own work and begin leaving too. Some are crying, others look scared and lonely as they walk off the school campus.

The camp is unraveling.

I remember something Obi said to me when I first met him. He said that attacking the angels wasn't about beating them. It was about winning the hearts and spirits of the people. It was about letting them know there's still hope.

Now that he's gone, it's as if the hope went with him.

52

It doesn't make me feel any better to have to tell them to evacuate. I had assumed I could just tell Obi and he would tell them. But now it's on my shoulders.

I gather everyone into the school yard with the help of a few people. For the first time, I don't worry about being out in the open or making noise, because I know the hunt won't start until sundown. Despite the number of people who left camp, we cover most of the yard. We catch a lot of people as they're preparing to leave.

I could just tell a few people and let the word spread, but I don't want to risk a mass panic full of confusion about what's happening. It seems worthwhile to take twenty minutes to have a final, civilized meeting and let them know what's going on.

I climb slowly onto a lunch table, even though I know we should be in a huge rush. There's something about telling people that they're about to die that stiffens my muscles. Half, maybe most, of the people here won't be alive by morning.

It makes things worse that there are still dead bodies in the yard. But I don't expect this to take long, and it's pointless pretending that a bunch of people didn't get killed.

I clear my throat, trying to figure out what to say.

Before I can begin, a new group of people walk toward us from the parking lot. It's Dee, Dum, and about a dozen freedom fighters, all streaked in soot and looking around at the bodies spread on the ground.

'What's going on?' asks Dee. His forehead creases. 'What happened? Where's Obi? We need to see him.'

No one says anything. I guess everyone expects me to answer.

'The camp was attacked while you guys were gone.' I try to figure out how to tell him about Obi. I lick my lips. 'Obi . . .' My throat dries up.

'What about him?' Dum sounds suspicious, like he knows what I'm about to say.

'He didn't make it,' I say.

'What?' asks Dee.

The fighters look around as if asking for confirmation from the crowd.

Dee shakes his head slowly in denial.

'No,' says another fighter. He backs away. 'No.'

'Not Obi,' says another fighter covering his face with soot-smeared hands. 'Not him.'

They look dazed and overwhelmed.

'He was going to get us out of this mess,' says the first fighter. 'That bastard can't die.' He sounds angry, but his face crumples like a little boy's. 'He just can't.'

Their reactions shake me.

'Calm down,' I say. 'You can't help anybody if—'

'That's just it,' he says. 'We can't help anybody, not even ourselves. We're not enough to lead humanity. Without Obi, it's over.'

He's repeating the words I've been saying to myself in my head. It makes me angry to hear the defeat in his voice.

'We have a chain of command,' says Martin. 'Whoever's below Obi takes over.'

'Obi said Penryn should lead,' says a woman who helped carry the injured with me. 'I heard him. He said it with his last breath.'

'But the second in command—'

'We don't have time for this,' I say. 'The angels are coming. At sunset tonight, they'll hold a hunt that's a contest for the largest number of human kills.'

I wait for a response, but no one seems surprised.

They've been beaten, abused, and traumatized. They stand there in their rags, skinny and malnourished, dirty and beaten, looking to me to give them information and a direction.

They're in stark contrast to my memories of the perfect bodies and the gold and glitter of the angel gatherings. Many people in the audience are injured, bandaged, limping, and scarred. Their wide eyes are a window into their desperation.

A wave of anger hits me. The perfect angels with their perfect place in the universe. Why can't they leave us alone? Just because they're better looking and have better hearing, better eyesight, better everything than us doesn't make them worth more than us overall.

'A hunt?' asks Dee. He looks at his soot-streaked brother. 'So that's why they did it.'

'Did what?' I ask.

'They set a line of fire to the south end of the peninsula. The only way out is across the bay or by air.'

'We saw it through the surveillance cameras,' says Dum. 'We went down to try to fight the fire, but we spent half our time avoiding angels. It's completely out of control now. We were coming back to tell Obi.'

The implications hit me.

The bridges are in pieces from the earthquakes. Even if we manage to gather all the working boats and planes, only a tiny fraction of people would be able to get off the peninsula before sunset.

I'd assumed that because the hunt wouldn't start until tonight, we'd be free to run until then.

'The fire is moving up north,' says Dee. 'It's like they're corralling us.'

'They are,' I say. 'They're herding us for their hunt.'

'So we're sitting ducks,' says someone in the crowd. 'That's it then?'

'The best we can do is run and hide and hope they don't find us?' There's an edge of anger in their voices.

Everyone starts talking at once.

An anxious voice rises above the noise. 'Can somebody take this girl?'

We all look at the man in the crowd who yelled out his question. He's a skinny man with bandages across his shoulder and arm. Two girls about the age of ten stand beside him.

He pushes one girl behind him and the other in front of him. 'I can't feed and protect her if we have to go back out on the road.'

Both girls begin crying. The girl peering around behind him looks just as scared as the girl being pushed forward.

Some of us watch with quiet sympathy while others look on in horror. But even the most compassionate hesitate to step forward to take on the responsibility of feeding and protecting a helpless kid when everyone is either predator or prey.

Not everybody looks like their heart is being wrenched, though. A few watch the girl with cold, crafty eyes. Any second now, one of them will step forward to claim her.

'You're giving away your daughter?' I ask, stunned.

He shakes his head. 'I'd never do that. She's my daughter's friend who came with us on vacation to California just before the angels invaded.'

'Then she's your family now,' I say through gritted teeth.

The man looks around at the faces around him. 'I don't know what else to do. I can't protect her. I can't feed her. She'll be better off with someone else. My only other choice is to just abandon her. I just can't keep my family alive and her too.' He wraps his good arm around the crying girl behind him as if wishing he had hid her before he caught everyone's attention.

'She's your family too,' I say. I'm so angry that I'm shaking.

'Look, I've kept her alive all this time,' yells the father. 'But I can't do it anymore. I don't even know how I'm going to keep me and my daughter alive. I'm just desperate and doing what I need to do to try to protect me and mine.'

Me and mine.

I think about the dying man Paige found in the department store. What happened to his people? If we scatter now, are we each going to find ourselves dying alone in a dark place with no one to care if we're eaten alive?

The only thing that man had left was a crayon drawing made by a kid he loved. It dawns on me that in that moment, that kid, Paige, and the dying man were part of a spiderweb connection that spelled family. That's what saved the man from being eaten alive. That's what reminded Paige to fight for her humanity.

I finally understand what Obi was telling me. These people – these vulnerable, bickering, flawed people – are my family too. I want to curse Obi for making me feel this way. It's been hard enough trying to protect my sister and mother. But I can't watch my own people splinter off and die and maybe tear each other to pieces while they're at it.

'We're all your family.' I echo Obi's words. 'You're not alone. And neither is she.' I nod toward the trembling girl standing in the middle of the yard with no one beside her.

'Take a deep breath,' I say, trying to sound the way my dad used to sound when I was freaked out about something. 'Calm down. We'll survive this.'

People look at me, then at the rest of what's left of the Resistance. There's a whole world of emotions swirling in the crowd.

'Yeah?' asks one of the fighters. 'Who's going to save us? Who's crazy enough and strong enough to hold everyone together while we ram our heads against this impossible enemy?'

The wind flaps the jackets of the dead around us.

'Me.'

Until I say it, I hadn't really believed it.

At least they don't laugh. But they stare at me for an uncomfortable amount of time.

I shrug. It's awkward talking about yourself. 'I know more about angels than just about anyone else alive. I have an . . .' I remember I don't have Pooky Bear anymore. 'I've made friends with . . .' Who? Raffe? The Watchers? They're going to hunt us like animals. 'Anyway, I have one hell of a family.'

'You have brains, and you have a family,' says a man with a gash on his head. 'That's your special power?'

'We can all go our separate ways and die alone.' My voice becomes firm, and I try to inject steel into it. 'Or we can stay together and make our final stand.'

Whether I want to or not, I'm going to lead what's left of Obi's Resistance.

'Instead of scattering and hiding, we're going to work

together. The healthy and strong will help anyone who has trouble moving. We'll collect as many boats and planes as we can, and we'll begin getting people across the bay as soon as possible. We need volunteers to drive the boats and help get everybody across.'

I doubt that there are any planes available and, if there are, that anyone will be brave enough to take to the air while there are angels around. But some of these people might know how to pilot a boat.

'We can't get everyone across before sunset,' says someone in the crowd.

'You're right,' I say. 'We're going to keep ferrying them for as long as it takes, because some of us will create a diversion and keep the angels occupied.'

'Who's going to do that?'

I think about that for a minute before answering.

'Heroes.'

53

It doesn't take long for people to decide whether to stick around and help or to take off and take their chances solo. A third of the people leave after they hear me in the yard. But the rest stay, and that even includes some able-bodied people who could have left.

The healthy ones who stay behind help the injured into cars. Even if they can't be moved very far, we need to move them out of here, because this is the first place the angels will come tonight.

We'll have to leave the dead behind. That bothers me more than I can say. Even the Fallen managed to give Beliel a burial ceremony.

'How far away is the fire?' I ask the twins as we walk into the adobe-style building that Obi used as his headquarters.

'The south end of Mountain View was starting to get smoky when we left,' says Dee. 'We can check out the surveillance videos and see how far it's gone.'

Surveillance videos.

'Can we make an announcement through the surveillance system?'

The twins shrug. 'We could probably make an announcement through the laptops and cell phones that we use as cameras. We'd have to talk to the engineers to make sure, though.'

'Are any of them still here?'

'They never left the computer room,' says Dee.

'Can you get them to set that up? Let's get the word out,' I say as we walk down the hallway to the computer room. 'People need to know what's going on.'

The computer room is cluttered with piles of portable solar panels, cables, cell phones, tablets, laptops, and batteries of all sizes and shapes. The trash can is overflowing with empty instant-noodle packages and energy-bar wrappers. Half a dozen engineers look up as Dee-Dum begins explaining what happened in the school yard.

'We know,' says one bleary-eyed guy wearing a T-shirt with a picture of Godzilla crushing Tokyo. 'We watched it through the cameras around the yard. A couple of the guys left, but the rest of us want to help. What can we do?'

'You guys are the best,' says Dee.

It doesn't take long before the engineers are ready for me to make an announcement. As the last of the camp abandons Paly High, we record my speech so that they can loop the message.

'The angels are coming at sunset tonight,' I say into the mic. 'They're hunting as many people as they can. The south end of the peninsula has been cut off by fire. I repeat, the south end of the peninsula has been cut off by fire. Go to the Golden Gate Bridge – we're sending people there to help you cross. If you're willing and able, come to the East Bay Bridge to distract the angels and give the others a chance at life. We could use all the fighters we can get.'

I take a deep breath. 'For you gang members out there – how long do you think you can last on your own? We could use some good street soldiers.' It hits me that I sound like Obi. 'We're all on the same side. What's the point of you surviving today when tomorrow they'll just come and wipe you guys out? Why not band together and have a real shot? At the very least, let's go out with a bang and show them what we're made of. Come join the fight at the Bay Bridge.'

I steel my voice. 'Angels, if you're listening, everyone will know you're shameful cowards if you go after the helpless ones. There would be no glory in that, and you'll just embarrass yourselves during the blood hunt. The real fight will be at the East Bay Bridge. Everyone worth fighting will be there, and I promise we'll have a good show for you. I challenge you to come find us.'

I pause, not sure how to end it. 'This is Penryn Young, Daughter of Man, Killer of Angels.'

That phrase, Daughter of Man, will always remind me of my time with Raffe. Raffe, who will be hunting all of us tonight along with his buddies who I thought could be my friends too. But that's like a child expecting a hungry lion to be her fuzzy pet instead of being her killer.

I think I sounded confident, but my hands feel frozen and my breath comes out trembly.

'Ooh, I like the killer of angels title,' says Dum, nodding.

'Are you sure this will work?' asks Dee with a frown. 'If they go after the Golden Gate—'

'They won't,' I say. 'I know them. They'll come where the fight is.'

'She knows them, man,' says Dum. 'It's cool. They'll come after us at the Bay Bridge.' He nods, then frowns as the implications hit him. 'Wait a minute . . .'

'Are you sure that people will listen?' I ask.

'Oh, they'll listen,' says Dee. 'If there's one thing that us humans are good at, it's gossip. Word spreads – and everybody's heard of you.'

'They've heard of your mom and sister too,' says Dum. 'But that's another story.'

'They'll come,' says Dee. 'You're the only leader we've got.'

54

I get into an SUV big enough to have two backseats. I slide into the back and notice the soft leather, the tinted windows, the first-class stereo. Things we took for granted that we'll never have again.

Paige is flying in the arms of one of her three locusts, while Mom is riding on a bus with a bunch of cult members who swear they had nothing to do with my kidnapping. I don't know what to make of them, but if I were going to worry about the safety of anyone on that bus, it'd be them, not my mom.

My recorded announcement tells people that we have a plan. But we don't, not really. All we know is that some of us will distract the angels at the Bay Bridge while everyone else crosses the channel spanned by the Golden Gate Bridge.

I squeeze into the backseat with the last remaining members of the old council that Obi was putting together. One is a woman who managed global distribution for Apple, and the other is an ex-military guy who calls himself the Colonel.

The Colonel keeps throwing suspicious glances at me. He's made it clear that he doesn't believe a word of the wild stories going around about me. And even if any of it is true, he still thinks I'm a 'mass hallucination preying on the desperate hopes of the people.'

But he's here to help as best he can, and that's all I can ask for. I just wish he'd stop giving me those looks that remind me that he could be right.

Doc and Sanjay slide into the seats behind us. It's not surprising that the two of them get along since they're both researchers. Sanjay seems to have no worries about being seen with Doc.

The two council members objected to Doc being here, but no one else has Doc's knowledge of angels and monsters. Doc's bruises look just as bad as the last time I saw him, but there are no fresh ones. People are too busy surviving to mess with him right now.

The twins slide into the driver's and passenger's seat in front of us. They have newly dyed blue hair. It's not entirely blue but streaked and splotched over their blond as if they didn't have enough time to do it right.

'What's up with your hair?' I ask. 'Aren't you worried you'll be spotted by angels flying above with all that blue?'

'War paint,' says Dee, fastening his seatbelt.

'Except it's in our hair instead of on our faces,' says Dum, starting the engine. 'Because we're original like that.'

'Besides, are poisonous frogs worried about being spotted by birds?' asks Dee. 'Are poisonous snakes? They all have bright markings.'

'You're a poisonous frog now?' I ask.

'Ribbit.' He turns and flicks out his tongue at me. It's blue.

My eyes widen. 'You dyed your tongue too?'

Dee smiles. 'Nah. It's just Gatorade.' He lifts up a bottle half-full of blue liquid. 'Gotcha.' He winks.

'"Hydrate or Die," man,' says Dum as we turn onto El Camino Real.

'That's not Gatorade's marketing,' says Dee. 'It's for some other brand.'

'Never thought I'd say this,' says Dum, 'but I actually miss ads. You know, like "Just Do It." I never realized how much of life's good advice came from ads. What we really need now is for some industrious soul to put out a product and give us a really excellent saying to go with it. Like "Kill 'Em All and Let God Sort 'Em Out."'

'That's not an advertising jingle,' I say.

'Only because it wasn't good advice back in the day,' says Dum. 'Might be good advice now. Attach a product to it, and we could get rich.' He turns and arches a brow at his brother, who turns and arches an identical eyebrow back.

'So does anyone have a good survival strategy, or is there no hope for getting out of this nightmare?' asks the Colonel.

'We came up with a big, fat zero. I don't know how we're going to survive the blood hunt,' says Dee.

'That wasn't the nightmare I was referring to,' says the Colonel. 'Death by stupid comments is what I was talking about.'

The twins look at each other and make an O with their mouths like little boys telling each other they've been busted.

I grin in spite of it all. It's good to know I can still smile, if only a little.

Then we get down to business.

'What's going on with that angel plague you were working on, Doc? Any chance we could go pandemic on their asses?' asks Dee.

He shakes his head. 'It'll take at least a year, assuming that we could get it to work. We don't know anything about their physiology and don't have anyone to test it on. But if we're lucky, it'll take a few of them out soon anyway.'

'How?' asks the Colonel.

'The angels were creating another beast for the apocalypse,' says Doc. 'The instructions were very specific. It had to have seven heads that were a mix of animals.'

'The sixer?' I ask. 'Yeah, I saw it.'

'If it has seven heads, why do you call it a sixer?' asks Sanjay.

'It has the number six-six-six tattooed on its foreheads.'

Dum looks at me with a horrified expression.

'The angels called it the beast,' says Doc. 'But I like your sixers name better.'

'The seventh head was human, and it was dead,' I say.

'Was the sixer alive?' asks Doc. 'Did any of the angels around it look sick?'

'Oh, it was definitely alive. I didn't notice anybody looking sick. But then again, I wasn't looking at them. Why?'

'We had three of them.'

'There are three of those things?'

'All variations of each other. With that many animals mixed together in one body, things are bound to go wrong. At the same time they were making them, Laylah, the lead physician, was working on an apocalyptic plague. It was supposed to be for us humans, but there was a lot of experimentation to make it as gruesome as possible. Somehow, one of the strains got passed on to the sixers.'

I remember Uriel talking to Laylah in his suite before the last aerie party. He was pressuring her pretty hard to cut corners and make the apocalypse happen faster. I'm guessing she's been cutting corners all along to meet his demands.

'The sixers infected the angel doctors. They got sick, then about a day or two later, they were exposed to the sixers again, and that massively accelerated the disease. They bled out in the most horrible way. It looked excruciatingly painful too. It was everything they were trying to do with a human disease, only it killed angels and locusts instead. The human lab workers were fine, and so were the sixers. They were just carriers of the disease.'

'Do you have one in a cage somewhere?' I ask.

'The infected sixers were all killed. I was ordered to dispose of the bodies. Angels don't do dirty work like that. Before I burned them, though, I managed to sneak two vials of their blood. I used one to infect the new batch of sixers that they created. I was hoping it might cause some random damage.'

'Did it?' I ask, thinking about Raffe even now.

'I don't know. After the accident, they separated the projects to avoid further contamination, so I lost track of it.'

'What did you do with the second vial of blood?'

'I kept it for study. That's what we've been using to try to come up with an angel plague.'

'But no luck?' I ask.

'Not yet,' says Doc. 'Not for a long time to come.'

'Time we don't have,' says the Colonel. 'Next idea.'

Our goal is easy to identify – we need to come up with a way to survive the onslaught tonight. But we just talk in circles, trying to figure out how to do it. For all we know, we could be the only freedom fighters showing up at the Bay Bridge.

As we drive up the peninsula, we talk.

And talk.

And talk some more.

I'm trying not to yawn, but it's not easy. It feels like it's been a week since I slept.

'The angels might not even know which bridge is the East Bay Bridge,' says the Colonel. 'We need a lure or something that will attract them away from the Golden Gate.'

'What kind of a lure?' asks Dee.

'Should we dangle little babies from the bridge?' asks Dum.

'Sadly, that's not funny,' says Doc.

I rub my forehead. I'm usually not prone to headaches, but all this desperate talk of coming up with a plan is killing me. I'm not really the planning type.

My eyes drift to the window, and I become mesmerized by the drone of the adult voices in the car and my own sleepiness.

We're driving along the bay as we head north to San Francisco. The water sparkles like a field of diamonds waiting to be picked if only you could reach in with magic hands and grab them.

The wind picks up, floating leaves and trash by the side of the road. I don't remember seeing trash by the freeway in the World Before, but a lot has changed since then.

My eyes lazily follow a piece of paper as it flitters across the road. It dances in the breeze, floating up and down, then pirouetting on the wind. It lands in the water, causing a ripple of sparkles around it.

In my half-dreaming state, it looks like one of the twins' talent show flyers.

'Come one, come all to the greatest show of all.' Isn't that what the flyer says?

I can see the twins standing on an apple crate, wearing striped suits and hats like barkers at a carnival. They're calling to the ragged refugees. 'Step right up, folks. This will be the biggest fireworks show in history. There'll be bangs, there'll be screams, there'll be popcorn! This is your last chance – your last chance to show off your amazing talents.'

Then it all comes together.

I sit up, as wide awake as if I'd been zapped by my mother's cattle prod. I blink twice, tuning back in to the conversation. Sanjay is saying something about wishing he knew more about the angels' physiology.

'The talent show.' I look at the twins with wide eyes. 'Who could resist a talent show?'

Everyone looks at me as if I'm nuts. That puts a slow grin on my face.

55

By the time we arrive at Golden Gate, it's noon. We have about six hours until sunset.

The famous bridge is in shambles like all the other bridges around the bay. Several of the suspension cables swing in the air, tethered only at the top. It's broken in four sections, with a big chunk missing just past the middle. One of the sections leans precariously, and I wonder how long it'll be before it falls.

The last time I saw the Golden Gate, I was flying in Raffe's arms.

The wind chills me as I get out of our SUV, the salty air tasting like tears.

A meager group of people mill about by the water's edge beneath the bridge, waiting for someone to tell them what to do. I didn't expect thousands of people, but I was hoping that more would be here.

'We're the ones who rescued the people off Alcatraz,' Dee shouts. He acts as if there are hundreds of people here. 'You've heard of that, right? Those same boats are coming here. When they arrive, do what you can to help. It's the nice thing to do.'

'If you're not inclined to do the nice thing,' says Dum, 'then meet us at Bay Bridge. Let's show the angels what we're made of!'

I look around and see that there are more people here than I realized. Small movements of clothes, hats, bags, and weapons shift all around us in the trees, the cars, and the wreckage of ships washed up on shore.

People are hiding nearby, listening, watching, ready to disappear at the slightest sign. A few yell questions out to us from their hiding places.

'Is it true that the dead are rising?'

'Are there really demon monsters coming after us?'

I answer the questions as best I can.

'Are you Penryn?' someone yells from behind some trees. 'Are you really an angel killer?'

'Hell, yeah!' says Dum. 'Come see for yourself tonight. You too can be an angel killer.'

Dum nods his head toward the car. 'Go on,' he says to

us. 'I'll spread the gospel about the talent show here and catch up.'

Dee grins. 'Do you have any idea what the betting pool will be like tonight?'

'It's gonna be *epic*,' says Dum as he struts into the crowd.

I follow Dee back into the car. The woman from Apple and the Colonel stay to oversee the evacuation while the rest of us go to the Bay Bridge to prepare for battle.

'What are the chances that our men just grabbed the boats and took off?' I ask. My stomach turns at the thought as we drive through the city.

'I'm guessing at least half of them will do us right. We picked guys who had family among this crowd.' He nods at the people standing by the water where Dum is already circulating in the crowd, getting the word out about the talent show.

'By random luck,' says Dee as he drives around a fallen electrical pole, 'we happen to have stowed away the grand prize on the other side of the Golden Gate.'

'What grand prize?'

'For the talent show.'

'Duh,' says Sanjay in a good impression of Dum.

'We wanted it away from people who knew about it,' says Dee. 'But in the end, we couldn't have planned it any better if we had known what was about to go down.'

'What's the grand prize?'

'You haven't heard?' says Dee.

'It's an RV,' says Sanjay, sounding bored.

'What?' Dee glares at Sanjay through his rearview mirror. 'It's not just an RV. It's a custom-made, bullet-proof, luxury recreational vehicle. And that doesn't even describe it all.'

I raise my eyebrows and try to look interested.

'Fear not, my little padawan. You will understand the awesomeness of the Tweedle Twins when the time comes.'

'Whatever it is, I'm sure it'll at least be entertaining.' This time, rather than sounding like Obi, I sound like a patient mom. I crinkle my nose at that.

Dee holds up a set of keys. 'Of course, the winner has to survive the talent show and then tear the keys out of my cold dead hands.' He grips the keys and makes them disappear.

'But there's no doubt it'll be worth it,' I say.

'See?' says Dee. 'That's why she's the leader. The girl knows what she's talking about.'

But I don't. When we reach the East Bay Bridge, there's nobody there.

My shoulders sink as I see the abandoned streets and empty waters. My announcement is looping throughout the peninsula, and everyone who was at the Resistance camp knows to come here if they're willing to fight. I didn't expect a large group, but I'm devastated that no one has shown.

'No time to stand around,' says Dee as he gets out of the car. 'The guys have already started dropping off the supplies.'

I look to where he points. There's a pile of lumber waiting by the water. 'And that must be our ride now.'

Dee nods at a ferry moving our way. It used to be white once upon a time, but it looks like someone threw dark paint all over it to try to camouflage it.

'Well, at least there will be four of us in the fight.' I try to sound extra cheery.

'Three,' says Sanjay. 'I'm just here as the expert. Guys like me, we're lovers, not fighters.'

'You're a fighter now,' I say, pulling him toward the water.

By two o'clock, Dum comes back with a smug grin, strutting like he just accomplished something big. There are also enough people now who have come out of the woodwork for us to have a real working crew. Lumber, hammers and nails, stereo equipment, and lighting are all being ferried and put together on the island chunk of the Bay Bridge that we've selected for our final stand.

By three o'clock, the first gangs roll up to the shore. By this time, there is a respectable number of refugees and freedom fighters. We've collected some of Obi's old citizen soldiers who heard our announcement.

'Better to go out like a man than run like a cockroach,' says one bearded guy leading a bunch of others with gang tattoos as he struts into the group.

If the other survivors weren't already scared, they'd be at least a little afraid now. These are the guys the rest of us avoided on the streets.

Although the new guys may have decided to join the good fight, as soon as they come, they're more interested in establishing who's boss. People get shoved, told to leave the shade for the gangs, tolerate food being snatched on the way to their mouths.

Everyone is exhausted and afraid, and all they seem to want to do is fight each other. Honestly, I don't know how Obi managed all this. I wish I could figure out a way for all of us to run and hide, but we can't do that with this many people in all their various conditions. So once again, I'm back to the last-stand concept.

I don't like the sound of that phrase, last stand. Did I inherit the Resistance only to see it go down on my watch?

As new gangs walk into our area, they begin clashing with the other gangs. If it's not the color of their shirts or the shape of their tattoos, it's some other seemingly random choice of who's on whose team as the gang population gets bigger. Some are divided down racial lines while others are split among regional lines – the Tenderloin gangs versus the East Palo Alto gangs, that kind of thing.

'This is an explosive combination. You know that, right?' asks Doc who has volunteered to be the field medic despite his arm still being in a sling. We all know he would have been rejected by the Golden Gate crowd had he gone there. There are too many Alcatraz refugees there to leave him in peace.

'We don't need to keep it together for very long,' I say. 'They're healthy fighters, and we'll need them tonight.'

'When Obi asked you to take over, he might have meant that maybe you should take over for longer than you're considering.' Doc sounds like one of my old teachers, even though he looks more like a college student.

'Obi knew exactly what he was doing,' I say. 'He asked me to keep people from dying. If they bruise each other while I'm trying to keep them alive, that's just something we'll have to deal with.'

The twins nod, looking impressed at my tough love attitude.

'We'll take care of it,' says Dee.

'What are you going to do?'

'What we always do,' says Dum.

'Give the masses what they want,' says Dee as they walk over to two growing crowds facing off with each other.

The twins walk right into the middle of the face-off with their hands in the air. They talk. The crowds listen.

A large man struts forward from each side. One of the twins talks to the two large men, and the other twin begins taking notes as people from the crowd call out. Then everyone steps out into a circle, leaving the two large men in the middle.

As if on cue, the combined crowd begins shouting and jumping for a better view. They've closed the circle, so I can't see what's going on inside, but I can guess. The twins have started an *official* fight and are taking bets. Everybody's happy.

No wonder Obi kept the twins around and put up with their antics.

By four o'clock, we have as many talent show contestants and audience members as fighters. I'm so busy I hardly have time to think about Raffe. But of course, he's always in the back of my mind.

Will he do it? Will he kill humans in order to be accepted back into angel society? If we have to fight each other, will he hunt me like an animal?

The end of the world hasn't exactly brought out humanity's finest qualities. Raffe has seen people do the worst possible things to each other. I wish I could show him the other side – the best that we can be. But that's just wishful thinking, isn't it?

There are familiar faces among the volunteer fighters. Tattoo and Alpha from Alcatraz are there. Their real names are Dwaine and Randall, but I'd gotten used to thinking of them as Tattoo and Alpha, so I keep calling them that. Others are picking the names up, and if they don't stop it soon, they'll become their permanent nicknames.

It seems that half the group goes by nicknames. It's as if everyone feels like they're different people now, and so they shouldn't have the same names as they did in the World Before.

I look up when people step aside to let a man in a suit and chauffeur's hat walk up to me. Everyone stares at his exposed teeth and the raw meat where skin should have covered the bottom half of his face.

'I heard your announcement,' he says in his tortured way. 'I'm glad you made it out of the aerie alive. I'm here to help.'

I give him a small smile. 'Thank you. We could use your help.'

'Yeah, as in right now,' says Sanjay, waddling by us, trying to hold up his end of a stack of wooden planks. My ex-driver rushes over to help.

'Thank you,' says Sanjay with much relief.

I watch them load the planks onto a boat with easy camaraderie.

I feel like I have a lead submarine in my stomach when I think about all these people who will probably die because they believed me when I told them this was worth fighting for.

56

The sun flashes off the dark water of the bay below us. Even though it's still afternoon, the sky has a fiery tinge with dark tendrils reaching across it. In the distance, the fire on the south end of the peninsula billows smoke into the air.

It's not quite the reddish glow of the Pit, but it reminds me of it. Instead of being suffocatingly red, though, our burning civilization is ironically beautiful. The sky is alive and in motion with the reflected colors of the fire in hues of maroon, orange, yellow, and red. There are plumes of dark smoke shifting through the air, but instead of blotting out the colors, the sky blends and absorbs it, darkening some while contrasting with others.

Here on the concrete island that was once part of the beautiful Bay Bridge, the excitement is palpable. It throbs from every direction in the crowd – and it is a crowd now – as people mill around on the broken connection between San Francisco and the East Bay.

Everyone is helping set something up. Shirtless gang members show off their tattooed muscles as they climb to the highest points on the suspension bridge. The different gang factions race to fasten an enormous set of speakers and spotlights. The winner of the race claims some victory over the others for a prize that Dee and Dum have made worthwhile.

An impromptu stage is being built while people practice their talent show performances all around it. Crates have been stacked and are being nailed together for a fast and sloppy set of stage stairs.

Men in gray camouflage walk past me with their rifles. They wear large headphones around their necks and night vision goggles on their heads. I have headphones around my neck as well, but not the goggles. And instead of a rifle, I carry a pair of knives. There are plenty of guns, but the bullets are reserved for the experts.

A couple of them wear elaborate tentlike camouflage with bits of random stuff attached to it that makes me think of swamp monsters.

'What are they wearing?' I ask.

'Ghillie suits,' says Dee-Dum, walking by, as if that explains everything.

'Right, of course.' I nod as if I have a clue what that means.

I look around to see if I can be useful and find that everybody has their task and is busy doing it. Dee is handling the details of the show while Dum is organizing the audience, which is practicing the escape drill. The Colonel and the other council member who I'm starting to think of as the logistics lady weave through the throng, directing projects and keeping people on task.

Doc is handling the makeshift med station, which people avoid unless they've really hurt themselves. I admit, even I'm a little impressed with Doc's dedication to people, even if I'll always think he's a monster for the things he did.

On the broken edge of the bridge where the rebar sticks out into the air, my sister sits with her legs dangling over the edge. Two of her scorpion-tailed pets lie curled up beside her while the third flies in loops in front of her. Maybe it's catching fish. They are the only ones with space around them, as everybody gives them a wide berth.

I feel sick about having her here when I know she'll be in danger. But as hard as I tried, both Mom and Paige refused to leave me. It twists my insides to have them be part of the fight, but on the other hand, I've learned that when you separate from people you love, there's no guarantee you'll ever see them again.

Raffe's face pops into my head like it's done a thousand times today. In this memory, he has a teasing look in his eyes as he laughs at my outfit when we were at the beach house. I shove the memory back. I doubt he'll have a teasing expression when he slaughters my people.

My mom is nearby with a group of sheet-draped cult members. They all have amnesty marks on their shaved heads.

My mother tells me they are committed to making up for their sin of betraying me, but I wish they weren't here at all. Still, if they want to show their commitment to the cause, sticking with my mother is a good way to show it. It keeps them out of the way, and I'm pretty sure my mom is making them pay their penance.

It looks like the only group that could use my help is the stage crew. I pick up a hammer and get on my knees to help build the stage.

The guy next to me gives me a rueful smile and hands me some nails. So much for the glory of leadership.

I don't know what all those power-hungry people like Uriel are thinking. As far as I can tell, a leader ends up doing all the worrying and still needs to pitch in for the regular work.

I hammer, trying to settle my mind and keep from freaking out.

The sun is beginning to set, adding a golden glow to the water. Wisps of mist begin creeping over the bay. It should be a peaceful scene, only my blood feels like it's freezing by the second.

My hands feel cold and clumsy, and I keep expecting to see vapor from my breath. It feels like I don't have enough blood in my body, and I can feel my face turning pale.

I'm scared.

Until now, I really believed that we could pull this off. It sounded good in my head. But now that the sun is setting and things are coming together, I'm freaked out by all these people who believed me when I said this was a good idea. Why would anybody listen to me anyway? Don't they know I can't plan worth two pennies?

There are far more people here than there should be, and they continue to swell the ranks as ships continue to ferry them to our broken bridge. We don't need them all, just enough to make the angels believe that coming here instead of the Golden Gate Bridge is worth their time. But we put the call out, and more and more people are arriving. It never occurred to us to put a limit on the size of the audience, because we thought it would be a miracle if we had three people who showed.

They know the angels are coming. They know this is our last stand. They know we will most likely be massacred.

And yet they keep coming. In droves.

Not just the able-bodied – the injured, the children, the old, the sick – they're all here, crowded onto our little island of broken concrete and steel. There are too many of them.

This is a death trap. I can feel it in my bones. The noise, the lights, a *talent show* for chrissake, at the apocalyptic End of Days. What was I thinking?

Despite the crowded conditions, the audience maintains a respectful distance from the curtains and dividers that have been set up as a makeshift dressing area beside the stage.

Dee thunks onto the stage and bounces on it. 'Good job, guys. I think it'll hold for a few hours. Good enough.' He cups his hands over his mouth and calls out to the crowd. 'The show starts in ten, people!'

It's a little odd that he doesn't yell to the dressing area but rather to the crowd at large. But I guess he's right – everyone here is performing tonight.

I work my way up to the makeshift stage, feeling the panic. The last time I was on a stage, the angels went berserk and decided they were going to kill everyone and feel righteous about it.

This time, I'm in front of an equally charged crowd of humans. But the emotion they're charged with is fear and barely contained panic, not bloodlust like the angels.

In front of me is a standing-room-only crowd with hardly enough room to maneuver. The only thing that limits the number of people is the dimensions of the concrete island we chose.

People are too close to the edge of the broken bridge, where the rebar hang like dead arms reaching toward the dark water. They have children sitting on their shoulders. Teenagers and gang members are hanging off the suspension cables that rise to the sky and disappear into the wispy fog gathering above.

The thickening mist has me worried. Very worried. If we can't see them, how are we going to fight them?

57

There must be a thousand people here. I can tell from the twins' expressions that they didn't expect such a large showing either.

'I don't understand,' I say when I reach the twins onstage. They're dressed in matching patched-up hobo outfits complete with clown faces and exaggerated bed-head hair. They each hold microphones that remind me of huge ice cream cones.

'Why are there so many people here?' I give them a baffled look. 'I thought we made the danger clear to them. Don't they have an ounce of common sense?'

Dee checks to make sure his mic is turned off. 'It's not about common sense.' Dee surveys the crowd with some pride.

Dum also checks to make sure his mic is off. 'It's not about logic or practicality or anything that makes a remote amount of sense.' He sports a wide grin.

'That's the whole point of a talent show,' says Dee, doing a spin onstage. 'It's illogical, chaotic, stupid, and a whole hell of a lot of fun.' Dee nods to Dum. 'It's what sets us apart from monkeys. What other species puts on talent shows?'

'Yeah, okay, but what about the danger?' I ask.

'That I don't quite have an answer for,' says Dum.

'They know it's dangerous.' Dee waves to the crowd. 'They know they'll only have twenty-five seconds to evacuate. Everybody knows what they're getting into.'

'Maybe they're sick of being nothing more than rats rummaging through the trash and running for their lives.' Dee sticks his tongue out at the kids sitting on shoulders. 'Maybe they're ready to be human again, if only for an hour.'

I think about that. We've been scratching by since the angels got here. Everyone, even the gangs, has been afraid. Constantly worried about food and shelter and basic human necessities. Worried about whether friends and family will survive the day, worried about monsters jumping out in the middle of the night and eating us alive.

And now there's this. A talent show. Silly and nonsensical. Stupid and fun. Together. Laughing. Being part of the human race. Knowing about the horrors that have happened and will happen but choosing to *live* anyway. Maybe there's an art to being human.

Sometimes I feel like a Martian in the middle of all this humanity.

'Or,' says Dum, 'maybe they're here because they're all lusting after the' – he turns on his mic – '*amazing*, magical *recreational vehicle!*' He sweeps his arm to the stage backdrop.

There's still enough light to make the projection behind him dim, but it's a picture of a scratched-up RV.

'Yes, you can believe your eyes, ladies and gentlemen,' says Dee. 'This is an unbelievably high-end recreational vehicle. In the old days, a beauty like this would run you – what – a hundred thousand dollars?'

'Or a million,' says Dum.

'Or ten million, depending on what you want to do with it,' says Dee.

'This sweet baby is completely bulletproof,' says Dum.

The crowd goes quiet.

'Yes, you heard that right,' says Dee.

'Bulletproof,' says Dum.

'Shatterproof,' says Dee.

'And zombie-proof windows grace this beauty of a moving home,' says Dum.

'It comes complete with an early intruder system, three-sixty-degree video capability for watching your surroundings at all times, remote motion sensors so you'll know if someone or something is near. And best of all . . .' The photo projected behind them changes to the interior of the RV.

'Absolute luxury of the World Before,' says Dee. 'Leather seats, luxury beds, a dining table, TV, washing machine, and its own bathroom complete with shower,' says Dum.

'For those of you wondering what the TV is for, why, we've made sure it comes with its own enormous movie collection. Who needs broadcast or streaming when you have a generator built in to your home?'

'It took us a week to get the paint to look as dirty and grimy as possible. And believe me, it broke my heart to have to dirty this beauty up, but it's a huge advantage not to look like a rich kid on wheels.'

'Speaking of wheels,' says Dee. 'It can go twenty miles on four flat tires. It can climb up hills and over other cars if need be. This is an all-terrain vehicle of the wet dream kind, ladies and gentlemen. If we ever loved anything more than this, we must have called her Mommy.'

'Hang on tight to your raffle tickets,' says Dum. 'They could be worth more than your life.'

Now it makes more sense. I'm sure some people came to stand by other humans in a final fight for survival, but I'm equally sure that some came for a shot at winning the World After RV.

The RV projection turns off. Huge spotlights turn on that make the stage glow. I cringe at the beacon, then remember that it's supposed to be showy.

The speakers crank up with a whine that turns into a piercing shrill as the feedback blasts throughout the broken bridge.

I scan the dusky skies and see nothing but the beautiful sunset coloring the wispy mist. The peekaboo sky is a magical backdrop for the show, which seems miraculous in itself.

Dee and Dum dance a jig onstage, then bow as if they're expecting a Broadway-show response. At first, the applause is muffled and scattered, timid and afraid.

'Whooo-wheee!' Dee shouts into his microphone. It reverberates through the whole crowd. 'Damn, it feels good to make noise. Let's all get it out of our system, people.'

'If we're going to rebel, we might as well rebel with noise and gusto!' says Dum.

'Everybody, let's take a moment of joy by screaming out whatever you've been feeling all these weeks. Ready? Go!'

The twins let out a holler through their microphones that releases all kinds of stored up energy ranging from excitement to anger, aggression to joy.

At first, only one or two echo the twins' yells. Then more people join in. Then more. Until the whole crowd is screaming and yelling at the top of its lungs.

This may be the first time anyone has spoken loudly since the Great Attack. A wave of both fear and cheer is released into the crowd. Some begin crying. Some begin laughing.

'Wow,' says Dum. 'That's a big ol' mess of humanness right there.'

'Respect!' Dum thumps his fist to his chest and bows down to the audience.

The noise goes on a little longer, then settles down. People are jittery and anxious, but excited too. Some have smiles on their faces, others have frowns. But they're all here – alert and alive.

I settle into my spot at the corner of the stage and look around. I'm on the ground crew, which means I'm one of the lookouts for tonight until there's action on the ground. I scan the horizon. It's getting harder to see in the thickening mist, but I don't notice any hordes of angels.

On the water, two boats are throwing buckets of chopped fish and venison innards into the water all around our chunk of the bridge. A pool of blood spreads behind the boats.

Onstage, the twins stand tall with goofy smiles on their faces. 'Ladies and gentlemen, and the rest of you who fit into neither of those categories, I am your master of ceremonies, Tweedledee.' He bows. 'And here's my co-MC, my brother and my bane, Tweedledum!'

The crowd whoops and hollers. Either the twins are extremely popular or people really like being able to make noise again. The twins take deep bows with a matching flourish of their hands.

'Tonight, we have the show of a lifetime for you. It is unfiltered, unmanaged, and certainly undeniably awesome!'

'We take no responsibility for any of the bad things that might happen tonight,' says Dum.

'And take all the credit for the fabulous, fantastic, and fun-filled things that will definitely happen tonight,' says Dee.

'And without further ado,' says Dum, 'let me introduce our First Annual World After Talent Show contestant. The San Francisco Ballet!'

There's a stunned silence as everyone takes a moment to make sure they heard right.

'Yup, you heard that right, folks,' says Dee. 'The San

Francisco Ballet is here to perform for you tonight, you lucky dogs.'

'I *told* you we had talent on the streets,' says Dum.

Three women in ballet tutus and four men in matching pink tights come out onstage. They walk with the grace of professional ballet dancers. One of the ballerinas walks up to Dee as the others get into their ready stances. She takes the mic and stands in the center of the stage until everyone quiets down.

'We are what's left of the San Francisco Ballet. A couple of months ago, there were over seventy of us. When the world collapsed, many of us didn't know what to do. Like you, we stayed with our families and tried to find the ones we loved.

'But for us dancers, the ballet company is our family, and so we searched among the rubble of our theater and dance studio for those of us who fell. In the end, twelve of us found each other, but not all of us made it this far.

'This dance is the one we were practicing on the day the world ended. This one is dedicated to the members of our family who are not here today.' Her voice is clear and strong. It carries through the crowd like the wind caressing our necks.

The ballerina gives the mic back to Dee and steps into position. The dancers take what looks like random places in a line. I can almost fill in the rest of the line in my mind with the other dancers who are not here tonight.

The music begins, and the lights follow the dancers as they leap and pirouette across the stage. It's a strange yet graceful postmodern kind of a dance with most of the performers missing.

There's a move where a pair of dancers – a man and a woman – come up to center stage and dance together while the rest stand back and float in the air on their toes. Their motions are graceful and romantic.

Then a dancer comes forward to replace the pair. It's clear by the empty air between the dancer's arms and the sad line of his body that his partner is missing. He dances his part of the duet with empty arms.

After him, the remaining dancers come up to dance – one by one, dancing with a ghost partner.

They caress the air where the face of their partner would have been. They spin and land on the floor with their arms stretched out in longing.

Alone in a world of misery.

I watch the beautiful performance with an ache in my chest.

Then, just when I can't stand the sadness anymore, a dancer floats out from the side of the stage. A dancer in ragged clothes, filthy and half starved. He's not even in ballet shoes. He's just barefoot as he glides out to take his place in the dance.

The other dancers turn to him, and it's clear that he is one of them. One of the lost ones. By the look on their faces, they weren't expecting him. This is not part of the practiced show. He must have seen them onstage and joined in.

Amazingly, the dance continues without a missed beat. The newcomer simply glides into place, and the final dancer who should have danced solo with her missing partner dances with the newcomer.

It is full of joy, and the ballerina actually laughs. Her voice is clear and high, and it lifts us all.

58

When the performance is done, the crowd goes wild with their cheers. There is total abandon with their clapping, whistling, and shouts of bravos.

It's amazing.

I've never felt so moved by a performance before. It's not like I've been to a lot of ballets or any other live performance at all. But the sense of camaraderie here tonight leaves me breathless.

Like true professionals, the dance troupe takes its bow first before the dancers converge on the newcomer onstage. The hugs, the tears, the cries of joy are a wonder to see.

Then they spread out into a line, hold hands, and bow again. Everyone is up on their feet, and none of us worry about the noise we're making or what we might bring upon ourselves.

The twins are right. This is *life*.

No one can really top that ballet performance, and I assume no one will try. Everyone seems happy to have been a part of it.

The twins get up onstage to clown around and entertain people. I'm guessing they're giving people time to absorb what they just saw so that someone else can get up the nerve to perform. They do a magic act that's almost professional. They fumble a few times, but I know they're doing that for comedic effect, because I've seen their work and it's amazing, as good as any professional stage magician.

After that, a young guy walks up onstage carrying a battered guitar. He looks like he hasn't had a shower in days, his face is covered in scruff, and his shirt has a splatter of dried blood.

'This is a song sung by the late, great Jeff Buckley called "Hallelujah."' He begins strumming his guitar, and he quietly transforms into someone who I'm sure would have been a celebrity at any other time.

The bittersweet chords ring over the bay as his voice softly builds momentum. People begin singing along with his mournful crooning. Some of us have tears drying on our faces in the cold wind as we sing 'Hallelujah' in broken voices.

When it's over, there's a moment of quiet. We're left wondering about life and love and other things that are messed up and broken, yet somehow still a triumph.

The clapping is subdued at first but quickly builds into a wild cheer.

After that, the singer strums his guitar aimlessly until he hits on a familiar tune. He begins to sing a pop song that's light and fluffy and upbeat. Everyone sways and hops and bursts out in song.

We're nowhere near as good as the angels I heard singing at the aerie. There are enough of us singing off-key that we could never be considered good, much less perfect like the angels. But all of us singing together – the cults with their greasy amnesty marks, the rival gangs on the suspension cables, the angry freedom fighters, the parents with their kids on their shoulders – that's a feeling I'll never forget for as long as I live. However long that will be.

I hold on to the feeling and try to lock it in the vault in my head where I know it'll be safe and with me forever. I've never put anything good in there before, but I want to make sure it doesn't get lost. Just in case this is the last big human show of any kind, ever again.

And then, I hear it.

The thing I dread. The thing I've been expecting.

There's a low buzz. And the air begins to stir.

Far too close to us, the mist boils.

They're coming.

The sky blacks out with their bodies, and the mist swirls with the wind of a thousand wings. Either no one spotted them coming in the gathering fog, or we were all too mesmerized by the show.

A voice over the speaker starts a countdown. That's supposed to be a signal for the audience to run and for everyone to get into position.

'Five . . .'

Five? It's supposed to start at twenty-five.

Everyone wastes a precious second realizing that we're already out of time.

'Four . . .'

Everyone scrambles. People shove and run in panic. The overcrowded audience and the show contestants have only four seconds to evacuate to the hideaway lattice and net beneath the bridge.

The singer onstage keeps on singing as if neither hell nor high water nor apocalyptic angels descending on us will stop him from giving the best performance of his life. He's finished his catchy pop song and is now singing a love song.

'Three . . .'

I have to clamp down hard on the urge to run like everyone else. I keep my position and put heavy-duty earplugs in my ears, leaving my noise-canceling head-phones around my neck. I see others doing the same around the edges of the stage, the rafters, and the suspension cables.

'Two . . .'

There are too many people rushing in the same direction. The hideout lattices we set up can only handle so many people below the bridge. It's utter chaos, with everyone running and screaming.

'One . . .'

As the crowd drains, they leave behind camouflaged gunmen who scramble into position.

A cloud of locusts swoops in from the mist faster than I expect in a flurry of stingers and teeth.

Locusts?

Where are the angels?

59

Shots blast into the locust swarm, but we might as well be shooting at the clouds for all the good it does. The locusts must have been attracted to the lights and sound that were meant for angels.

They're landing on all fours around us. Gunfire shoots off everywhere as the ground crew kicks into action.

I pull out my knives just as a locust drops down from the sky in front of me. Its stinger looms over its head and jabs at me.

My arms automatically come up. I slice and stab. I'd give anything for Pooky Bear right now.

That thought makes me all the more vicious. I voluntarily gave Raffe his sword back.

I slice again.

The stinger whips out of the way of my blade.

The scorpion in front of me is doing its best to kill me. It's moving its stinger so fast I have to wonder if it was a tap dancer in its previous life.

I'm drenched in sweat in seconds as I evade and try to fight at the same time. These little knives aren't going to do anything but annoy it.

I spin to the side and give it my fastest side kick. My foot slams into its knee with a crunch.

The locust screeches and leans to the side as its knee breaks.

I bend low and swipe the other leg. The monster crashes down.

'Stop!' My sister runs to the middle of the bridge flanked by her pet locusts, yelling at everyone around her.

It's a war zone with bullets zinging by, and she still runs out in the middle of all the chaos with her arms out. My legs almost give out at the sight of her.

'Stop!'

I'm not sure who stops first – our fighters or the locusts – but both sides pause to look at her. Hope and wonder rise in me as I watch my sister stopping a bloody battle with just her conviction.

I don't know what she would have done next, because a huge locust lands beside Paige.

The white streak in his hair is unmistakable and so is his demented anger. This time, Raffe isn't here to intimidate him. He grabs Paige's pet locust and lifts him into the air above him like a squirming baby.

'No!' Paige's hands reach up like a little kid trying to get her ball back from a bully.

White Streak slams the smaller locust down against his knee, breaking the beast's back with a snap.

'No!' Paige screams. Her crisscrossed face turns red, and the cords in her neck stand out.

White Streak tosses the broken locust onto the concrete. Ignoring my sister, he stalks around the broken beast.

The injured locust pulls itself forward by its hands. It tries to get away from White Streak, dragging its dead legs behind it.

White Streak is making a show of it, puffing up and standing tall for all to see as every scorpion-tailed monster watches. He clearly plans to show that he's the king of the locusts and no one else can challenge him.

That means he's going to have to kill Paige.

I sprint toward my sister, weaving through the spectators. Although the air boils with locusts, no one else is fighting on the bridge. Doc had warned them that some locusts might be on our side. Now no one seems sure what to do. Everyone on the bridge – locust and human – watches the drama unfold.

Paige's face crumples as she watches her pet locust drag itself helplessly on the asphalt, unable to move its legs or tail. She starts sobbing.

The sight seems to enrage White Streak. He swipes at her with his tail.

I scream. Every time I've seen my sister win a fight, she's had the element of surprise on her side. But this time, White Streak knows she's a threat and is out to kill her.

Then someone shouts over the loudspeaker, 'They're coming!'

The dark mass of locusts shifts and churns above the bridge, blotting out the sky. Between the stingers and iridescent wings, I catch glimpses of an ever-growing tide of bird-of-prey wings.

The blood hunt is starting.

60

I try to slam my fear and anxiety into the vault in my head, but they're too big.

When I look back down from the sky, Paige is ripping her teeth into White Streak's arm. She's alive and fighting.

I run toward her, trying to be as small as possible in case there's a stray bullet.

In the center of the bridge, White Streak swats and tosses Paige onto the ground like a rabid dog, then he stomps his foot on her chest, keeping her struggling form down as he looms over her.

My sister is unrelentingly furious and thrashing beneath him. Watching her pet be crippled and crawl helplessly must have triggered something in her, something so violent and intense that it might just choke her.

Just as I get close, her remaining two locust pets fly into White Streak. They're no match for the monster, and he tosses them aside easily.

The rest of the scorpion-tailed locusts fly in nervous, agitated loops above and in front of me, going in every direction and just barely avoiding crashing into each other. They seem confused and upset.

I can't get past them and have to back off from their shifting barrier.

White Streak lifts his enormous stinger, getting ready to strike at my little sister, who is still thrashing under his foot.

I try to dart in between the swooping locusts, but their stingers are everywhere and I can't get past. On the other side of the fight, I see my mom having the same problem.

White Streak's stinger whips down toward my sister.

I scream and take a step toward them. A locust flies right into me, slamming me down onto the concrete.

Amazingly, Paige reacts faster than the stinger. She twists her body out of the way. The stinger jabs into the asphalt, embedding the tip in the bridge.

Before White Streak can pull it out, she bites into his

tail. Blood bursts out around her mouth as if she bit into an artery. She rips out a chunk of his tail before he can swat her away.

This time, when he hits her, there's desperation in his motion. This time, when he hits her, a locust drops from the sky and stings his neck.

White Streak swings and blindly grabs at the traitorous thing. He snaps its neck and tosses its dead body onto the street.

Another locust hits him with his body in a fast flyby. White Streak staggers, taking his foot off Paige for a split second. It's long enough for her to scramble up.

From above us, two locusts dive to attack Paige.

She ducks from one and runs headlong into the other. My blood freezes as White Streak's locust shoots its stinger toward my sister.

A shotgun blast hits Paige's attacker.

The locust falls writhing on the ground. The shooter stands nearby, looking familiar.

Martin nods to Paige, with his rifle still aimed at the bleeding locust. If he keeps this up, I might even forgive him for lassoing Paige for being a monster.

Paige turns around and leaps to rip into White Streak's throat.

Locusts begin swarming on Paige's side, swirling above her as she rages. They're drawn to her furious cries despite whatever influence White Streak has over them.

Another group of locusts swarms on White Streak's side. I wonder if there is going to be an all-out war among them.

The ones hovering above Paige spin off to attack White Streak. The ones above White Streak drop to attack Paige.

Martin shoots at Paige's attackers as they come for her.

Locusts clash midair, crashing and stinging until there's a horde of them engulfing White Streak and Paige.

I can't see what's happening as they get buried under a mass of wings and stingers.

I think I stop breathing for a minute. I can't see anything beyond the seething giant that is the swarm.

The locust cloud lifts from the bridge into the air as everyone watches. The wind generated from their wings buffets our hair and clothes, whipping us all. They float up into the sky until they blend into the mist, making it look like the sky is boiling.

They drift off over the bay, and I can't see Paige or White Streak anywhere.

There's nothing I can do for her now.

I have to accept that my sister has to go through her

own fight. I just need to survive and be here for her when she gets back.

Don't think about the possibility of her not coming back.

61

As soon as the locusts leave, I can see the sky filling with angelic warriors.

I catch myself automatically scanning the sky for Raffe, but I don't see him in the mass of bodies.

I put my noise-canceling headphones on and shut my eyes to brace for what's about to hit.

Even through my closed lids, I can see the blindingly intense spotlights turning on everywhere. The lights stab my eyes as soon as I try to open them.

I have to squint and blink several times to adjust to the brightness.

The angels shield their eyes behind their arms and pause in their flight. Several of them crash into each other. Many turn around to get away from the blinding light and fly straight into their buddies.

The lights stab my merely human eyes. I can't imagine how painful it must be for the angels.

Then the giant speakers screech their feedback – the loudest and most piercing feedback I've ever heard, even through my noise-canceling headphones. All that intense noise blasting straight into the angels' hypersensitive ears.

The angels slam their hands against their ears. With their eyes and ears assaulted, they're staggering in the air, neither attacking nor flying away.

The angels' exceptional night vision and sharp hearing is working to our advantage. Their superior abilities are their weaknesses now. They can't turn it off. The intense lights must be killing their eyes. And that noise – hell, it almost makes *my* ears bleed with the sharp blast.

It helps to have Silicon Valley geniuses in your crew.

Freedom fighters with rifles pop up everywhere – beside the stage, along the bridge walkways, and behind the bridge supports. Although I can't see them, there should also be snipers settled beside each spotlight and on platforms hidden beneath the bridge.

Gunshots ring through the night.

While the angels are staggering in midair, trying to see and think enough to get away from the god-awful noise, our fighters are shooting them down into the water. After what I saw when we fought angels in the sea the other day, it's a good bet that most of them can't swim.

By now, the great white sharks of Northern California should have found their way to the bloody bait we cast into the bay during the show. Here, sharky, sharky . . .

The feedback from the speakers changes and begins blasting death metal music so loudly into the sky that I swear the bridge suspensions are vibrating.

The twins were in charge of the music selection.

I catch sight of them on the side of the bridge, each with an arm raised, holding up their forefingers and pinkies in a devil sign, head-banging to the beat. They're mouthing the words to the garbled voice screaming over the intense electric guitar and drums blasting out of the speakers. They might look pretty badass if it weren't for their hobo clown outfits.

It's the loudest party the Bay Area has ever heard.

62

Those of us on the ground crew help reload the bullets for the gunners. The goal is to try to knock the enemy out of the sky and into the shark-infested waters, but if some of them happen to fall onto the bridge, we'll be ready for them.

I hope.

The lights turn off all together, plunging us into darkness. Doc and Sanjay insisted the lights flash to keep the angels from adjusting to the light and to continue to keep them blind. So the lights are on timers to turn off and on according to their guesses as to the angels' ability to adjust.

Our snipers have infrared goggles to see in the dark, but there weren't enough to go around to the ground crew. With all the death metal blasting through the air and my double-layered soundproofing, I can't hear anything either.

We're in the middle of a battle for our lives – blind and deaf. I freeze, desperately trying to sense something. It feels like we stand vulnerable in the dark forever.

Then the lights turn back on, blasting our eyes with their intensity. I squint, trying to see through the blinding glare.

Angels begin to fall onto our bridge. We work in groups to shove them off the edge while they're still debilitated. Let the sharks sort them out while they thrash in the water.

I'm hoisting a net with a team of guys, ready to toss it over an angel, when I see my mom wandering around in the middle of all this, shouting to herself. I drop the net, letting the three other guys handle it, and run over to frantically try to get her under cover.

She's too busy to listen to me. After a few seconds, I realize she's shouting commands to the shaved cult members.

The cult members are tackling the newly landed angels off the edge of the bridge. Their robes flutter in the air as they wrestle and fall over the edge with them.

They also swan dive from the bridge as the angels fly low and get near. They grab onto the angels in midair like human projectiles. The angels, not expecting the extra weight of someone dragging on their wings, plunge into the water – pinwheels of arms and legs and wings. I hope those bald people can swim.

My mom shouts out commands like a general in battle, even though no one can hear her. Still, her message is clear if only because of her arm motions as she rhythmically dispatches her people into graceful swan dives off the bridge.

For those who dive, there's good motivation in catching themselves an angel, because the angel will slow down their fall, and they will have a chance of surviving the dive. The ones who miss their aim are on a suicide mission.

I worry about my mom diving as well, but she seems to have no shortage of volunteers waiting for her command. The woman has a job to do in the middle of all this battle, and she doesn't look like she's about to abandon it.

Hopefully, her job will keep her from obsessing over what's happening with Paige. As worried as I am, I know that if my sister weren't fighting to win over the locusts, they'd be attacking us right now along with the angels.

We're doing way better than I imagined, and I'm beginning to let myself believe that we might have a shot at winning this battle. I can almost hear the people cheering in my imagination when I see the sky darken with more angels.

It's a new wave of them. And it's a much larger group than the one that's already here.

On the way toward us, some of the angels swing low over the water, capsizing boats and giving their drenched and wounded comrades a hand. The winged warriors in the bay climb onto the capsized boats as the humans frantically swim away. They cling on awkwardly like drowning hawks, shaking their wings out and spraying the bloody water off them.

The gunners follow the new angels with streams of bullets. Angels continue to get shot out of the sky and into the shark-infested bay, but the new group hovers out of reach like spectators. They see what's happening with their fellow warriors, and they stay back.

I'm wondering what they'll do next when I notice that the angels are split into three groups. The first is the one that came right after the locusts. I catch glimpses of Uriel shouting in that group. The second is the mass of wings hovering at a higher altitude than Uriel's group. I can almost feel their cold eyes glaring down at us, watching and judging.

Then there's the smallest group. Their wings are dark and tattered. They could hardly be called angels. A white-winged Adonis swoops across them.

It's Raffe with his Watchers.

If one group is Uriel's and the other is Raffe's, then who are the others? Are they spectators here to watch the blood hunt?

It hits me that the real battle is only just beginning.

Even if Uriel wanted to back off and try again another time, he can't now, not without everyone in the host knowing that he backed down. What kind of blood hunter would he be?

Uriel and his angels must realize it at the same time I do, because they suddenly dive-bomb us.

The music is still blaring. The closer they get, the louder it is for them, but they commit to their attack.

The lights turn off, pitching us into the dark.

I feel the makeshift stage thunking with the weight of bodies landing hard around me.

The lights turn back on.

Around me are three angel warriors. They leap up, punching blindly as they spin in place with their eyes shut. They can't see, and the noise must be pounding their heads into mush, yet they're ready to fight.

Angels land all over the bridge. Some are crashing, lying broken on the concrete. Enough of them make it, though – uninjured enough to kill the nearest human even as they're adjusting to the light and recovering from their impact.

A bloody fight erupts on the bridge. People everywhere are running or fighting. The gunners aren't sure what to do, and they stutter in their aim. They can't open fire on the bridge without hitting our own people, and the angels above us are mostly out of easy range.

The angels don't even pull out their weapons. Either they're worried about my little trick with the sword I no longer have or they're so confident that they don't bother with weapons.

We can't beat angels one-on-one. We had anticipated the ground crew having to fight some angels who landed or fell onto the bridge, but not the entire angel host. That was as far as our planning skills and time allowed.

People are getting slaughtered as angels punch our fighters off the bridge or break their backs or kick them into oblivion. People use their handguns or rifles to shoot at the angels despite the risk of hitting other people.

I raise my knife against an angel who heads my way. It feels really flimsy compared with the sword I used to have. I don't know if he can see me now or not, but he has murder in his eyes. He knows he's going to kill. It's just a question of who.

If I'm super lucky, I might be able to fight him off and

maybe even the warrior after him, but it's not a long-term survival strategy. By long-term, I mean the next ten minutes.

We're screwed.

63

Knowing we signed up for this doesn't help even if we all knew our chances of survival were close to zero. Actually being faced with death is totally different.

My hands are trembling and clumsy as I brace for a fight. I try to calm down so I can fight effectively, but adrenaline screams through my veins, making me jittery.

As I calculate my best options, I see motion out of the edge of my vision. Another angel has snuck up on me. His wings are golden and his face chiseled, but he looks at me with the cold eyes of a killer.

Before I can figure out what to do, snowy wings blot out the angel.

It's Raffe.

And he has two of his Watchers backing him up.

My heart races even though I thought it was already going full speed. He has his back to me as if completely confident I won't attack him, despite the fact that we're enemies.

He punches the attacker, then grabs him and tosses him off the stage.

I let out a deep breath. My hands shake with relief. Raffe is fighting another angel, not humans.

He whips out his sword, ready to strike. I step back-to-back with him, slicing at the other angel coming at us. His Watchers step to each side of us, making a defensive perimeter around us.

The angel I'm fighting leans back to avoid my slice. I swipe my feet under his, and he goes down, landing hard. He's probably not used to fighting on his feet.

My opponent rolls away from me, blindly finding a new place to fight.

Raffe turns to me.

It's the first time I've seen his face look less than perfect. He's squinting in pain and blinking rapidly.

He came to help me.

Through all the screaming noise and blinding lights, he came.

I dig into my pocket and pull out a handful of industrial-strength earplugs. He looks at the orange plugs in my hand, then back at me. I grab one and push it into his ear.

He understands and puts one into his other ear. I know they don't help a lot, but they must help some, because his face relaxes a little. He gets the attention of the two Watchers beside us who also pluck earplugs out of my hand and put them in their ears.

I give Raffe a quick hug. I don't care who sees me at this point. Raffe might, though.

As if to prove it, he glances up at the sky. The rest of his Watchers and hellions are hovering above the fight where the noise is less. And beyond that is the cloud of winged spectators. I'm sure it's just my imagination, but I sense the arctic winds of disapproval coming down at us from the spectators above.

He came down to help us rather than hunt us even though the entire angel host was watching.

Raffe makes a twirling gesture to his two Watchers. They nod.

The two Watchers jump into the air and make the same twirling gesture to the rest of the Watchers hovering above.

Raffe's entire crew dives down through the painful noise and blinding lights and lands on the bridge.

When angel meets Watcher, they're like two feral cats meeting each other in an alley. They raise their feathers, making their wings look spiky and larger than before.

At first, our freedom fighters assume that there are just more enemies to fight and withdraw into a more defensive position against them. But when they see the Watchers attacking Uriel's angels, they waste a second, watching the scene unfold with slack jaws.

I raise my arms and whoop even though no one can hear me. I can't help it. With Raffe's group, we now have a fair shot of fending off Uriel's attack.

Everyone else must feel the same way, because all around me, people shout and raise their arms in a war cry.

The lights turn off again, throwing the world into utter darkness.

I stand still, not having anywhere to hide while the angels can see and we can't. Someone brushes by me in the dark. I want to hunker down and cover my head, but I just have to trust Raffe and the Watchers to keep me alive.

When the lights turn back on, Raffe is fighting beside me. He and his two winged opponents flinch as the light hits them.

There are more people alive than I'd hoped. The Watchers did the fighting for us while we were blind. Now they're all blinded, and it's our turn.

I rub Raffe's arm to let him know it's me and take the sword out of his hand. During the disorienting few seconds while the angels are covering their eyes, trying to adjust back to the light, we humans attack.

I cut and slice the angels closest to us while other people attack single angels in groups large enough to overwhelm them. Raffe's Watchers fought while we were helpless. Now we fight while they're debilitated.

We're working together as a team, Raffe's group and my people. We bridge their weaknesses and they bridge ours. We're a weird, ragged, mismatched group compared with the perfectly formed, powerful, beautiful angels, but we're still beating them back.

Adrenaline is pumping through my blood, and I feel like I can fight ten of Uriel's angels. Screaming my head off in a war cry, I run for the next squinting angel who is shielding his eyes.

Raffe falls to the ground wrestling blindly with two angels who are working together to hold him down. I stab my blade through one's back, and Raffe kicks off the other.

I feel like we have a real shot at beating them back with all of us working together.

But the glorious elation ends too soon.

The cloud of spectator angels begins coming down on us, hard and fast.

64

It's not surprising that the spectator angels are jumping into the fight now that Raffe and his Watchers are defending humans against other angels.

As the spectators begin diving, the fog around them begins churning. The angels falter in their flight and look around.

A cloud of locusts bursts out from the fog surrounding the angels.

I search the chaos for a glimpse of my sister but don't see her in the swarm of wings and stingers.

A bloody body drops from the center of the locust cloud.

There's a heart-stopping moment when I can't see any details. I want to shut my eyes in case it's Paige. Instead, my eyes are glued to the body as it falls.

I can't see anything until the body gets close enough. When it does, there's just enough time for me to see who it is.

Iridescent wings flutter in the wind. A scorpion tail. A white streak in flowing hair.

Then he smashes onto the asphalt.

I can breathe again.

Paige. Where is she?

In the sky, the swarm of locusts closes in on the angels. Paige sits regally in the arms of a locust followed by the rest of the swarm.

We all stare. Paige is covered in blood. I hope it's mostly White Streak's. She drips blood from her mouth. She's chewing something.

I don't want to think about that. I'm careful not to look too closely at White Streak, who lies broken on the bridge.

The old leader is dead.

I can't get my mind around it. My baby sister – queen of the locusts.

Paige lashes out with her voice and hand with a fury that reminds me of Mom. I can't hear what she's yelling, but she sweeps her arms, and the cloud of locusts follows.

They crash with the spectator angels in a tumbling mash of perfection and monstrosity. Blood starts raining down on us as stingers and swords clash.

My sister is keeping the spectator angels from coming down on us. Doc and Obi were right about her.

A surge of pride and fear swirls inside me. My baby sister is a savior.

Then the lights turn off again, and we're plunged into darkness.

I feel a hand grabbing Pooky Bear out of my grasp, and I know Raffe has the sword again. I crouch down low to stay out of the way and cover my head. I just have to trust him to keep me alive while I'm blind and deaf.

Behind my closed eyes, I see the impression of my sister riding a locust in battle.

65

When the lights turn back on again, I see someone trying to climb up the broken edge of the bridge from below. He has his mouth open in a frantic scream. Whatever it is he's trying to get away from is worse than what's on top of the bridge.

I run over to help him up. His hand is sweaty, and he's trembling. I can't hear a word he says, so I lie on my stomach at the crumbling edge and look down. I can see the bottom of the hideaway net strung below the bridge.

The net is broken. People cling to it in clumps, as if trying to get away from something. They're all staring wide-eyed at the turbulent water below.

The sea churns and explodes as a multiheaded sixer beast shoots up in a cascade of water. Its six living heads all have their mouths open like a misshapen fish jumping for bugs.

One of its heads sees me and snaps its jaws.

The apocalyptic monster grabs and bites several people with its six live heads. It then disappears back into the bay with the bleeding, squirming victims.

The dark water splashes and swirls as the last victim's hand disappears into the vortex.

Everyone below the bridge is in a panic. They crawl over each other, trying to get away from the spot where the sixer appeared.

How long has this been going on?

Jumping up, I rush over to the ladder that was pulled up to try to keep the talent show audience hidden beneath the bridge. A thought pops into my head – what if Doc was wrong and humans are not immune to the sixer's plague?

I can't let all those people die just because there's a chance of something going wrong. I unlatch the ladder and drop it down the side. They need to get out of there. They are now almost literally the low-hanging fruit in this war.

Our people scramble to the edges of the nets, some of them climbing over each other. There are as many people who fall into the water trying to escape as there were people who were taken by the monster.

The water churns again, and another sixer jumps up from the water. The distance they can jump is astounding. It greedily grabs people with its six jaws and drags the screaming, squirming people down below, into the depths.

'Come on! Get back up here!' I wave to the nearest people on the nets. They may be safer on the battlefield than where they are now.

As people begin climbing back up, I run through the chaos to the other escape routes around the bridge and lower the ladders. People begin streaming up the ladders as soon as they're in place.

The music stops.

We all look up. Even the angels and locusts pause midfight to look. What now? When this is all over, I never want another exciting moment in my life ever again.

Someone in a white suit flies above the stage. It's Uriel. His wings look off-white in the bright artificial light with a web of stark shadows.

My ears ring from the lack of sound. I peel back my headphones.

'The trial by contest is over.' He speaks in a regular voice, but in all this silence, it sounds like he's shouting. 'Raphael has proven himself a traitor. I am now the undisputed Messenger.'

Just as he says that, someone screams. A sixer climbs over the edge of the bridge. People back away as soon as they see the six heads with the seventh lying limp on its shoulder.

An angel near the sixer crashes onto his knees. His face is turning red, and he's sweating. Blood dribbles out of his mouth.

Another sixer climbs over the other edge of the bridge.

More people scream as they frantically try to get away from the sixers, but we can't go far on our bridge island. We herd together like frightened animals.

Two locusts near the sixer begin coughing. Then choking. They try to flap their wings, but they tumble to the concrete.

Blood begins dripping out of their mouths, their noses, their eyes. They make pitiful mewling and choking noises as they writhe on the bridge.

It's the apocalyptic pestilence.

66

'Raffe!' I try to get his attention. 'Get off the bridge! These monsters have angelic plague!'

A low-flying angel falls out of the sky, moaning like his insides are churning. Blood drips out his mouth, ears, nose, and eyes as he writhes on the concrete.

Angels take to the sky, avoiding the sixer. The words *angelic pestilence* are whispered in the air along with the whoosh of wings.

Every winged creature flies off the bridge, away from the infected angels and locusts. But only the winged ones can get away from the sixers.

If Doc is right, we humans are immune to this plague. But we're certainly not immune to a sixer killing us by force.

'Penryn!' Raffe calls to me from above, floating on his snowy wings. 'Jump off the bridge. I'll catch you.'

I rush over to the edge of the bridge where my mom is. Maybe the Watchers can catch her and whoever else is willing to jump. Luckily, my sister is in the air, far enough away to be safe.

An angel who hovers too close to the bridge screams. He convulses in the air as he begins crying blood tears.

Another sixer climbs over the edge of the bridge near Mom. She runs toward the center of the bridge like everyone else. How many of these monsters are there? I scramble to the side, yelling for my mom to head for a different part of the bridge.

'And his number is six hundred threescore and six,' says Uriel from the air, his voice booming through the panic. If he's surprised by the plague, he's not showing it.

As I near the edge of the bridge, I see more of the bay. The bloody seawater is peppered with sixers swimming toward us.

Two more climb over the edge. All around us, more sixers reach up and climb on top of each other to get on the bridge.

Six hundred sixty-six. It's not just the number tattooed on their foreheads. It must be how many of them there are.

I look up.

Raffe floats above me.

The angel just below him begins to writhe in pain. His nose begins bleeding.

I wave to Raffe to get away. 'Go!'

Raffe hovers. Two of his Watchers grab his arms and drag him up.

All around, people run every which way. Guns fire. Screams everywhere.

'I'll save your Daughter of Man's head to graft onto one of the beasts,' says Uriel to Raffe. He's flying well above us where he has a good view of the slaughter.

Sixers pour in from every edge of the bridge.

We humans back into the center as they lumber toward us. I have my knives out, but they might as well be toothpicks pointed at an army of grizzlies.

'Penryn!'

I look up to see Raffe watching me with anguish in his eyes as his Watchers hold him at a safe distance from us.

Raffe grabs the dried fruit hanging off his neck and brings it to his lips.

He bites into it.

It bursts between his teeth, oozing what looks like thick blood down his lips.

67

The bitten fruit smokes.

The smoke takes shape into the Pit lord we fought in hell.

He looks worse than I remember. Although the pieces I sliced have grown back, his wings still look like old charred leather, now covered in layers of scars. There's a new chunk missing out of one wing, and he has a gnarled gash through his lips that makes him look like he has two mouths.

He leans over to Raffe in midair as the Watchers bristle and form a protective line near Raffe.

After that, I can't watch anymore. The sixers are attacking around me.

For a while, I'm lost in the screams and sprays of blood

from the massacre. Bullets fly everywhere, but I don't have time to worry if I'll get hit by a stray as I slash at a sixer's head with everything I've got.

The screams intensify. At first, I assume people are getting slaughtered. But there's something about the pitch that sounds inhuman.

The sixer that I'm fighting suddenly gets hit with three whip heads.

I have to blink to make sure I'm seeing what I'm seeing. Are those the Consumed whip heads from the Pit? I look around, trying to see what's going on.

Under the spotlights, the shiny sea is covered with the Consumed propelling through the bay. They converge on the sixers that are still in the water.

Heads shoot up out of the water, screaming with their razor hair shooting out in front of them.

Their teeth latch onto the sixer in front of me and immediately begin chewing their way in.

The sixer writhes in pain, trying to scrape off the heads. More land on its shoulder and burrow.

Everywhere, the sixers are being attacked by whip heads. They're ignoring the people around them as we huddle in the center.

I look up. The Pit lord with the charred wings looks down at us with a satisfied look on his face. He's very pleased with himself.

Beside him, Raffe watches me. I can't read his expression. What did he do to make this happen?

'Are you all right?' he shouts.

I nod. I'm covered in blood and cut up, but I can't even feel the pain, not with all this adrenaline flowing through me.

All around, the whip heads are chewing their way out of the sixers. The sixers' living heads are being chewed off and are thudding to the concrete. In their place, the whip heads sprout, taking over the bodies.

Their screams turn into shrill laughter. Mad. Intense. Gleeful.

The possessed sixers lumber off the bridge and into the water.

It occurs to me that if the real apocalypse ever starts, these Consumed sixers might come back from the bloody sea as the real beasts of the apocalypse.

68

'A pair of archangel wings *and* a new army,' says the Pit lord.

'What have you done?' Uriel flies over to Raffe. 'Do you know how hard—'

Raffe whips his sword across Uriel with intense fury. Uriel barely manages to get his own sword up to block, but he gets hurled by the force of Raffe's blow.

Uriel tumbles out of the sky, landing hard on the bridge.

He staggers up, bleeding and holding his shoulder. It looks crushed. Before he can regain balance, a crowd of people rush him.

A woman slaps him, screaming about her children. Then another comes and kicks him. 'That's for my Nancy.' She kicks Uriel harder. 'That's for little Joe.'

Another person jumps in and begins wailing on him as a fourth runs up and begins plucking his feathers. After that, Uriel disappears under a mob of angry humans.

Feathers fly. Blood spurts. Knives slash up and down in the spotlights as arms pump, covered in blood.

Everything else has stopped – the music is off, the lights stay on, the angels have stopped fighting, and the Consumed sixers have quieted.

There's only the eerie glow of the spotlights beaming in every direction and Uriel's screams.

The angels look confused, unsure of what to do next. Maybe if Uriel's supporters had actually been loyal and cared about him, as opposed to following him because of what he could do for them, maybe they would risk themselves to save him. But before the uncertain angels can make a move, the crowd over Uriel begins to disband.

Several people hold up grisly parts of him as trophies. Bloody feathers, clumps of hair, a finger, and other parts too bloody to recognize.

Okay, maybe we're not the most civilized beings in the universe, but then, who is?

69

'I've fulfilled my end of the bargain, Archangel,' says the Pit lord. His burned wings sweep back and forth lazily in the air. 'I saved your pitiful Daughter of Man and her family. Now it's your turn.'

Raffe hovers on his beautiful feathered wings in front of the Pit lord. He nods with a grim expression.

'No.' The word slips out of my mouth as I watch, mesmerized.

Two hellions with black axes fly in from the dark outside the spotlights. Their axes are stained with layers of old blood. They position themselves behind either side of Raffe's wings.

There's a moment when I think Raffe will come up with a way out of this as he stares down the Pit lord.

Then he gives a single nod.

Without warning, the two hellions simultaneously lift their axes and slice through Raffe's wing joints.

They lift their axes and slice through Raffe's wing joints.

They lift their axes and slice through Raffe's wing joints.

They lift their axes and slice through Raffe's wing joints.

They . . .

. . . his wings . . .

I don't know if Raffe yells out in his pain, because all I hear is my own scream.

Raffe falls.

Two of his Watchers swoop down and catch him before he can crash onto the bridge.

Raffe's snowy wings land with a thud on the concrete.

A second after that, his sword clatters onto the ground, cracking the concrete with its weight.

70

The morning light tinges the sky above the San Francisco skyline. It's forever changed, but I'm starting to find it familiar, if not comforting.

Boats roam the bloody bay, collecting the last of the drowning angels and humans. The boat guys wanted to put the rescued angels into cages and shoot them to debilitate them for a while. I'm sure they would have been happy to gauge how long it would take for them to recover and maybe even see whether they can recover on their own without food and water. But not surprisingly, Josiah and the Watchers insisted that the best they can do is deprive them of blankets and the warm drinks the rescued humans get.

Now that Uriel is dead, they have a shortage of

archangels. Raffe seems to be unofficially in charge by default, only he's going in and out of consciousness as we race down the bay to the nearest working – or at least standing – hospital.

The Watchers are executing Raffe's orders and reporting back to him when he's conscious. The angels are so shell-shocked that they're just following orders.

I get the impression that so long as it sounds reasonable to them, they'll do what Raffe says, at least for now. This is a group that's so used to following orders that they probably wouldn't know what to do without someone in charge.

The humans have mostly left the bridge. I'm using Josiah and the Watchers to relay messages for me too, just because it's easy for now. I'm too worried about Raffe to help much with the logistics of making sure the humans get to shore. In theory, they're following my orders, but in reality, they're doing whatever the Tweedle Twins tell them.

I glance over at Raffe for the hundredth time as I huddle with Pooky Bear beneath a coat that someone gave me. I'm shivering as if it's zero degrees, and no matter how much I hug myself, I can't get warm. I can barely see his dark hair blowing in the wind among all the Watchers and angels surrounding him. He's lying on one of the bench seats of the speedboat that the twins found for us.

The angels and Watchers move aside and look at me expectantly. Then they all take off into the blue sky. Raffe is conscious and looking at me.

I walk over to him. I've been trying not to be a big baby by insisting on holding his hand in front of the angels, but the urge is strong. I don't want to embarrass him even when he's unconscious.

But now that the others are gone, I sit beside him and hold his hand. It's warm, and I pull it to my chest to warm me up.

'How are you feeling?' I ask.

He gives me a look that makes me feel guilty for reminding him about his wings.

'So? What's the deal? Are they making you the new Messenger?'

'Hardly.' His voice is raw. 'I fought against them, then conjured up a Pit lord. That's not much of a campaign for election. The only thing that saves me in their eyes is that they think I sacrificed my wings to save them from the angelic pestilence.'

'You could have had it all, Raffe. Once Uriel was out of the way, you would have been back with the angels. And they might have voted you in as their king.'

'Messenger.'

'Same difference.'

'Angels shouldn't have a Messenger who used to have demon wings. It's unseemly.' He winces and closes his eyes. 'Besides, I don't want the job. We've sent word out to Archangel Michael to get his stubborn ass back here. He doesn't want the title either.'

'There sure was a lot of fuss over a job that no one wants.'

'Oh, lots of angels want the job, just not the ones who should have it. Power is best held by the ones who don't want it.'

'Why don't you want it?'

'I have better things to do.'

'Like what?'

He opens one eye and looks at me. 'Like convince a stubborn girl to admit she's madly in love with me.'

I can't help but smile.

'So if it's not a pig farm that you want, what is it?' he asks.

I swallow. 'How about a safe place to live where we don't have to scrounge for food or fight for it?'

'It's yours.'

'That's it? All I have to do is ask?'

'No. There's a price for everything.'

'I knew it. What is it?'

'Me.'

I swallow. 'I need you to be very clear right now. I haven't slept in forever, and I've been living off of adrenaline, which isn't the best lifestyle for humans. So what are you saying?'

'Are you really going to make me spell it out?'

'Yes. Spell it.'

He stares deep into my eyes. It makes me squirm but also makes my heart flutter like a schoolgirl's. Oh, wait. I *am* a schoolgirl. I blink a few times, wondering if that's how I'm supposed to bat my eyelashes.

'What are you doing?'

'What?' Ugh. I suck at this.

'Are you batting your lashes at me?'

'What, me? No, of course not. What . . . spell it.'

He squints his eyes suspiciously at me. 'This is awkward.'

'Yes, it is.'

'You're not going to make this easy on me, are you?'

'You'd lose all respect for me if I did.'

'I'd make an exception for you.'

'Quit stalling. What are you trying to say?'

'I'm trying to say that I . . . that I . . .'

'Yes?'

He sighs. 'You're very difficult, you know that?'

'You're trying to say that you're what?'

'OkayIwaswrong. Now let's move on. Where do you think would be the best place for the angels to stay until they leave?'

'Whoa.' I burst out laughing. 'Did you just say that you were *wrong*? Was that the word? *Wrong*?' I smile at him. 'I like the sound of that coming out of your mouth. It's lyrical. W-r-o-n-g. Wroooong. Wrrrrong. Go on, sing it with me.'

'If I didn't love your laugh so much, I'd kick you off this extremely noisy and bumpy vehicle and let you shiver in the freezing water.'

He loves my laugh.

I clear my throat. 'What were you wrong about?' I ask in all seriousness.

He throws me a glare, looking like he might not answer. 'About Daughters of Men.'

'Oh? We're not all freakish, repulsive animals who sully your reputation?'

'No, I was right about all that.' He nods. 'But it turns out that's not always a bad thing.'

I give him a sideways glance.

'Who knew?' he says. 'I had no idea that someone could be such a thorn in your foot during a death march and still be irresistibly attractive in some magical, undeniable way.'

'So is that what people call sweet nothings? Because somehow, I expected it to be a little more . . . complimentary.'

'Don't you know a heartfelt declaration of love when you hear one?'

I blink dumbly at him with my heart pounding.

He caresses a lock of my hair out of my face. 'Look, I know that we're from different worlds and different people. But I've realized that it doesn't matter.'

'You don't care about the angelic rules anymore?'

'My Watchers have helped me realize that angelic rules are for angels. Without our wings, we can never be fully accepted back into the fold. There will always be talk of taking a newly Fallen's wings and transplanting them onto us. Angels are perfect. Even with transplanted wings, we'll never again be perfect. You accept me just the way I am, regardless of whether or not I even have wings. Even when I had my demon wings, you've never looked at me with pity. You've never wavered in your loyalty. That's who you are – my brave, loyal, lovable Daughter of Man.'

My heart beats so fast I don't know what to say. 'You're staying?' *With me?*

He moves to kiss me but winces. I lean over to him and pause just as our lips are about to touch. I like the heat and electric tingles on my lips from his closeness.

His warm lips press against mine. My hands spread out over his hard chest and slide down around his taut stomach to his lower back, trying to avoid the cuts. We hold each other close. He feels so good. So warm. So solid.

I want this moment to last forever.

'Aw, true love.' Howler lands on the boat, rocking it. 'It makes me want to puke. Doesn't it make you want to gag too, Hawk?'

'I never thought it was a good idea in the first place,' says Hawk as he lands beside Howler. 'Eternal damnation is what I get for listening to you lot.'

'How's the flesh wound, boss?' Howler shows off his forearm that glistens with his raw, skinless muscles. 'Want to compare and see who gets bragging rights?'

I don't want to ask, but I have to. 'What about the angels?'

'They'll find Michael,' says Raffe. 'They'll go back home and elect him as the new Messenger. They should manage to corral him eventually. He'll make a fine Messenger, even if he doesn't want to.'

'We'll be safe from them?'

'They'll all be gone soon. Your people can start rebuilding your world.'

'What about the Watchers?'

'They've chosen to stay with me. They never had the prejudices against Daughters of Men anyway, which was their problem to begin with. I'm afraid your people might have their hands full with them.'

'But only because the women will prefer us over their own men,' says Howler.

'Is that right? You're so sure we'll all want an ex-angel over regular ol' men?'

Howler shrugs.

'We may not be as perfect as we used to be,' says Raffe, 'but it's all relative.'

I try to give him a dirty look, but I can't help but laugh. 'Yes, I'm laughing at you.'

Raffe pulls me closer and kisses me again. I melt into his taut body. I can't help myself. I'm not even sure I should try.

My whole world turns into Raffe sensations as our lips explore each other.

EPILOGUE

I walk down the center of the street in our old neighborhood. I recognize the cracked building with the graffiti
of an angel that has the words 'Who will guard against
the guardians?'

Every door now has a feather dipped in red paint nailed
to it. I guess one of the gangs won the turf war since we
left and it's all their territory now. I suspect there are still
regular people hiding in attics and basements, though.

This is now the southernmost end of the peninsula
that hasn't been burned down by the fire from the blood
hunt. Many of the walls are dark with soot, but the
buildings still stand.

My sister rides ahead on one of her locusts. She calls
out to people that the angels are leaving and that they

can come out of hiding. She's been talking more as her stitches heal, letting her move her jaw more freely. She'll always be scarred, but at least her body will be fully – well, more than fully – functional.

She's regaining some weight now, finally moving beyond broth and eating solid foods. Laylah worked on her, hoping that Raffe would say a good word for her to Michael when he takes over. Whatever she did to Paige, it seems to be working. My sister still prefers raw meat and doesn't like vegetables, but at least she's not picky about what kind of meat or whether it's dead or alive.

My mother clatters behind me, rolling her grocery cart. It's full of empty soda bottles, old newspapers, blankets, flyers, and cartons of rotten eggs. People come out of hiding more for the rotten eggs that she passes out than the flyers, but Dee and Dum have assured me that that will change when people start feeling more human and less apocalyptic rat.

Mom is convinced that the hellions and demons will be taking over soon, and by the look of the small crowd that follows her around these days, a lot of people believe her. They flank her with their own grocery carts full of junk and rotten eggs. They have no idea why Mom carries the garbage around, but people are guessing it could be useful someday the way her rotten eggs were useful, and they don't want to take chances.

As I leave a flyer under a windshield wiper, I catch sight of Raffe gliding with Beliel's old demon wings above me. He refused to take part in such 'human work' as leaving flyers on cars and doors but keeps an eye on us anyway.

The flyer is for another of the twins' shows. This time, it's a minicircus. They're convinced that a freak show will bring everyone together, and have there ever been more freaks than at the End of Days?

My mom yells at someone behind me. I spin with my hand on Pooky Bear, ready to pull out my blade. But it's just my mom throwing rotten eggs at someone who took an empty soda bottle without asking.

I run my fingers through the bear's soft fur, telling myself to stop being so jumpy. The war is over now. It's time to bring the survivors together and rebuild.

Even Pooky Bear still needs some convincing to trust. She still hasn't let Raffe hold her since the blood hunt, but we're making progress. He says she'll eventually figure out that just because he doesn't match the perfect image of an angel anymore, it doesn't mean that he's not worthy.

A horn honks down the street. The twins wave out of the window of their grand prize RV. There was an official winner, but somehow, they managed to end up with it anyway. I didn't ask for details, but I'm pretty sure it involved gambling since their new slogan is 'The House Always Wins!'

My mother is conking the thief over the head with the empty plastic bottle he tried to steal.

'Mom!' I trot back to see if I can keep the peace.

Acknowledgements

Many thanks to my fabulous beta readers, who helped take the book to the next level: Nyla Adams, Jessica Lynch Alfaro, John Turner, Aaron Emigh, and Eric Shible. And of course, a huge thanks goes out to the readers of the Penryn & the End of Days series for their wild enthusiasm and support.

Enjoyed this book?
Want more?

Head over to

CHAPteR 5

for extra author content,
exclusives, competitions – and lots
and lots of book talk!

Our motto is
Proud to be bookish,

because, well, we are ☺

See you there . . .

f Chapter5Books 🐦 @Chapter5Books